RAFAŁ WOJASIŃSKI

TEFIL

PUBLICATION SUBSIDIZED BY
THE POLISH BOOK INSTITUTE

THE ©POLAND
TRANSLATION
PROGRAM

BOOK INSTITUTE

©POLAND

TEFIL

by Rafał Wojasiński

Translated from the Polish and introduced by
Charles S. Kraszewski

First published in Polish as *Tefil* in 2022

**This book has been published with the support
of the ©POLAND Translation Program**

Proofreading by John Nicolson

Introduction © Charles S. Kraszewski 2024
© Glagoslav Publications 2024
© Rafał Wojasiński

Cover art © Stanisław Baj, 'Stanisław Wawdejuka
ze wsi Dołhobrody', 1997

Back cover photo by Katarzyna Pizoń-Wojasińska

www.glagoslav.com

ISBN: 978-1-80484-138-9
ISBN: 978-1-80484-139-6

First published in English by Glagoslav Publications in June 2024

A catalogue record for this book is available from the British Library.

RAFAŁ WOJASIŃSKI

TEFIL

TRANSLATED FROM THE POLISH AND INTRODUCED BY
CHARLES S. KRASZEWSKI

GLAGOSLAV PUBLICATIONS

Rafał Wojasiński

Contents

SECULAR FUNGALISM:
THE TERRIFYING COSMOS OF TEFIL

Charles S. Kraszewski

We all know the story of Oedipus. A young happy man in Corinth, son of Polybus and Merope, prince and heir to the city founded by Ephyra, all is going swimmingly for him until once, at a banquet, a drunken boor begins mocking him. 'You are not the son of your parents!' he tells him. And although both Polybus and Merope assure their son that, yes, indeed, they are his parents – and they are not lying, when you think of it: it's not the physical act of procreation that creates a family, but the mutual love of parents and children; on the part of the former, the hard slogging of raising the child in love and security that makes parents parents – but Oedipus is not satisfied. He goes off to Delphi to get the 'truth' from the horse's mouth, i.e. the oracle of the god Apollo. One would think that it wouldn't be hard for the person with a line to the god of divination to give a straight answer, Yes or No, to the simple question: 'Are Polybus and Merope my parents?' But that's not how things turn out, and instead of getting satisfaction, one way or the other, to his original question, Oedipus is presented with even more horrible news than uncertain parentage. 'You're going to kill your father and sleep with your mother,' the oracle tells him.

In Rafał Wojasiński's engaging masterpiece *Tefil*, we come across a similar situation. A young, relatively good-looking, and well-preened man named Rozmaryn finds a photograph depicting his mother in the company of a stranger. He seems to have lost both his parents at an early age, and may never even have known his mother at all. So he sets off in search of that stranger, and it leads him to one of the most articulate, yet eerie and possibly mentally handicapped characters as can be found anywhere in literature: Tefil. A balding and somewhat odiferous inhabitant of a garret flat in a sleepy town somewhere in the Kujawy region of Poland, never married, who spent his working years as a village factotum, employed at tasks ranging from the sweeping of the grounds at a veterinary surgery to carting potatoes in a rickety handcart without tyres, he now exists as something of a self-interested Oxfam bin collecting the clothes of the dead (except for his linens, which he takes from a local church's charity box, and female clothing: he's no cross-dresser, though he did once come across a blouse, which 'really suited him'). He also goes to extreme lengths to avoid paying back insignificant debts (200 złoty; some thirty-seven pounds, forty-six dollars, forty-three euros) and cadging pastries and coffee, and sometimes alcoholic dinners, from passers-by to whom he attaches himself like a tick. It is to just such an oracle that Rozmaryn arrives with simple questions: Is this your picture? Did you know my mother? What can you tell me about my mother? and Tefil, true to the nature of all oracles, shamans, and other weird folk, replies with:

> Black mould in the corner of the ceiling of my flat in the garret. Mould will outlive us all… The history of humanity, of religion, of the nation, of our language, is nothing but clippings from the history of mould… Nations and religions are not immune… Nor is language… Mould is immune, even to the atomic bomb… Mould shall liberate us from being what we are… […] Did you know sir, that the mushrooms you've digested and evacuated from your

body are still able to live? You also heard that, sir? Is it true, or no? As they travel along the sewers, somewhere they are born again, and on and on endlessly. Mould, sir, you know, can live even two thousand years, eight thousand years. It can transform every poison into healthy nourishment for itself. It's more clever to be a mushroom than a man. Mould lives upon us, it eats us. Mould absorbs us, Rozmaryn, sir. Our intelligence is no help at all here. Reason constantly deprives us of reason. A mushroom never loses its reason. You know, sir, what I'm getting at.

Does he? Do we? The answer to that question is more crucial than it seems at first glance.

To return to Rozmaryn's distant cousin Oedipus, as we know from the most familiar telling of his story by Sophocles, the fact that he actually does end up killing his father and 'ploughing the furrow from which he sprang himself' cannot be blamed upon fate, the gods, or a family curse. It's really his own fault, for not being able to control his tragic flaw: impetuosity.

On the one hand, Oedipus does exactly what he ought to do. He accepts the information handed him, and starts off in search of a way out from underneath the catastrophe looming over him. The problem is neither his strategy – finding a rational way to avoid killing his father and sleeping with his mother – nor the tools with which he seeks to achieve his liberation: he prides himself on his reasoning powers, and, after all, it was him who finally solved the riddle of the Sphinx. The problem, as we say, is his impetuosity, his rashness in seizing the first solution – so often the wrong one! – that occurs to him. For example, as soon as he receives the horrid warning from the oracle at Delphi, he sets off for anywhere except Corinth, checking his progress by the stars to make sure he's avoiding the city where Polybus and Merope live. Now, wouldn't it have been better for him to *return* to Corinth, and to set the matter clearly before the couple who raised him? If they had 'lied' to him before, for whatever reason, would their response not have been different this time, had he said 'Look, I really need to know: are you my parents or not? Because I received this oracle that says I'm to kill my father and sleep with my mother, neither of which things, of course, I would ever wish to do!' One assumes that at this juncture, Polybus and Merope would have done what any normal human beings would: 'Listen, Oedipus. Since you put it that way, know: you *are* our son; we've loved you and raised you as our son, but, in fact, you are adopted. Does that oracle have to do with your biological parents? If so, it has nothing to do with us.' And presto! It would turn out that the *safest* place for Oedipus is Corinth! Had he remained there, chances are, he would never have come across Laius at the place where three roads meet, the Sphinx would have devoured all of Thebes, including Iocaste, whom he never would have met even had she escaped the murderous riddle. Living in Corinth, having a horror of both patricide and incest (which we know to be a fact from what he says in his play), it's rather a sure bet that Oedipus would have lived out his life in peace, going off to his eternal reward, at last, sighted, dreading not to meet up with his parents in the underworld. And even had he decided to return to Corinth from Delphi and pose that question once more, still unsure as to whether Polybus and Merope were his parents or not, surely he would be able to control himself for that short space of time, avoiding the running through of Polybus with his short sword and the jumping of Merope until he'd received his answer?

But that's just his problem. Let's consider this again. What's the one sure way of avoiding the fate of killing your father and sleeping with your mother if you do not know who those two worthies are? Well, obviously, *kill no one*. That can't be all that hard, can it? Take a vow of *ahimsa*. Why offer anyone any violence? The person who kills no one will never kill his own father. The person who sizes up a situation of threat before acting – This fellow who's being nasty with me; grey-haired, my build... that can't be my father, can it? – will hesitate before pulling out the weapon. But no, in the first documented case of road rage in our culture, shunted aside there at Phocis, Oedipus just loses it and slays the whole bunch of men who had collided with him at the place where three roads meet, increasing thereby the chances of doing exactly what he wanted to avoid – killing his father – some dozen-fold; and indeed, that 'grey-haired' gent who was 'about his build' was, indeed, papa.

And as for sleeping with Mum? Why, that's not so hard, is it? Even in a society in which girls married early, even given the fact that Iocaste might still be a very attractive thirty-two year old when Oedipus meets her (if he were, say, eighteen at the time and she'd given birth to him at fourteen), well, think a bit, Oedipus, before giving that rash 'Sure!' in answer to the offer of the grateful Theban people: 'Hey, listen – we're down a king. Would you like to take his place, marrying the widow?' It's not all that hard to judge a woman's age. If Oedipus had determined never to sleep with a girl who was older than him... Correct again, contestant number one! Oedipus beats fate.

The point we're driving at here is, at least as Sophocles presents it, the oracle is no historian of future events, saying: This is going to happen to you, and there's nothing you can do about it, but a warning: This is going to happen to you, unless you can find a way out of it. As we've just seen, there were several options open to Oedipus upon his reception of his oracle, and with a little elbow grease of the ratiocinating powers, he would have come out on top.

The issue with Rozmaryn and his oracle, Tefil, is a harder nut to crack. Reading Wojasiński's novel, we are as a matter of course confronted by the oracle ourselves. And since what Tefil reveals pertains not only to Rozmaryn but to all of humanity, all of existence, indeed, like it or not, we all find ourselves in Rozmaryn's shoes. Instead of a straight answer to a question about the past of one's mother – which may or may not have a visceral significance to the questioner – we receive the news that the world is absurd, and that the destiny of mankind, all mankind, from the drunken clochard zonked out in the weeds near the food store in Tutberg to Shakespeare and Pope St John Paul II (we dare reach no higher in our examples!) is to become food for all-conquering, undying, immortal mould:

> In our books, symphonies, inventions, words, holy scriptures, there really isn't anything at all. Nothing. They might as well not be at all. And once they were not. For quite a long time. And when some new humanity makes its appearance, out of sheer pride they will once again create that product for which there are no interested clients, and which must be forced upon them.

God as fungi. What on earth are we supposed to do with that? Compared to the riddle with which Tefil presents us, that of Oedipus is a piece of cake.

TEFIL THE NIHILISTIC COCKROACH IN LOVE WITH REALITY

So who is this Tefil? In all things, we must consider the source. Is Wojasiński's protagonist a guru worth heeding, or is he a crank? In 1934, Karel Čapek brought out one of his most interesting, and innovative novels: *Obyčejný život* [An Ordinary Life], the story of a grey man: a railroad retiree and impassioned gardener, who has done nothing special at all in the course of the life he has decided to record for posterity. It is the life of a *hodný člověk* – a good, solid fellow, and that's all. Čapek's novel, and its reason to be: the record of the life story of the marvellous average of good people, who through the critical mass of their ordinary, good-hearted lives, somehow steer the human race away from the final catastrophe we perhaps so richly deserve, cannot but call to mind the oeuvre of Rafał Wojasiński. *Tefil*, presented here in English, is the latest coastline mapped in Rafał Wojasiński's periplum of the neglected corners of his homeland. The eponymous character is no important person, as the world sees important persons, which is not to say that he is not extraordinary. As I mention above, Tefil lives in a garret flat in a provincial backwater, taking on odd jobs and giving a 'second life' to the clothes of the departed. Writing of Wojasiński's earlier novel *Olanda*, Dariusz Jaworski, director of the Book Institute (and therefore, a critic professionally concerned with the propagation of Poland in literature) comments that, through his work 'Wojasiński [...] brings us to the world of the provinces, which, so often, we contact only through the window of a train or during walks beyond the city centre. These are dynamic pictures of today's Poland, ambiguous, fascinating.'[1] Echoing Jaworski, Marcin Kube says:

> We find in [these works] a gallery of figures which, on the face of it, are not very attractive – drunks, village idiots, shopkeepers and retirees. The doubting and the humble, who fill their time alternately with garrulity and attention to the words of others. They are immersed in sadness but not in despair.[2]

....

[1] Dariusz Jaworski, *New Books from Poland* (Warsaw: The Book Institute, 2019), p. 3A.

[2] Marcin Kube, 'Rafał Wojasiński: Przestrzeń na smutek,' *Rzeczpospolita*, 3 April 2019 <https://www.rp.pl/literatura/art1401051-rafal-wojasinski-przestrzen-na-smutek> [accessed 13 May 2024]

So far, so good, as far as Marek, the hero of *Olanda*, is concerned, or Old Man Kalina, around whose character one of Wojasiński's most important stageworks revolves. But as for Tefil? The world with which we are presented in this novel is that of Anna and Wilhelm Sasnal's *Z daleka widok jest piękny* [It Looks Pretty from a Distance, 2011], that horrifying account of life on a country scrap-heap which displays the provinces of Poland as one of the more irking circles of Hell. If Tefil himself is not submerged in despair, there's no guarantee that the reader won't be, at the conclusion of his story.

The thing that both Jaworski and Kube notice about the people and places described by Wojasiński in his writing is their devotion to the palpable, the authentic, the real. This is what animates Tefil – the savour of existence:

> The real world. The charm of reality. To gaze with delight upon the clouds racing through the sky, on spruces bent by the wind, the sun poking through, throwing shadows... The wind's up a bit... A blast of breeze burls through the air around us. You hear it, sir?

As he puts it elsewhere:

> Shakespeare posed a rather weak final question, there. Decidedly. It's my own I prefer, completely. Not any to be or not to be. But: what is this? What is all this? What does all this mean, my dear sir, Rozmaryn? You. Me. Your mother. Litental. Prodige. Tutberg. Garbarska. What is it?

The love of sensual reality, the de-metaphysicalised world that surrounds us, which can be seen, heard, touched, smelt, and tasted, is a constant that runs through Wojasiński's writing, and *Tefil* is no exception to the rule. In one of the more interesting passages of the book, when Tefil is describing to Rozmaryn scenes from his early childhood, there occurs the

14

intriguing passage of a child's innocent exploration of the world: 'There were other children there besides me. Two, three at most. Who also canvassed the area on all fours. Looking for something, sniffing out something, drawing into themselves smells, colours, sounds.' One of the words that is constantly on Tefil's lips is *wchłonienie* – absorption, osmosis. Absorption is the child's approach to the world – eyes, ears, and nostrils wide open, little hands ever eager to reach out and touch, feel, take, and raise to his lips. The child is a sponge, actively allowing him- or herself to be acted upon by the world, without, however, giving anything back. The child's approach to the world is a one-way affair: reception, not creation – there will be time for that later. This of course begs the question: does Tefil, that uncritical lover of tactile reality, ever grow up? Does he ever give back to the world, transformed, the creative synthesis of what he earlier received from it, after having digested it?

One wonders which would be worse: Tefil the eternal child, satisfied with the passive experience of reality, or Tefil the teacher, who 'gives back' a synthesis of reality to which not many of us, I reckon, are willing to ascribe. The noun digestion, referred to above, immediately calls to mind those mushrooms, that mould... My mushroom, my executioner...

Fascination with reality is the most human of traits. It is familiar to anyone who ever examined a fly's wing for the first time through a child's microscope. It is shared by Rozmaryn, seemingly the more stable of the two main protagonists of Wojasiński's novel:

Rozmaryn twisted the cap off the neck of the bottle and began pouring the vodka. In even portions. He squinted one eye, first the left, then the right, because he had that ability, although not every human person has the ability to squint both the left eye and the right eye, leaving the other wide open. At last he placed both shot glasses next to each other. And it looked like he was successful, maybe a millimetre of a difference remained, not more (but sometimes a millimetre can be the difference between life and death). Then, between the millimetre of a difference and the rim of the shot glass Rozmaryn noticed a fingerprint. The print of a human being, some filth transferred, maybe, from the horse market. And that trace once more reconciled him with existence. Reality. Relief.

That being the case, a fascination with the concrete, a directing of the reader's eyes to wonders often passed over, is neither a distinctive trait of Tefil's, nor is it enough to command our interest. We want the child – the big baby? – to take the next step, and creatively transform that reality, to evaluate it for us. To refer back to the Greek stage, we're not expecting the 'author', i.e. Tefil, to make up anything new for us. We know the story. What we want is an interpretation that helps us look at ourselves from a new and different perspective. And it is here that, frankly, Tefil gets scary.

His fascination with the natural world is not that of a John Muir or a William Wordsworth. It is not even enough to say that Tefil loves nature because it is inhuman; he loves it because it is *anti*-human: 'Trees or a lake have no human talent and that's why they never bore me. They're always beautiful. They use no words, they draw nothing, they compose no music.' How different this is from the 'inhuman' philosophy of Robinson Jeffers who, even if he will not acknowledge man as a being separate, and above, botanical and zoological nature, still sees man as a 'part of that organic whole', whose role is to be the senses, both physical and intellectual, which allow his somewhat pantheistically conceived Deity to understand Himself. For even being only part of an organic whole is not a diminishment of human dignity, but an emphatic recalibration of the same, which sets it in its proper context. As he wrote in a letter to Sister Mary James Power, who was writing on the religious sensibility of contemporary English poets:

> I think it is our privilege and felicity to love God for his beauty, without claiming or expecting love from him. We are not important to him, but he to us.
>
> I think that one may contribute (ever so slightly) to the beauty of things by making one's own life and environment, beautiful, so far as one's power reaches. This includes moral beauty, one of the qualities of humanity, though it seems not to appear elsewhere in the universe.[3]

One of the ways that man – whom Jeffers, after his mentor Thomas Hardy, disdains at times for his cruelty to other forms of life – can 'contribute to the beauty of things' is through his engagement in words, in drawing, in composing music, three perfectly human traits that Tefil rejects. What is even worse, while Jeffers also acknowledges man's capability to achieve 'moral beauty', it is that very thing which we find completely lacking in the moral anarchist Tefil. In his lyrical extrapolation of the last words of humanity, enunciated by the woman behind the counter in a butcher's shop, Tefil's spokeswoman says:

> Pig's feet three fifty (not on sale). For meat jelly. You'll be able to have a little party on Saturday night. Mama, Dad, Unkie from your Mama's side, Unkie from your Dad's. My sister'll be there as well with her husband; we'll turn the lights down, fill up the shot glasses with vodka, and we'll feel alive in our flat. Splendidly alive. Splendidly, because individually, each for him- or herself. Each alone with the

....

[3] Robinson Jeffers, letter to Sister Mary James Power, dated 1 October 1934. Cited by James Karman, *Robinson Jeffers: Poet of California* (San Francisco: Chronicle Books, 1987), p. 70.

meat jelly and his or her own shot glass. The savour of feeling individually happiness comes from the individual, only from there. It's true that the living has to kill the living and consume it in order to sense a certain savour. That's no extraordinary discovery. Nothing extraordinary tells us that.

What is 'splendidly alive' here is a haphazard gathering of carnivores, each intent on nothing but the plate of meat before him. The splendid quality of life is unsharable, for the only communion it intimates is that between the devourer and the devoured. The little human society described in these lines is nothing different from a swarm of cockroaches feasting on some slab of decomposing flesh, minute individuals who take no note of their fellows unless they intrude on the inch of protein on which they are gorging themselves. The fact that the people described in Tefil's account are related – Mama, Dad, Unkie, and the rest – is entirely irrelevant. Even cockroaches are 'related' in some way. The important thing is that, as Tefil sees it, 'Nothing exists but parallel beings.' As we know from physics, parallel lines never meet; in much the same way, this philosophy teaches us that there can be no real contact between people. Perhaps, indeed, that is the reason why Rozmaryn gets no answer to his question; why Tefil never tells him what he knows about his mother. There is no sense in making connections between things – people – who are disconnected naturally. And so, as we continue on through the thought espoused by Wojasiński's hero, there can be no civilisation, no culture:

Man is a garbage dump. He'll remember all the things that mess him up with desires, hankerings, but which offer him no means of fulfilment. And then he has to carry that load of rubbish around with him for ages on end. As if those ages of his meant anything more than the ages of a dead fly.

CHARLES S. KRASZEWSKI

Tefil is, at least, honest enough not to set himself apart from the humanity he despises. He has his meaningless 'hankerings' as much as the other man, who is only as important to him as a host is to its parasite: 'There are so many people who can still buy me cheesecake. It seems to me that there's still a lot of such folk left here and there, hiding in odd corners and not yet revealing themselves. But they'll show up and treat me.'

I reckon that most of us would leave Tefil right then and there after this admission, which is, in the context of Rozmaryn's traffic with him, an evaluation of his human worth. Even though Tefil can't do simple arithmetic, to him human dignity is reducible to dollars and cents. He'll keep Rozmaryn hanging around, spinning his yarns that lead nowhere, as long as Rozmaryn has enough cash for cheesecake and coffee, schnitzel and vodka, a couple cold beers.

Rozmaryn is no great shakes himself. There's something creepy, in an adolescent way, of his leery voyeurism, his overcharged libido that likes peering into the cleavage of waitress or barista, his unwillingness to advert his eyes when he chances to glance into an occupied changing room. And yet – as imperfect as he is – there is something heroic about his character. Tefil may be an anarchist, a nihilist, yet Rozmaryn, in his dogged determination to hold out to the end, in hopes of at last receiving some insight from this Diogenes in dead men's clothes, enunciates thereby an implied faith in a sense-filled universe. There is truth, and he who searches for it, even banal truths about one's nearest relations, will find it. The problem is, he's really barking up a wrong tree here. Tefil has nothing to offer him, nothing to teach. In an admission that reflects back on the atomised world of parallel beings, Tefil says about his incessant jawing:

> As soon as I took up one of my topics, immediately it turned out that none of them could be a topic in common… That there exists no possibility for the topic of

socks, trousers, or Prodige to become a topic in common... No possibility. Then, with the last of my strength, I tried to move the topic of felt-lined boots sliced low. To prove that I was right in slicing low those felt-lined boots... And nothing.

In the context of the novel, which portrays Tefil as something of a trickster, a bottom-feeder of a conman whose game is to wheedle pocket-change and pork chops out of his victims, this hand-spreading about a congenital inability to communicate may be nothing but a dodge, a way for Tefil to keep away from addressing the question of Rozmaryn's mother. But then again, it might be a flash of truth that the incautious reader passes over, like daft Faustus standing before the truth-telling Mephistopheles: 'Come, I think Hell's a fable!'[4] Whereas Tefil is screaming at this point: *I have nothing to say. I am not interesting. You are wasting your time listening to me.*

Curiously enough, Wojasiński chose a line from Dante's *Purgatorio* as the motto for *Tefil*: 'Follow me, and let the people talk on' (V:13).[5] That motto, on page one, is the first red herring of several in the novel. For this 'Dante' (who is Rozmaryn), cannot learn from the dead, as they are incommunicado. Tefil-Virgil leads him to no living spirit, but only to the dead, mute, deaf matter of the grave:

> You know, sir, I adore pondering whether to go up the hill where the pine remembers the Jewish cemetery, of which only the faintest traces remain underground, or

....

[4] To which the devil replies: 'Ay, think so still, till experience change thy mind.' Christopher Marlowe, *The Tragical History of Doctor Faustus*, scene 5.

[5] Thus the translation of the Polish *Pójdź ze mną, a ludzie niech mówią dalej*. The original Italian reads *Vien dietro a me, e lascia dir le genti* [Come on behind me, and let those people talk].

CHARLES S. KRASZEWSKI

to go to the Catholic cemetery and visit the graves of my two splendid friends who committed suicide, or to go to the Lutheran cemetery and stand on one of those little mounds that signify that there are corpses beneath it, and to feel like a corpse upon corpses, living upon the dead – such an exchange of generations.

Even worse than the sentiment that these words convey is the obvious satisfaction of the speaker when enunciating them.

TEFIL THE ANTI-BUDDHA, BENEATH THE DRY-ROTTEN BO TREE

Tefil makes no claims to Virgilian splendour or wisdom. Although Marcin Kube feels that 'this bitter, anti-civilisational Jeremiad lies bare our self-satisfaction, ridicules our canons and ideals and unmasks our embarrassing chase after immortality,'[6] one is tempted to respond: Is that all that's on offer here, then? Instead of Chartres, Goethe, and the Tympanum Giselberti with its warning and promise of the last judgement, we're to be satisfied with a two-metre square smokehouse, Tefil, and the scattered bones of desecrated graves? How much can be expected of a man who is so lacking in metaphysics as to claim 'The profundity of thought and the life of the spirit in comparison with the profundity that is found in money is nothing at all. The spiritual life of man is money'? Neither Virgil, nor all the more so Dante, would agree to this pearl of spiritual wisdom:

I, you know, sir, Rozmaryn, sir, am just as much of a believer, just as immortal, in the same state of grace as my

....

6   Marcin Kube, 'Upajający brak wiedzy,' *Plus Minus*, 22 July 2022 <https://www.rp.pl/plus-minus/art36738721-upajajacy-brak-wiedzy> [accessed 13 May 2024]

dog Prodige. In the same way I am just as much of an unbeliever and just as mortal as my dog Prodige. Do you think, sir, that you, sir, or I am capable of believing any-thing more or disbelieving anything more than Prodige?

Readers of the *Bhagavadgita* may start to attention at this statement of Wojasiński's protagonist. There seems to be at least the faintest of echoes of Krishna's sermon to the an-guished Arjuna on Kurukshetra Plain, before the epic battle of Pandavas and Kuravas, when, in the course of his teach-ing on disinterested action and the yoga of the dispassionate kshatriya, he says: 'Wise are they who see no difference be-tween a learned, well-mannered brahmin, a cow, an elephant, a dog, and an eater of dogs.'[7] However, the similarity is only illusory. Whereas Hinduism, especially in its Krishnaist ele-ments, is outwardly expansive, ennobling non-human life to the same level of participation-in-being shared by humanity,[8]

....

[7]   *The Bhagavadgita in the Mahabharata. A Bilingual Edition*, ed. and trans. by J.A.B. van Buitenen (Chicago: University of Chicago Press, 1981), p. 93 [27 (5) 19].

[8]   Eastern philosophy is generally more inclusive in this regard than what we are used to in the West. Witness the popularity of animal tales in the Buddhist tradition, in which the Buddha is not exclusively concerned with the (self) salvation of men and women, but with the enlightenment of entire creation. For that reason, the Bodhisattva of-ten withholds himself from advancement through reincarnation in order to preach to the animals, as an animal himself. In the West, such inclusivity is a cardinal tenet of Robinson Jeffers' idea of 'Inhumanism'. In the Christian tradition, for me it was enunciated most satisfyingly by Prof. Rio Preisner, who stated that animals must be in Heaven, for if Heaven is the sum of all happiness, most men who attain Heaven would not be perfectly happy without animals. The Christian sense, however, is that animals are inherently good and innocent – and as such are in need of no spiritual instruction or enlightenment, wheth-er Christian or Buddhist. Animals are pure merit. Tefil takes the op-posite view. Far from an apotheosis of the dog Prodige, his words

CHARLES S. KRASZEWSKI

Tefil's statement is clearly reductive. Once more, he is attacking the very idea of humanity by reducing its range of moral and intellectual action to that of a canine.

We share in the same life as animals, and that life is devoid of any higher plane. Tefil has nothing in common with any sort of theist – he is an atheist, the lowest common denominator of a rationalist.

It is true that Tefil – like a prestidigitator – expresses himself at times in ways that approach metaphysical experience and spiritual wisdom. The greatest example of this is his description of the brick smokehouse built by the 'Lutheran cantor', in the house of whom he and his parents took up residence after the war:

> In building that smokehouse, that genius constructed the only temple that ever spoke to me. It created no illusions that there can be any greater accomplishment than beginning. Repetitive, quickly passing, unconscious in the face of the unconscious, eternal existence of all matter. In building the smokehouse, the genius made it so that I should become like unto the smoke emerging therefrom, like the lilac branch that hangs there near the fence. I became a part of all being and eternity for I lost the consciousness of being myself. An exit from humanity through a smokehouse built by a man. [...] His great work of genius, which elevated me for a moment above the prison I carry about within me, wherever I go or wherever I am herded. I'm always sitting in a slammer. A more or less pleasant one. A tunnel... Life sentence... Eternity... No journeys west or east. Beginning... The

....

here are a confirmation of the worst sort of rationalist considerations, which see animals as little more than self-animated machines – and it is to such a level of soulless mechanics that he would reduce men and women too.

discovery of the fascinating, overpowering mystery of space. Mystery…

Buddha had his bo tree, Tefil has his smokehouse. But again, the similarity is misleading. Gautama receives a revelation that leads from a realisation of the causality of being to the determination, through compassion, to lead men past suffering,[9] Tefil's experience is one of *anti*-enlightenment, as it is a revelation of the supposedly 'unconscious, eternal existence of all matter'. Sitting on his stump, meditating, becoming 'like unto the smoke' that rises from the cherrywood slowly being reduced to ash (is it any wonder why Tefil so frequently ponders cremation and determines to frame a will to be cremated and scattered?) he becomes like unto the sausages and hams being cured on the hooks above the fragrant fire-pit – once more, life is nothing but a cycle of devouring and being devoured. The final victory belongs to the mushrooms.

Supposedly, Tefil engages in long theological disputes with the rector of the Catholic parish and his vicar. But notice again at what, he imagines, those disputes will arrive:

> But I believe in myself, in the vicar, and in the rector. And I'm certain that, someday, in this discussion of ours, we'll soar far away. We'll rise above the wonderful roofs of Litental and reconcile the irreconcilable. We shall find solutions such as overthrow all patterns heretofore acknowledged as true, and arrive at the place where zero becomes incarnate in the mystery of beginning…

....

[9] For the most succinct and satisfying description of Gautama's experience of enlightenment in English see Joseph Campbell, *The Hero with a Thousand Faces* (Princeton: Princeton University Press, 1973), pp. 31–33.

CHARLES S. KRASZEWSKI

This is no progress, philosophical, moral, or otherwise. It leadeth not to the peace that passeth understanding, to that realm where all tears will be wiped away – it leads to 'zero' becoming 'incarnate in the mystery of beginning'. Whatever that means. Even the eastern metaphor of mokṣa being the return of a drop of water to the sea is crystal clear – and much more hopeful – in comparison to this. The only time when Tefil will actually 'rise and soar' is after his death, and that elevation has nothing of the spiritual about it:

> Let the wind puff the rest of my ashes against what remains of the cemetery walls and the fields around the cemetery fragrant with freshly ploughed earth or stubble. Let them fall on the feathers of the crows crouching on the balk; let them fall, carried by the wind, onto the fur of the fieldmice, the stray dogs, the foxes out in search of conquest.

When Rozmaryn is sent back to Tefil's flat to retrieve the old man's eyeglasses, 'He [catches] the scent of violets, as if in the house of a saint.' This is another red herring tossed the reader's way by Wojasiński, the prankster novelist. For if Tefil is at all pungent, it is not with the odour of sanctity, nor is he a sage. He has nothing to teach us:

> Now we're talking rubbish... And that's why we're sticking it out together... Patterns, patterns, patterns... Estimating, overestimating, descriptions of nature, of love... Descriptions of the fates of entire families, villages, and nations... We recount stories, anecdotes... We search out boobies... To listen to us... All we can do is chunter and babble... In search of wonder... Shh! Hush now! All you gotta do is wait, nobody'll give a toss about the stains. Nothing will remain of people that'll be worth anyone's

notice. Not a single sentence! Everything discovered turns out to be mistakes and glitter! All you gotta do is wait.

TEFIL THE LINGUISTIC NIHILIST

It's hard to see why the quotation from Dante's *Purgatorio* should have been chosen as the motto for *Tefil,* a book without a traditional spiritual arc to its journey, a novel in which hardly anything happens, and for all the talking – sometimes beautiful, engaging talking – nothing is really ever said. A better motto for the book might be found in the story itself. Describing one of the little anabases of Tefil and Rozmaryn, circumscribed by the limits of the tiny, insignificant town somewhere in the backwaters of Poland (a town that Tefil can 'never leave'), the narrator says:

> The road that Tefil and Rozmaryn were taking was short, but it took them a long while. They had already been going like that some few dozen minutes, and still they hadn't gone farther than the public pump placed some hundred metres from the crossroads.

What a perfect thumbnail description of the novel. It's short enough to be considered a novella – the original Polish edition is a mere 175 pages – and the action is framed, not by the classical one revolution of the sun, but a mere fraction thereof: a few hours to both sides of the meridies. And still, for all the talking that takes place, all the dead air that Tefil stuffs with his unending yarns, we get 'no farther than the public pump' before, suddenly, the novel ends and the two interlocutors vanish back into the mists from which they originally emerged.

That being the case, the manner in which the novel progresses, or does not progress, calls to mind one of the great classics of the Modernist period: James Joyce's *Ulysses.* When asked about his opinions concerning Joyce, Wojasiński stated:

> For me, Joyce is an opening of the tongue. For me, *Ulysses* is the one book which is closest to 'reality'. For reality is not about something, it *is* something. Life is not the story of something, a tale. Life is essence. Life can do 'everything' possible with life. Only life. Not man. And I think that Joyce was the one writer who set himself to creating everything he wished with language. He did what he wished in a dimension in which others were not successful. And for that reason he is exceptionally inspiring to me, especially dramaturgically, in the dimension of language. He and Ezra Pound tell me that literature is something worth cultivating, irregardless of whether or not someone reads what one writes. For life is also cultivated no matter what anyone thinks of it. In actuality, life isn't at all concerned with what man thinks of it. Life is that, and only that, which it is. Without any regard for the opinion of any human mind.[10]

Here, I reckon, we have both the essence and the magnificence of Rafał Wojasiński's *Tefil*. Everything that has gone before in this essay, during which I have evaluated the character of Tefil, judged him, tried to make some traditional sense out of what he says and does, what philosophy he presents, is, when seen through this prism, worthless. Because the story is not important here – there is no story, in any traditional sense. Rozmaryn's quest for information about his mother is not a plot, it is a framework, an excuse to kick-start Tefil, to give him an audience, a sounding-board, against which to reveal – not his thoughts but himself. 'Each mortal

....

[10]   Rafał Wojasiński, Letter to the writer, 4 September 2023.

thing does one thing and the same,' Gerard Manley Hopkins proclaims in a sonnet philosophically far removed from Tefil the nihilist:

> Deals out that being indoors each one dwells;
> Selves – goes itself, *myself* it speaks and spells,
> Crying *Whát I dó is me: for that I came.*[11]

It is as if Wojasiński were saying to us: 'Hey, you really ought to see this strange chap who wanders the streets of my town. He is the essence of the idiosyncratic,' and that's exactly what we proceeded to do: to observe the life of Tefil *in flagranti* for four hours or so. In this sense, *Tefil* is not a story at all, it is reportage, and not even that, for reportages often arrange the documentary evidence they present to us in a way that leads us, gently and logically, to the point of view of the reporter. It is, rather, that raw material recorded by camera, microphone, or pen, before processing.

It is striking what Wojasiński says concerning Joyce and language in the fragment of his letter quoted above. It is in this, I feel strongly, that the greatness of the work consists. *Tefil* is, like another of Joyce's works, *Finnegans Wake*, above all, poetry broadly understood: the shaping of sounds and ideas through wordplay. *Tefil* is a joy to read aloud. The Polish original has a marvellous cadence to it; the text itself is full of anaphoras, alliteration, clever rhymes and puns. The reader will excuse me for not offering many examples here – it is his or her job to determine, whether or not he or she is able to compare the translation with the original text – how far this is true of the translation, and to draw his or her attention to any particular portion of the English version would seem, I reckon, a bit too much like patting myself on the back. Perhaps

---

[11] Gerard Manley Hopkins, 'As Kingfishers Catch Fire', 5–8.

CHARLES S. KRASZEWSKI

one short paragraph, chosen at random, will give the reader some idea of the rhythm and construction of his phrasing:

> Everything is real, even when it talks rot. Protruding bones say: think what you like, but, all the same, reality will consume everything. Mozart, Bach, Gide, Miłosz, Pessoa, Wittgenstein, and Bernhard. The lawn mower, the chaff cutter, the harrow, the castra, and the rotavator. Reality will swallow Galileo, Newton, and Copernicus. The quern, the chimney on the roof, the warm stove lid in the kitchen, and the skillet unscraped of fried eggs. Beginning. My poking bones in my pale drying skin. Even schizophrenia won't liberate you from reality. Nothing will free one from it. No faith in any God, in any state, in any art, in any language and love.

Passing over the name-dropping – which true to form, is only introduced here in order to strip human authority of any significance – one is arrested by the piling up of concrete images, from agricultural tools to a dirty skillet, which arouses the evocative immediacy of an Imagist poem. And when aloud, passages like this (Wojasiński is especially drawn to litany-like lists) introduce an incantatory flavour to the narrative which grips the reader strongly, whatever he or she might think of the protagonists or the story itself.

There may be better examples, even in the English translation, of Wojasiński's manner of toying with language, but in all honesty, I feel that they would all seem inadequate in comparison to the original. The translator in me takes comfort in the fact that Tefil (and perhaps his creator Wojasiński) finds all language to be inadequate:

> Language. The word 'stone' does not name the stone. The word 'roof' does not name the roof. The word 'Marynia' does not name Marynia. The word 'Prodige' does not

name my dog. Counterfeiting. Falsification. Falsehood. [...] There isn't a single good name. That's why I'm not satisfied with one single thought of this world, why language has never satisfied me. The barking of a dog satisfied me, the chirping of a sparrow, the snorting of pigs, the rustle of the wind and the little waves on the lake.

From this perspective, it seems as if all of Wojasiński's writing, and in particular *Tefil*, is an exercise in somehow expressing the inexpressible: the nature of the stone, or roof, or Marynia, which words are incapable of conveying. The incommunicable essence. Incommunicability. The essence of our species, our communion (or lack thereof), is: 'It is impossible to say just what I mean!'[12] Have we not all repeated, more than once, the words of that other great Modernist idol of Wojasiński's? I see it clearly, but you cannot, and I cannot present it to you. Maybe there's something deeply true in Tefil's idea of parallel beings after all?

Perhaps. But such is the mind of man and woman – of any man and woman who has passed by the 'absorptive' stage of childhood, which seems still to grip old, balding Tefil – that it cannot stop at merely recording phenomena; it must push on past cataloguing to interpretation. And so even the lists that the voracious visible perception of Wojasiński's protagonist strings out tell us something about the perceiver:

These differences between the species really throw me in a loop. Tail. No tail. Claws. Fingers. Eyes. No eyes. One gender. Two genders. Beauty. Lack of beauty. Beginnings. One foot, two foot. A little crouch, decline, ascent. Scratching the back. Beginnings. Stranger and friend. Danger, the end. Calculation. Miscalculation. Numbers.

....

12   T.S. Eliot, 'The Love Song of J. Alfred Prufrock', 104.

The God of the majority. Beginning… Choking to death on a walnut, being run over by a car, freezing to death, drowning in the lake, tripping on a high kerb.

A fascination with the variety of life forms, innocent and laudable enough, suddenly swerves into a fascination with the variety of death that lurks on these living things. And this cannot but induce the sensitive reader's hackles to rise in the presence of a creepy sort of chap who seems to be something of a borderline necrophile:

> When I was nine years old and went to school, I'd linger around that cemetery often. The graves dug up, skeletons laid out on the slabs, skulls at the foot of the trees, telltale signs in jaws of gold teeth having been prised out. […] Once there was this tin coffin. The tin was nothing worth: a chisel does the trick and the lid is bent back. I had a peek into the coffin. It's hard not to look into a coffin. That was my one encounter with the universe, for I'm not going to fly off to the Moon or to Mars, after all. A stranger's skeleton, the remains of a skeleton, a shoe…
>
> Nothing tempts me as much as a coffin. Really, it's hard for me to think of anything more interesting. Perhaps if nature had better developed my sexual inclinations, I'd have a different point of view, but in this situation, the only one that is available to me… Well, the coffin, especially the coffin pried open a crack, is the most interesting fragment of reality.

Uh-oh.

Voyeurism is a problem with Tefil. Consider another cataloguing of chance material items: those found in a dead, old woman's flat. This is one of the most unsettling episodes in the novel. Tefil, in flashback, reminisces about catching sight of an old woman at the end of a leaf-covered path he had been raking, back when he was working as a porter at the local veterinary surgery. Something makes him drop his rake and follow – one almost wants to say pursue – the old woman all the way to her flat, where, after being 'invited in' by her faint voice, he finds her lying in bead near a window-sill – dead. And then, amidst the strange conversation shared by these two extraordinary parallel beings, Tefil has a look around the flat:

> Candles, which remained on the table. Gloves and stock-ings thrown to the side in haste. Tiny grey shoes in the corner not far from the window. A sugar bowl with a crust of sugar. A shrivelled fly on the windowsill. Two piles left by a dog, resting on the floor-slat nearest the door, had been saved. The remains of a shrivelled mouse beneath the bed had been saved. The overcoat on the hanger hooked high on the door of the armoire. Forks and knives in the drawer. Rubbish, which no one had taken out now. A wet stain on the ceiling which had now grown to the size of seven large watermelons. A wedding por-trait on the wall. Photographs of two little girls in white dresses had been saved, tucked in the chest of drawers be-neath some bedclothes gone mouldy. Banknotes in a roll beneath the floorboards under the door. Bills of exchange, notes, receipts, and debts entered in a small notebook. A wedding ring, an engagement ring in the lower drawer of the chest of drawers.

If the reader hasn't felt uneasy in the presence of Tefil yet, it's a strong stomach that doesn't feel the first butterflies of a turn now. When does an interest in reality become snoop-ing? When does the 'recycling' of the clothes of dead persons donated to one by the surviving family members, those no-torious slashed felt-lined rubber boots and thirty-year-old trousers, become a borderline criminal rifling through the drawers of an absent person, in a stranger's flat? It's one thing to glance at a wedding portrait hung on a wall for all to see, and quite another to rummage through a chest-of drawers and pull out communion photographs of children not one's own, opening another drawer to uncover jewellery, and... prising up a floorboard that catches one's eye to extract some hidden banknotes!

What is Tefil *doing* there? Who is that old woman? Is she really there? If so, is she dead? And... how did she die...?

Wojasiński is at the top of his game here. If, like Tefil, he doubts in the ability of human language to convey truth, here, in a masterful way, he leads the reader to a shifting wasteland of language, in which nothing certain can be ascertained. Is it possible to be led by a ghost to a deserted apartment in which the ghost's former flesh is slowly mummifying? Is it possible to have a conversation with a corpse? Did this ever happen, or is Tefil making it all up? And if that's the case with this episode in the strange tale woven by Tefil, what about the rest? Where does the truth lie? What is a lie? What is the truth?

TEFIL SAYS THERE IS NO GOD.
THE READER ASKS: IS THERE A TEFIL?

Through even such a brief consideration of Wojasiński's language (and we are far from done with it) we have now arrived at a place of utter discomfort for any traditional literary criticism. Is there anything subjectively true in *Tefil*? Other than, perhaps, the evident truth of Wojasiński's perspective on reality, which can be boiled down to the following statements: 1) Reality exists. 2) It can be perceived and should be perceived as it is, without seeking to find any 'meaning' it might contain. 3) Whatever we experience in our contact with reality, it is our own personal property, and cannot be shared with any other being parallel to our own; certainly not through language.

In this sense, then, Rafał Wojasiński's linguistic jaunt of a novel *Tefil* is the subjective work of art *par excellence*. It is as close as one can come to 'absolute literature' in the sense of 'absolute music' or 'non-representational art'. Bach's Little fugue in g-minor is not programme music; it does not tell a story. It is simply an arrangement of sound and auricular colouration moving through time. While listening to the fugue, one person might 'see' a group of Lipizzaners prancing about, and another might 'see' a flock of swallows darting about at twilight. But neither of these visions are objectively found in Bach's fugue; he did not intend them, and neither can they be the starting point for any criticism. Similarly, one viewer might stubbornly insist on seeing a stained-glass window in Piet Mondrian's *Composition in Red, Yellow, Blue, and White* and another the grid-like map of city streets, but neither image is anywhere else than in the mind of the subjective beholder. Mondrian's non-representational canvas is simply what it claims to be: a visual composition in various colours (actually more than the four mentioned in the title), and criticism of the canvas as a work of art cannot pass beyond matters of colour, line, volume, and shape. It is 'absolute' painting.

In the same way, *Tefil* is, or seems to approach, 'absolute' writing. We cannot be sure if anything in the novel is objectively real, beginning with the eponymous hero himself. Remember the importance of considering the source. Tefil, the conman out 'in search of boobies', invites us to call him a liar. We should trust him only as far as we can throw him. He uses his pathological mother, who, by his own admission, had the most influence on him,[13] to enunciate his relativistic approach to reality and its communication to others:

....

[13] 'I also had a mother. I remember her, not like you... She could gripe like nobody's business. She had such a talent for griping that she could go on for hours. And how! I get that from her... That's the only trait of mine I like.'

CHARLES S. KRASZEWSKI

To deceive, to delude, to poison, and to give antidotes in proof of goodness. It's best to go stupid and make others stupid… And to take a beautiful park alley amidst the songs of skylarks beneath a blue sky, in the aroma of flowers and perfumes… One technique.

How are we to know when such a person is telling us the 'truth', or 'deluding and poisoning' us? To make matters worse, we can't even trust the narrator of the novel, whose voice intrudes on Tefil's monologue from time to time, in order to set the surroundings of his blather in the concrete reality of a forenoon-afternoon in Litental:

Tefil tried to button his blazer because a cool wind suddenly blew up. Unfortunately, there wasn't a single button to be found on his blazer, so he buttoned his trench coat. Rozmaryn was standing right next to Tefil, to his left. So close that he probably caught the odour of the older, balding man.
[…]
Then, walking alongside the little park, they slowed down. Tefil half-closed his eyes, probably because the sun was so strong.

'Probably'? What's with these 'probablies'? Does the third-person narrator not know whether or not Rozmaryn's olfactory nerve was affected by the proximity of Tefil's body? Does he not know why Tefil half-closes his eyes, and can only assume it was on account of the bright sunlight? The lack of an omniscient third-person narrator only further complicates the uncertainties facing the reader in search of something firm to grip onto. Reading *Tefil* with the intent of arriving at some objectively truth-based interpretation is like trying to cross a river by hopping on styrofoam rocks.

Neither Litental nor Tutberg exist. They are fictive places, behind which may exist some real locality from the Kujawy region of Poland known to the author, just like Hardy's Casterbridge is a fictional town, beneath which the real Dorchester's heart beats. But in any novel of Thomas Hardy's, the reader can wilfully suspend disbelief and enter into the believable, trustworthy, fictional reality of the story. Not so with Wojasiński's *Tefil.* Consider this third-person description of Rozmaryn sitting across the table from Tefil in the 'famous restaurant':

> The colours of the rainbow appeared on the little panes of the windows on the door of the famous restaurant. Rozmaryn felt as if he were floating off somewhere. From the dark corners of his mind and memory some images came to him: a lake, a boat, and a forest on a hill past the lake. They penetrated the narrow veins and passageways of his brain. Recollections. Revelations of memory. And yet too weak to be grasped.

Here the narrator, whether omniscient or not, tells us something concrete. He categorically states that images from his memory: 'a lake, a boat, and a forest on a hill past the lake', pass through Rozmaryn's mind. Then, the scene shifts outward, and it is Tefil speaking: 'What were you dreaming of, sir, when you were pouring out the vodka? I noticed the expression on your face... Of little waves breaking on a beach, right?' What? How did he know that? As far as the reader knows (and the reader can't make any suppositions as to what happened in the fictional world of the characters before the book began, what conversations they may have had) Rozmaryn never told Tefil about that lake. He drifted off here, his eyes going glassy. Not only can't he communicate with Tefil (according to what we know of parallel beings), he wasn't even trying to. And so Tefil read his mind?

CHARLES S. KRASZEWSKI

We never hear Rozmaryn say a word in the novel. We see how he reacts to outward situations and people; through the narrator, as here, we are from time to time privy to his thoughts and emotions. But he never takes voice – at least we never hear him do so, though Tefil sometimes reacts as if to a comment of his companion's – and so we never hear him relating that memory of the lake to Tefil, or anyone else. And yet, a little further on in the novel:

> And again you've got that lake in your head. It's getting tiresome – said Tefil. – I can tell from the expression on your face. Constantly the sound of those waves (I hear it too), tensing. And that smell of water that invades the lungs. There's some hidden violence in all that. [...] And. I've got it just like you, sir. Nothing else. I see the same thing in my head. Enough! Enough already! Cut it out, sir! Are you incapable, sir, of cutting it out? You're disrupting! You're disrupting, sir! Stop disrupting, sir! Enough already! I say enough! Cut it out with that beautiful lake of yours!

How can this be? There seem to be only two possibilities here. One, that Tefil is a mindreader, which must be discounted from the get-go by anyone – I reckon the majority of real human beings – who doesn't really believe in telepathy. Two – that Tefil and Rozmaryn are one and the same person. That Tefil is creating Rozmaryn, or Rozmaryn Tefil, or that Tefil (or Rozmaryn?) is the narrator of the story he's making up – that there is only one voice in the entire novel. This is not as far-fetched as it sounds, considering the 'end of the world' speech, which Tefil imagines being delivered by the woman behind the counter in the butcher's shop, in which he refers to himself – Tefil – in the third person, speaking in the voice of the tired and lonely hawker of animal flesh. If he creates that narrative, what's to say he hasn't created the whole show?

Curiously, for a writer like Wojasiński, who confesses himself to be under the spell of Pessoa, nearly all the characters in *Tefil* speak with the same voice. Consider the following passage:

> Well, what'll it be? Two beers? What else? Coming right up, young man. Laws of nature. Have you made the sign of the Cross today, sir? Have you lifted aloft any petitions? Can I be the answer to your prayers, sir? How does it go with you, as far as religion is concerned? And what about your loyalty? Are you faithful from time to time? And what about your ideological beliefs? Your roots? What sort of roots do you have, sir? Do you believe in anything at all? Do you hope, sir? Are you accompanied by such an ubiquitous, never-ending hope, such as is born from the nearness of bodies? Art thou fruitful, dost thou multiply, sir? Will you take up the question? What is it that you've lost?

That barrage of questions, that inveterate list-making, that semi-sarcastic tone – that sounds just like Tefil. And yet it's not. It is Amelia, the pulchritudinous waitress addressing Rozmaryn, pouncing upon him in the same smart-alecky fashion as does the balding parasite. And again:

> Outside, life seemed a little bit lighter and cleaner. There was a hope, that if you kept on looking like that, there'd be more, more of something after all. A sliver, a millimetre, a second more. He was engulfed by a fragment of the area that could be seen only through the window. An image. Not the whole, but a clipping. A clipping. A piece of life, a piece of the world. Not a whole. Not everything. A tiny little part. The joy of existence. A scrap of what is true and irrefutable. You can't touch the whole, you can only touch thighs, breasts, knees, elbows, cheeks, a belly,

an eye, a mouth. You can touch a piece of bark, but not the whole tree; you can catch sight of several thousand stars, but not all of them. The whole cannot be sniffed nor tasted. Pork chop has a smell, as does a violet. Sweat has a taste; toast, cheesecake, and coffee. The whole falsifies, kills, terminates. The theory of everything. The theory of the whole. The Left. The Right. Ecology, Vegetarianism. Carnivorousness. God. The lack of God. God in the lack of God. In God the lack of God. One speech, two speech.

Tefil? No – the narrator this time, going on in the same style of the character he (we assume) has created, all the way down to that characteristic Doctor Seuss-like 'one speech, two speech', redolent of Tefil's belaboured traipsing up and down the stairs: 'one foot, two foot, handrail, pause'.

The cold of the water penetrated deeper and deeper into Rozmaryn's body. It helped him to come into contact with himself. With that unclear mixture in which he searched out his soul and the extraordinariness of the phenomenon of what was supposed to be his mind. Fiasco. Counterfeiting. The falsification of sausage, of thought, of activity, and the values of real estate. Fi. As. Co. And yet the coolness cleansed him. Cleansing, eliminating, burning down. Beginning.

Here again the narrator, and here again the exact same diction as Tefil's, all the way through his characteristic manner of emphasising ideas through syllabised pauses and his repetition of his favourite term 'beginning' (so suggestive of the nihilistic idea of the eternal return of the same).

Where does the narrator end and Tefil begin? Where does the narrator, or Tefil, end, and Rozmaryn, or Amelia, begin? In this stylistic non-differentiation we have a negative image of Wojasiński's aforementioned favourite author.

Whereas Pessoa was one man capable of creating a myriad of voices in constant interaction with one another, fake authors created by one man, Wojasiński creates three, or four characters (Tefil, Rozmaryn, Amelia, Narrator) all of whom speak in an identical voice. It is as if he wished to underscore the basic identity of all reality – we recall here Tefil's musings on metempsychosis when sniffing the cap he'd inherited from one of his dead neighbours – a reduction of all things and all persons to the very basic, atomic or molecular level of sameness. Despite the fact that, soon after this, Tefil confesses his terror of sameness – his fear that 'someday somebody will get into power who will want the whole world of people to be beautiful so that beauty should triumph.' That terrifies him, but reduction of all to a level deeper than ugliness: bland molecules, makes him ecstatic. And again, perhaps, although the most fruitful way of reading this novel is through the prism of language – Wojasiński's linguistic games – it would be no strange thing for me if the reader were to confess to being terrified him- or herself upon finishing the book, and setting it aside in unease.

TEFIL'S TUNNEL,
OR THE INESCAPABILITY OF SENSE

How then, do we deal with 'absolute' art? There is bald description of the object, such as we find in Ronald Alley's note concerning the Tate's purchase of Mondrian's *Composition* referred to above:

Painted during the period of De Stijl, the composition consists of a square divided up into a number of coloured rectangles of different sizes, like slabs of colour. Instead of the white and black and pure primary hues of his later work, the whole picture has a subdued, silvery tonality, with smoky yellows, pinkish reds, blues, greys, and black.[14]

There is also the more ambitious contextual study of Jack H. Williamson, who sets the non-representational painting against the background of the use of grids in art, from the late middle ages until the twentieth century:

> By 1920, Mondrian's pictorial vocabulary is established and consists of a white field through which travel continuous black horizontal and vertical bars that bound intermittently occurring rectangular zones of primary colour. The composition still implicitly extends beyond the borders of the canvas, and (according to Mondrian) the bars cross one another and overlap, but do not actually intersect.
>
> The resulting grid is of the line-based type and is thoroughly Cartesian in its presentation of an unchanging regular and isotropic universal field, ruled by logic and by the mathematical law that underlies the world of external appearance.[15]

While Williamson does not 'read into' the canvas any object that the artist did not intend to put there, and concentrates entirely on the abstract content of the artwork: volume, colour, shape, and line, he quite legitimately sets the physical design of Mondrian's grid within the context of the significance of grids in general. Such things do not exist spontaneously in nature. They are an invention of the rational hu-

....

[14] Ronald Alley, 'Mondrian's "Composition in Grey, Red, Yellow and Blue", 1920 (Tate Gallery)', *The Burlington Magazine*, Vol. 110, No. 781 (1968), 216–217 (p. 216).

[15] Jack H. Williamson, 'The Grid: History, Use, and Meaning', *Design Issues*, Vol. 3, No. 2 (1986), 15–30 (p. 22).

man mind, attracted to the idea of order, and represent man's comprehension of the orderliness to be found in creation.

Likewise, although we insist that the only legitimate manner of interpreting an abstract work of literary art like Rafał Wojasiński's *Tefil* is through a consideration of its stylistic bones, we too are called upon to study what the employment and arrangement of those bones signifies.

Just as Mondrian makes use of line, volume, and colour in order to comment, however subtly, on the cosmos we hold in common – the 'tunnel' in which we are all trapped, to use Tefil's own vocabulary – so does Wojasiński, or Tefil, make use of language in order to suggest some interpretation of his (or their) own concerning our reality. We have already noted the main character's distrust of the meaning-bearing capability of language, which is to such an extent profound as to exclude even texts generally accepted as the summits of human linguistic art:

> You can spend the night in the one little hotel here. Above the prewar cinema. A little hortello-bordello. My friend liked that rhyme, Rozmaryn, sir. Liked it better than Dante and Shakespeare, better than all phrases and descriptives known from literature, philosophy, and theology. He liked it, but he wasn't in awe of it. Maybe he liked petty things more than grand things. He liked the little flings of life? All that is grand is tiresome. And untrue to life.

Whatever Tefil means by 'truth', as we have heard him say before, it cannot be captured in speech. All speech, no mater how well intended, is falsification, counterfeiting:

> Language. The word 'stone' does not name the stone. The word 'roof' does not name the roof. The word 'Marynia' does not name Marynia. The word 'Prodige' does not name my dog. Counterfeiting. Falsification. Falsehood.

[...] There isn't a single good name. That's why I'm not satisfied with one single thought of this world, why language has never satisfied me. The barking of a dog satisfied me, the chirping of a sparrow, the snorting of pigs, the rustle of the wind and the little waves on the lake.

In an interview from 2020, when Wojasiński was working on this novel, he had this to say about language and its skewed relation to reality:

Justice is by definition absurd, because we are born into a world of unjust conditions. One person is born in a place where he has no chances for anything at all, another is born impaired, with genetic disorders, and another is born completely healthy. One is born with only three days to live, and will die without a language, without learning a single word. For this reason, instead of searching for justice, one should start with the assumption that the world has no human sense and doesn't need any. Because sense is associated with our language, and sometimes it stifles us, makes dangerous confessors of us.[16]

This interview was taking place on a walk near a famous institution for the blind, founded near Warsaw by the Blessed Elżbieta Czacka, a philanthropist and Franciscan nun. At one point, Wojasiński points out a large building on the grounds, and in response to the interviewer's question 'What is it?' he replies:

....

[16]   Marcin Kube, 'Rafał Wojasiński: Pogrzeby prawdziwsze niż we-sela', *Plus Minus*, 30 October 2020 <https://www.rp.pl/plus-minus/art8775211-rafal-wojasinski-pogrzeby-prawdziwsze-niz-wesela> [accessed 13 May 2024]

It's an institution for children who are deaf, dumb, and blind. The only contact they have with the world is through the sense of touch. And now here's the question: how can you communicate anything to a person like that, how can you teach him language, communication?

– *Is it possible?*

Whenever I find myself passing this place I think how little word and language is worth. For those children can't see, they can't hear, and they can't speak, and yet they're alive. In the face of the lack of these senses the word seems a faulty and secondary tool. And I arrive at the conclusion that, instead of helping us develop, language sets up obstacles before us, blocks us.

– *Surprising words, coming from a writer.*

Language is a fairly primitive tool, which chiefly aid us to pretend.[17]

Such being the case, Tefil, who, it should be pointed out, is both aware of the falsifying nature of language and glad to make use of the same, if it means a free meal, would like to be 'liberated' from language. In his rejection of verbal culture, which is tantamount to a rejection of all human culture, he would like to enter the world of pure reality, to be able to perceive, contact, and perhaps even produce 'real' sounds devoid of human meaning, yet fully expressive of the otherwise inexpressible meaning of existence:

Not a single sentence worth remembering will be left behind after humanity's gone. Mediocrity denuded. And yet the more these streets, blocks of flats, cemeteries, and the pastry shop in Litental hold on to me, the more certain I am that I shall finally emerge from all words. Each day,

....

[17] Ibid.

the walls of the buildings reconcile me to existence. The cup in the pastry shop, the oaken counter in the clothing store which remembers the hands of those that no one will ever recall by name anymore – all of this liberates me from language, from counterfeiting. From this it's easy to see that everything beyond Lithental is a squalid hole.

This, however – going beyond speech to some imagined, essential reality – is impossible to him or any other human, even though he, somewhat aspirationally, defines himself being 'what precedes humanity, not quite human yet'. It would be better to have been born a swine, to say nothing of a mushroom: 'I'm born. Well born. Almost in a sty. Chrum. Chrum. Chrum,' for the grunts of a pig are nothing more than the grunts of a pig – to the rationalistic, almost eighteenth-century mind of Tefil, completely devoid of expressive meaning, or, if expressive of anything, then expressive of the most basic passions and yearnings: fear, the sexual drive, anger, hunger, and thus much closer to 'reality' than those verbose windbags Shakespeare and Dante. This is why Tefil reminisces so fondly upon that childhood experience of 'absorbing' the foul-mouthed language of his next-door neighbour, which impressed him to such an extent that, in one of the only occurrences of the absorptive child squeezing something out of his sponge, he began to imitate her:

Then I cursed a blue streak myself for three days without pause. I used no other words. I did that when I was alone, in the barn or in the garden. And suddenly... I lost the power of speech. I stood there in front of the apple tree, dumb, and just stared out in front of me. No mistake. Not a single error. And then everything returned. Complete sentences. Grammatical clarity. The eternal, intractable, overwhelming, and pitiless forging of the truth. Rubbish. Rub. Bish.

He experiences the loss of speech – that is, the loss of communicability through the reduction of human speech to the saltiest of imprecations, disjointed swear-words with little more expressive potential than the grunting of a swine – not as a deprivation, but a liberation into some sort of freedom from interpretation, a communion with basic existence. Little Tefil becomes intellectually catatonic, as it were, a comatose person who can yet see, hear, smell, feel, and taste his surroundings. It is when 'everything returns' – the order of language, that 'net cast over the world' to use George Steiner's eloquent phrase[18] – that Tefil experiences a letdown. 'Grammatical clarity' returns, and with it, the 'forging of the truth', i.e. counterfeiting, i.e. 'rubbish'.

Tefil's distrust of language might be a result of pathology. At least twice in the book he describes himself in a way that leads the reader to wonder if he is not dyslexic:

> I grab a book and read. Though I don't understand a thing, because the letters mix around for me. You know, sir, 'e' mixes up with 'a', 'p' with 'b', 't' with 'l', and even 'k' with 'r', 'u' with 'a', 'p' with 'o', 's' with 'w', 'a' with 'x', 't' with 'l'.

Yet, considering the fact that he does read, after all – he has mastered (and rejected) Descartes, is aware of the great masters of the literary art he so hates, and even betrays a familiarity with Italian, this might be mystification too, one more red herring, and we must ask ourselves: is this 'true' what he's saying, or is he merely putting us on?

Once more, as an adult, and quite recently (as he refers to the experience as having taken place in his garret flat),

....

[18]   See the introduction to his *Penguin Book of Modern Verse Translation* (London: Penguin, 1966), or the magnificent *After Babel* (Oxford: Oxford University Press, 1981), which grew out of it – especially pp. 88–89.

Tefil undergoes a quasi-mystical elevation (or depression) into aphasia:

> Now, while I was sitting in that tub, I got very sleepy (maybe from the warm water), so sleepy that I seemed to be going unconscious. These sounds started seeping into my head, piercing it as if they were passing through cotton. They reminded me of individual syllables, and slowly they were transformed into something like words, but I couldn't understand them. All those sounds seemed so foreign to me, in my language, in Polish, but foreign, as if Polish had become a foreign language to me, completely incomprehensible. Purpossied, pwoysonnt, streeetifuld, shugcottony, brundchisy, dumisile, mournituble, lur, bg, blnkeet. Not a single Polish word in Polish. Everything in Polish but in a foreign language. I couldn't understand Polish anymore. Nothing. I don't remember when I heaved my wet backside out of the tub and fell into a deep sleep. And.

It is a moot question whether we are to pity Tefil in this state of his. It is curious to consider whether these episodes of aphasia, especially those of his adult years, are something intentionally triggered by the 'sufferer', or visited upon him by something he cannot control. The important thing for most readers, struggling with what to think of Wojasiński's Tefil, what to do with the 'interpretation' of our human reality that this backwater oracle offers us, is what he does with language when he is fully conscious. The most shocking example of a conscious deformation of language occurs at the end of the book. Tefil leads Rozmaryn into the abandoned Lutheran church (an eloquent symbol indeed, if *Tefil* is supposed to be a comment on spiritualia), where he takes his place in the deconsecrated apse, in front of the traces of the crucifix which no longer hangs on the wall behind him, and begins a travesty of the Mass:

Through the mystery... And...
Blessed are you... And...
Accept these... And...
Wash away... And...
Pray now... And...
Lift up... And...
We give you thanks... And...
It is truly... And...
It is truly... And...
Therefore... And...
Bless these offerings... And...
So that they become... And...
He... And...
Took bread... And...
Take this and eat... And...
Similarly... And...
Take this and drink... And...

This is no devaluation of Shakespeare or Dante. This is a travesty of something that, for many people, is the most sacred text ever conceived: the canon of the Mass, during which, through the agency of the priest, Christ Himself becomes physically present in the consecrated elements.

Now, in the end, as much as Tefil would like to attain the expressibility, or non-expressibility, of 'pure' nature — those sparrows or swine — this is impossible to him, as a man. And what he expresses, how he expresses himself in his fervour to deprive expression of meaning, is significant in and of itself, and open to our interpretation. And what we find here is that Tefil is not as innocent as he would like to have us see him. He's not simply an easy-going mystical layabout, 'absorbing' the world and singing its praises. He is an agent of decay, deforming language; his processing of reality, which he cannot avoid, is not creative, it is destructive. He does not build, he breaks down. In a word, Tefil is a mushroom, Tefil is mould, the rot that consumes everything. And if that's the sort of life that will outlive us all, you, me, and the shopgirl on her petty Patmos of the butcher's shop, this mould named Tefil — then God help us all.

Springfield, Va.
1 October 2023

TEFIL

Follow me, and let the people talk on
(Dante, *Purgatorio*, V:13).

Is it nice here? There's nothing in it – said Tefil. – One foot, two foot. Left foot, right. For a beginning. Not a metre higher, not a metre lower. Holding onto the handrail. Unpainted since forever, cold. Cold from the darkness? Going down the steps sagging from the tread of dozens of feet in shoes of different sizes. Hard soles, soft soles. Heels high and low.

I took over this flat from the chemistry teacher. She spent forty lonely years within these four walls. She lost her looks, her desire for a man, her appetite, and, finally, her life. There's a pastry shop downstairs. It remembers the days when the world was divided into Catholics, Lutherans, Calvinists, and Jews. They all had first names and last names in this town that's overgrown all other towns I've ever seen. Over all towns I've ever smelled, over the pavements of which I've wandered aimlessly.

Beginnings. Waking up every morning so that the sun might be seen, so that the cawing of the crow and the barking of the dog might be heard. The grace of incomprehension. Sitting, breathing, pulling on slippers, staring at the same things in the same old room for years upon end. Taming the cold stove in the corner, the slices of dried bread on the table, the crumbs on the floorboards, the milk bottle, and the glass unwashed of its tea stains. Beginnings. The domestication of what is dead inside us.

Yesterday I went to bed in my socks – said Tefil. – Too lazy to take them off. I only brushed my teeth. And I don't even always brush before going to bed. Ever more rarely, as a matter of fact. Ever more rarely I brush my teeth, ever more rarely I put on my pyjamas. I lay down in the shirt I've been wearing all day long. Extinction. From down below there arises the sweet and warm fragrance of the pastry shop. Can you smell it? I return to that pastry shop after each and every

RAFAŁ WOJASIŃSKI

stroll. And. And we'll eat some pastry – Tefil added as he was led down the steps by Rozmaryn.

My right leg's... bothering me somewhat. And my tailbone too. From walking down the stairs. That must mean something. That we've never had a tail grow out... What do you say to that, sir? Quiet. As the grave. You're out of breath. These differences between the species really throw me in a loop. Tail. No tail. Claws. Fingers. Eyes. No eyes. One gender. Two genders. Beauty. Lack of beauty. Beginnings. One foot, two foot. A little crouch, decline, ascent. Scratching the back. Beginnings. Stranger and friend. Danger, the end. Calculation. Miscalculation. Numbers. The God of the majority. Beginning... Choking to death on a walnut, being run over by a car, freezing to death, drowning in the lake, tripping on a high kerb. Beginning... One foot lower... one foot higher... Even when going downstairs... You've got to lift your feet. Something's in the air. From the mugginess? Mould? You smell it, sir? You're opening your mouth right wide. Short of breath? Breathe, sir, breathe, as long as you can. The smell of mould is the smell of life... Beginning.

I'm old.

Seriously now... no joking. At most a nice little walk... Nice... seriously... Achievement... Statues... One after another. The toppling, the sinking of monuments, rusting, oxidisation. Extinction... Natural loss... not a single statue... A statue to those who have fallen naturally... I want no solution... No way out... I don't want to know the way...

Beginning. One foot, two foot. Going down...

Have a look down below, sir. It's a little dark, eh?

And. I can't get pastries out of my head. I feel myself being drawn to that café on the square that still remembers forty-seven. And. Do the stairs in your building have an aroma, sir? One foot down, one foot up. You can hold on to something. Feel something. Smell something. The handrail, or you, Rozmaryn, sir. Feel. Smell. Or no. Better not. Not just now. Feel that draught? A window not fully closed? Or maybe a broken pane? I should have noticed a broken pane. Especially an old one. I don't see the new ones. I get used to the old ones; the new ones, no. I won't have anything new in my home. Maybe some fresh sausage or a new carton of milk. Sure. But a watch, a radio, an umbrella – no. For me, new means waste. New things aren't worth the trouble. They bring me misfortune. New things worry me – I worry about them getting scratched, getting broken, cracking, becoming less worthy. I prefer what's already scratched, rusty, chipped. Everything comes from something that existed before, even God. And the Big Bang. The new is just the old refurbished. Old walkabouts, old gasping, old pain in the hips. I prefer moving about at a slight shuffle rather than running; wandering the street, shuffling my feet, penetrating the wind and the alleyways between the buildings, on the lots and past the corner of Garbarska. So then, down the stairs, one foot, two foot, handrail, pause. Waiting.

Once I had a little wagon. A metal one. A neighbour of mine made it, welding it out of thick sheet metal and steel angle irons. He painted it brown – dark walnut brown. He got the wheels from an old motorbike. It was my father's before it became mine. I used it to cart potatoes from the field past the peat bog in Tutberg. I'd pile them up so high they'd be spilling off, and then I'd cart them into the courtyard, right up to the basement chute, and down they'd spill, right down onto the joined shelves waiting below. The carting of potatoes took me two weeks; with a horse and wagon I could've got it done in a day. I carted beets, carrots, apples, cinder blocks, fodder, wheat, pulp for the cows. First, the tyres went flat. One after the other. One wheel, then the other wheel. For a while, I pulled that wagon around on its naked rims. It wasn't easy; the wheels sank deep into the mud or the snow. They rattled along the road as if I were carting Death through the village, or news about the end of the world. Then I thought

RAFAŁ WOJASIŃSKI

about slicing some belts from old tyres, thick rubber ones, and stuffing my motorbike tyres with them instead of using inflated inner-tubes. Well, that worked for a bit. It was a little easier, but after a while the tyres went cockeyed, tilting left, tilting right, each one on a different skew, and that made the wagon entirely useless. So I went back to driving on the rims, and that's how it remained.

I don't know where that wagon is now, but back then it was my life-companion, a sign of presence. Cold hands and schlepping in front of it. The calming sound of the broken bearings, the echo of the clattering sheet metal sides when I'd pull the little wagon over rocks, or, on hot days, over the dry, the stone-dry ground. Not Mozart, not Bach. Rattling. I'd pause sometimes near the ditch connecting the two ponds and sit there next to the wagon, resting my back against a wheel. The rim would dig into my shoulder blade. The existence of that little wagon on its rims made me happy.

Tefil exited the building first, with young Rozmaryn tagging behind him, holding onto the long trench coat that Tefil had found in an attic cupboard. The sun blinded Rozmaryn; he lost his orientation. They walked along a wall, separated from the rest of the world by their reciprocal attachment. Suddenly, they found themselves in the pastry shop. The aroma of coffee and the conversation of two women at a table introduced a holiday sort of feeling to Rozmaryn's mood.

I've waited on you a long time, Rozmaryn, sir. And I'm so old that waiting becomes torture. I've never been a patient man anyway. Or humble, or modest – said Tefil, taking his place at a table by the window. – A double espresso, please, and apple charlotte: warm; and a Kraków cheesecake. I'll have more to order later.

Rozmaryn pushed his chair back from the table, stood up, and put his left foot out to the left, as if he were about to head in the direction of the counter, sliding his right foot somewhat under the chair. He stood like that, on widespread legs, for a bit, and only then did he set off to place the order. Then he brought the apple charlotte and the coffee back to the table on a little tray. He set the tray down on the tabletop and stood there, watching Tefil arrange the cup and the plate with the pastry. First the plate was closer to him, the cup farther off. Then it was the other way around. At last, the cup was to the left, the plate to the right. A moment of stillness, and the order was reversed once more. Cup to the right, plate to the left. A powerlessness appeared in Tefil's eyes. It was the look of a person in no condition to do anything, not the slightest thing. His chin trembled, and a coldness came into his eyes. He shut tight his lips.

What exactly was it you wanted to talk about, sir? Please, go on – about your mother? Come now, say what you want to say, but – brass tacks, please. At the moment, I'm not capable of listening to anything that's not to the point. As a matter of fact, I'm not capable of listening to anything, generally speaking – said Tefil. – If you're just going to stand there and stare like that, I'm not going to listen to anything. I'll have to go. Eat and go. Eating, talking, walking. Getting up, buttoning the jacket, clearing the throat, smacking the lips, hitching up the trousers. The most important things. Unassailable facts. Chicken soup. Eating chicken soup, let's say, on 16 February 1876 at four o'clock in the afternoon in the village of Łamięta. The essential taste, the temperature of the soup, the type of macaroni. Archaeological digs pass over all that – the taste of soup and the shape of the carrots in that soup. They say that there's already been over a hundred billion people on earth. How many of them ate chicken soup? Where and when? What happens to the essence of things when these things cease to exist? Is it all in the imagination? In the babble of nonsense left, and right? One hundred billion real persons… Like you and me, sir… You can rely on the sense of touch… The sense of smell… One hundred? Or maybe a hundred and seven? Or ninety-nine? Names, first and last names, address-

RAFAŁ WOJASIŃSKI

es, shoe sizes, height, age, gender. Information, please! Exact data. From the youngest infant to the oldest old fellow.

You and me. Unassailable, stubborn evidence of the existence of you and me. Where one lives. Circumference of the waist, gender, height, age, bank accounts. What is one hundred billion compared to your 'I' and my 'I' here, in this pastry shop, right now?

Beginnings. Go ahead sir, speak. Talk to me. Say it right now, now or never. Come on, word by word, get it all out. Open your mouth so that we can see your teeth and your tongue. Let's go. Beginnings. Speak. Get it all out, spill it. At long last, open your gob and have done with it. Starting with 'a' or with 'b', with 'c' or with 'u'. Whatever you like. Connecting first with second, third with fifth, seventh with zero. Speak, sir! Don't hold anything back. I'm waiting! And time is flying. Beat around the bush, babble, spit, lisp, mumble… Grunt, sir, squeal… Toothlessly. Straight from the shoulder. Who knows? Come on… bla, bla, bla… Ya, ya, ya, ya… Beginnings. Burying, unburying. Passing sentence. Verdicts. Death certificates, birth certificates, certified acts of mercy… The millwheels of government turn and turn… The eye of Providence never wearies… One foot, two foot… Absorption. Beginnings.

Did I know your mother? Or perhaps your grandmother? You're as old, sir, as my last pair of socks. Who was your mother? Your mother could have been my daughter, sir, or my granddaughter. Or maybe even something better… Am I supposed to keep guessing, man? Am I supposed to strain the brain, make the effort that draws me aside day after day? Lets me down…?

About your mother, your mother. I forgot my glasses. Hop off, little one, go get'em – they're on the table in my room.

Tefil veritably inhaled his apple charlotte. Presently, he began to search his pockets for something with those greasy hands of his. They moved slowly upwards, patting his stomach, caressing it somewhat, and then his fingers began rummaging, prying, slipping in between the buttons. They wandered higher, to his breasts. He pinched them, as if he were looking for something else. They went slowly still, stopped, slid down once more, apparently measuring the girth of his belly. They grabbed hold of it from below and tried to lift it upwards. When those hands began behaving somewhat more reasonably, concentrating on his sports coat, on its lower portion, Tefil noticed that two of the blazer's buttons had fallen off. When that happened, he had no way of remembering. He simply couldn't recall it happening. He knew that he'd never be able to, because recollection always leads to a full-on tensing of effort. Tension. Memory for show... Words like ground meat and fragments of images becoming a mass resembling a cutlet... Tefil ran his hand over the place where the button ought to be, exploring the hole through which that lost button ought to pass. It'd fallen away. Because of that enlarged stomach that won't let him get any closer to the table, to eat with elegance, with culture.

Meanwhile, Rozmaryn had run out into the street, rushing through the door of the building, after which he rumbled up the staircase. He was surprised at how little furniture there was in Tefil's flat. The floorboards leapt out at his eyes. They were painted over and over a deep walnut colour, with worn places at the table legs and by the chair; by the window, and beside the bed. Worn to the bare wood.

The eyeglasses lay on a cupboard covered with haphazard heaps of newspapers. The panes reflected the morning sun, and the lenses of the glasses enlarged some letters on the newsprint. Hor (illegible) pra (illegible) grip (illegible). Rozmaryn stood there, staring at the enlarged letters. Cont (illegible), sea (illegible), dar (illegible). Suddenly, he lifted his head and began rolling it on his neck, somewhat like the way a dog cocks his. He caught the scent of violets, as if in the house of a saint. There were no flowers to be seen, but the

RAFAŁ WOJASIŃSKI

aroma was coming from somewhere. First, Rozmaryn had a look inside a highly polished chest of drawers the colour of scrambled eggs. This was the same cupboard on which the pile of papers and the glasses were lying, but it had revealed itself to him anew. Ta (illegible) she (illegible) du (illegible) pre (illegible), for (illegible).

He had a look inside. A great volume of shirts, underpants, socks, and God knows what else tumbled out as soon as he opened the door. The scent swelled so overpoweringly that Rozmaryn opened the window and ran out into the stairwell. He ran downstairs with a loud rumble of feet. He pulled up at the door leading outside, hearing behind him the voice of a woman he saw from the corner of his eye. Fattish, in a frock with white dots and grey, very thick hair.

What's all that racket about? – she cried. – What're you thumpin' wid' those hoofs o' yours over our stairs? Maybe you'll be takin' your clothes off next? Who's that nut-job of a Tefil bringin' into our building now? To hell wid'im! He oughtta tumble a'ready into that grave what's been waitin' for 'im so long now! How can a body live wid a blighter like that around here? First wid' that dog so many years, and now it's one lad after another prowlin' around an' gallopin' down the stairs wid' them hoofs like draught horses! Tramplin' and treadin' down. Lemme not see you around here again, you scamp you! An' that there dog! The black one what drove ever'body balmy! Nobody'll forget that mutt! You make sure I never see you round here again!

Rozmaryn ran out into the street, but then he covered those few metres to the pastry shop at a slow, dignified pace. He was pretending to be someone else – which of course no one could notice. So he pretended to himself, which gave him joy, a more elevated sense of his own worth. He entered the pastry shop with an air of satisfaction.

Tefil was nodding off after the large dose of sugar in the coffee and the cake. He snored once, drew his right hand over his face from brow to double-chin, and turned a muddy gaze in Rozmaryn's direction.

And now a large coffee – he said. – and a cheesecake and... And. First the cheesecake. You need to know, my dear sir, Rozmaryn, that there are almost three thousand people living in this town. Go get me that cheesecake, will you? Because if even only a small percentage of those people decide to come here after work or after market – and today's a market day, you know – there'll be nothing left. Once, before the war, there were almost four thousand. There's fewer today, but that's no reason to become complacent. Not an inch backward! Or your place will be taken by someone else. Your shoes will be taken, your socks, belts, blazer, trousers, brassieres, crumbs of apple charlotte, the rust on the legs of the table in the pastry shop, the apron of the waitress. The Torah, the Koran, and the New Testament. Every thought, every word, every glance, every feeling, handshake, mathematical formula, every medicine. And.

Rozmaryn went up to the counter and asked the lady in the white apron and little cap – whom he hadn't noticed when placing the first order – for a large coffee and cheesecake for Tefil, and a cheesecake and tea for himself. He was hoping that the lady at the counter would bend over forward, because the blouse she was wearing was low-cut. And she did. Rozmaryn was in luck. He got an eyeful of almost one whole breast. He knew that, at that moment, nothing better might happen to him, all the more so in the presence of that fellow from the old chemistry teacher's flat. He returned to the table and waited for the order along with Tefil.

You're inspecting my blazer, sir? It's woollen. Wool from sheep who lived long ago, because the jacket is quite old – Tefil explained. – It was left behind by those who used to live in my flat. The chemistry teacher never threw it out. Forty years she kept it there. It was in a chest of drawers in the attic. A chest of drawers that was later brought downstairs to my room. No. It was a completely different chest of drawers. An exchange of chests of drawers. One of them burnt up for sure in the courtyard during a bout of evening merrymaking. I'm not sure what everybody was so happy about. I stood there, close enough to see the fire and the people lit up by the fire. It was early spring. Beginnings. Echoed voices: ha, ha, ha, ha, hee, hee, hee, hee, aaaa, uuuu, oooo, o Jesus, eh, stop whimpering, here, heel, one, one more, give that here, let that alone. The chest of drawers in flames. It was standing in the middle of the courtyard. The doors were open. All in flames. But the centre was black, an abyss sucking and sucked in turn by the beginning. The beginning consumed the chest of drawers. Every sound that was there, every voice, movement, every memory. Consuming. Chmmmmmmmmm... Aaaaach.

Cleaning up. It has to be clean, my mother used to say. Clean, in every corner, every cupboard. Cleaning, scouring, place after place. Patrolling and checking to see that not a trace of dust remained. Not a speck because then it'll be easier, everything'll come easier, each minute will pass by easier. My mother's head shining in an areole of cigarette smoke. It's got to be clean. She'd toss her fag into the coal scuttle, and then the place was entirely spic-and-span. All that remained was the fading aroma of tobacco. Beginning. Each and every time I have to descend the stairs and go back up, one foot up and one foot down, feeling up the handrail in the dark stairwell. I'm rooted there, fixed, and next to me plates are fixed, spoons, the chair, the table, the basin, and the bed. The moon – fixed; fixed the sun and the crosses on the churches Catholic and Lutheran. The poplar fixed by the bend of the road leading to the health centre and the fountain in the park.

It's got to be clean, my mother would say, and I'd sit there next to the coal scuttle while the bent fag lay snuffed on the briquettes. The flames were leaping in the kitchen, the light from the stove lids spread over the ceiling in mobile patterns. The fire dancing lively patterns on the ceiling in the kitchen of the Lutheran cantor, who lived there before us.

Step by step. Beginning. Going down the stairs in the block of flats that was standing in Litental already back in 1876. Step by step, dragging on up, crawling. Going down.

Tefil shifted back in his chair a bit. His stomach changed its shape. Rozmaryn watched him and listened, but he didn't know what he was hearing because Tefil constantly shifted his topic, always talking about something completely different from what had just gone before. You couldn't tell where something ended, and where something new began, where the middle was, the beginning, the end. The ending of the unending. The lunatic!, thought Rozmaryn. He's just a complete lunatic. A bonehead. But he couldn't tear himself away from Tefil's talking, from those endless beginnings. And it seemed to Rozmaryn that he also began again each time Tefil did. Was it a beginning to listen again? What was the beginning? What?

This cheesecake is miraculous! Tefil said, interrupting himself.

That hag from downstairs was screaming bloody murder. I heard her, but I didn't run to your rescue, sir. I don't know how to run. Running bores me from the break of day. I wouldn't run even if you gave me a thousand dollars. People run, but they don't survive. They're unable to. They vanish. Nobody knows how to survive. They run, build houses, drive, make visits, think up new engines, but they don't know how to survive. They die in the woods, in

RAFAŁ WOJASIŃSKI

houses, in hospitals, wherever it befalls them, they fall into the water, into wells... They die in dugouts, on crossroads, in utility tunnels... Beneath the wheels of cars, bicycles, motorcycles, under the hooves of horses... At the front... Wherever it befalls. Mass. Dying. One hundred fifty five thousand every day. Fifty six million five hundred seventy five thousand every year. Coffins are a growth industry. And there'll be more and more of us dying because there's more being born. Mass extinction. And that old hag screaming a blue streak, as always. That's how it goes. Some people don't do anything but scream. At everything. They take care of everything with a bellow. They don't know how to do anything else.

I heard her voice. I'd recognise it anywhere. It's a woman's voice, supposedly; one that loved in her youth as only one can love in one's youth 'cos then you have a different body, differently made, made of something else, but that screech of hers, why, it tears my head off – thus it is in my old age, and hers. She shouts like that because she's discovered nothing else all her life long, just like you, sir, and me. It's a wonder that I don't screech like that, left and right.

She says that I'm always bringing up boys for myself. Don't listen to her. It's entirely untrue. I don't bring up any of them, not a single one. It's true the young vicar comes by, but then again, so does the rector of the parish. We argue about theology, long into the night. And I have to say, he always loses. It's an ongoing discussion. A theological matter, yes. We're constantly returning to the same thing. Life can't be tampered into another form. You can change your sex, but, for now, you can't change your species... Yes, we've got to tread water, my dear sir, Rozmaryn, on this level. But I believe in myself, in the vicar, and in the rector. And I'm certain that, someday, in this discussion of ours, we'll soar far away. We'll rise above the wonderful roofs of Litental and reconcile the irreconcilable. We shall find solutions such as overthrow all patterns heretofore acknowledged as true, and arrive at the place where zero becomes incarnate in the mystery of beginning...

Tefil arose suddenly as if in response to an irresistible command. Carefully, he peeled off his sandy-coloured overcoat and hung it up on the back of the nearby chair. The one to his right. The window was at his left. He undid the button of his blazer, the last one remaining on him, and liberated that stomach of his restrained by his shirt, which stretched open somewhat in the region of the navel, uncovering for all to see a little clutch of grey black curly hairs. It was those hairs that caught Rozmaryn's attention. He knew in a flash that he would remember them for years to come. Perhaps until death itself? Rozmaryn was fascinated, always, by the human body. Unwittingly, as it were, beyond the participation of reason and will, so, unwillingly, naturally, divinely. Once, in a changing room, he caught sight of the *mons Veneris* of a woman trying on a bathing suit. That image gripped him for a dozen years at least. Things like that don't just evaporate. Your faith can evaporate; doubts concerning emotions and revealed truths, these can vanish; sense and hope can fade away; identity can disperse like air respired; personality can fall away, and historical memory submit to the sclerosis of hardened arteries, but images of body parts, especially intimate body parts, those never vanish. Perhaps this is the sole mystery of the soul. The *mons Veneris*. That other summit.

Rozmaryn undid the button at his throat for he'd gone a little weak.

'You're not eating?' Tefil asked. 'It's really splendid, little one. Delicious cheesecake. And this weather, ah, that lends beauty to the world, ever more beauty, even to people. Here – have a look at them through the window, out on the pavement there, which I polish as well, year after year, in other people's shoes. It's all important to me, I take it all in… I don't go about in new clothes, I take in the clothes of other people. Sometimes I don't even know where they come from, but sometimes from the concrete dead. Sometimes I go to visit the graves of people wearing the very same clothes they wore. Acceptance. Taking in. I talk to them as if they were alive.

I go there out of boredom. Or for a breath of fresh air, to make a quick turn off the main street, although I always turn right back onto it – 'cos I'm unable to leave the town. The people hereabout know that I take in the things left behind by the dead (except underwear and shirts – these I get from the church charity bins). And they give me them gladly. Sometimes almost ceremoniously. Widows give me the blazers left behind by their husbands, their suits and trousers. People simply push their old clothes into my hands. When they see me on the street wearing them, they smile. After all, when an old blazer comes walking down the street, it's like its owner didn't really wholly die. A well-respected widow knows this blazer. She's familiar with the feel of the material; she's sewn on a button or two. And so they watch me walking about in the overcoat left behind by Granddad, Daddy, or their son (I don't wear women's clothing, although there was this blouse once, with a collar, that really suited me). They stare at me as if I'd arrived from another world. As if I were evidence of the fact that life can go on after death. A shitty sort of evidence, but evidence nonetheless.

All of civilisation is made up of just such evidence. Everything we have is a hand-me-down… Reason, wisdom, faith. I collect things from the dead out of love… Nobody else in our town does that. And, most likely, it won't become a tradition. It will die out along with me. Swallowed by the mysterious and benevolent transformations that take place underground. Overpowered. Incapacitated.

I simply can't keep myself away from the clothes of the dead. They call to me, they domesticate the dead element within me. I have some trousers, sir, which have been living with me now for thirty years. Their owner is now nothing but white bones, but I simply can't part from these pants. And they still fit me. I'm getting fatter, and yet they somehow keep on fitting. The purchasing of clothes at the rate at which it goes on today indicates some sort of mental decline.

Dressing myself up in the clothes of the dead provides me with a feeling of security such as I don't get from money or from living people. People deprive me of a sense of security; they arrive and they deprive, they threaten me with their needs, their wisdom; they threaten me with the truth they're constantly and deliriously searching for; they knacker me with their terroristic need to succeed, to lengthen their days, to take care of their health, their foresight; they do me to death with their saving and scrimping life, all on behalf of death. The clothes of the dead comfort me, cuddle, me, defend me from the world of evil spirits like talismans. Wearing them, I feel like I'm in the right place. Where I belong. I take somebody's blazer, and I become fulfilment itself. I can flash along Garbarska of an evening as if I weren't there at all. I can turn right or left. And in this way I arrive at the joy which surpasseth all understanding.

I'm very taken with the fact that I can exist only in this town, in the clothes of the dead, with no possibility of exiting the labyrinth which is made up of the streets of Litental. I never leave here; leaving would mean abandoning the only possibility that I possess. The lack of leaving Litental. This more than anything gives direction to my life. It suffuses my meditations on the beauty of the sky, the wind, the scent of the pavements following a rain, lonely walks in the evening, the dimly lit groceries and clothing stores, stairwells and yards where you can find objects no longer needed cast away. Nothing fills me with such hope as castaways, abandoned things. A hope I am unable to share with others.

I don't want to leave here. Life beyond this town means annihilation. Past this annihilation lies The Battle. And fighting bores me, destroys my mind, destroys my 'me', destroys everything good in me. Fighting puts to death everything I've ever loved, whatever I could love. Fighting is treason. We've become mean, average, because without fighting we no longer know how to survive the next years that await us; we're average, bland, because we must do each other to death.

Existence beyond this town would be an unbearable torment for me. I'd fall into a cycle of still more profound illusions, counterfeits, and fakes. The reality of existence beyond this town would deprive me of my reason. Litental is my only path through life. Everywhere beyond Litental is unbearably repulsive provinciality. I'll never leave Litental.

This is your first time in our town, sir?

I know that man you were speaking of. That physician. He didn't only heal you, sir. He healed me as well. And then he healed himself. Unfortunately, he died. Just like that. He departed, as one says. One also talks about 'decease'. I have no favourite monicker. Perhaps 'shutting down'. People don't know how to survive. It's so mystical. Cosmic, almost, hovering high above the summits... The decease of an ant and a man, of a mouse and a grasshopper, of a daisy and a dog... I'm missing something here. Missing something... You feel it too, sir? Something's missing here.

Definitely. What's missing here, since everything is here, everything necessary for it to go on somehow, one foot in front of another, limping along, actually? But something's missing here for sure. The decease of a swine and a rabbit, of a grey crow and a louse, the decease of a bee and a human worm. I'm missing an element. There's a lack of one stain of blue on the little wing of a butterfly. A certain lack. Maybe that's why I carry out my activities, so as to supply the element that's lacking...

My fleecy rubber boots are chafing me. I cut them short. Bad idea. Stupid. I got those boots from an elementary school cafeteria cook. She brought them to me one spring afternoon, a few months after the death of her son. That Christmas, her son got up from the table, leaving his beets on his plate along with a third of his schnitzel, a spoonful of potatoes, and went off to the shed. And there he hanged himself from a beam. She stood there in my little garret and told me the whole story, point by point, holding those boots in her left hand. It was sudden, he got up just like that, in the middle of a conversation, well, actually not in the middle because we hadn't really even started talking yet, he got up and went out, leaving his fork on the tablecloth, his knife on the plate, I was lookin' at that food on his plate and I knew, I knew that something's not right, but I didn't follow him out. I sat there, eatin' and starin' at that plate. And I got worried. First that the food would get cold, but then I thought he's an adult I'm not gonna constantly flit there at his elbow tellin' him what he's gotta do, he's a free person, a grown man, mature, so I'm gonna tell him not to do – what? I can't follow him like that, I gotta give him that space of freedom, that personal space like they say, everybody's got a right to be free on this earth...

An' I was even proud of myself that I'm givin' him freedom like that, such a great freedom that I was even lettin' his dinner get cold. I conquered my urge and didn't go, the dinner was gettin' cold, so what?, I can take it. And I waited an hour, two hours, and I'm thinkin' he's wandering about the woods somewhere, he's a free man, he's gone off to that abandoned forester's shack where he liked to sit for hours on end, he's lookin' up at the sky, delighted with the winter and the meadows there in the woods he was always so de-

RAFAŁ WOJASIŃSKI

lighted with. He chiefly delighted in wide-spreading fields, the sky, the forest, and that abandoned forester's shack. As a matter of fact, that's the only thing that delighted him in life... He loved that, and I loved myself for permittin' him such freedom that he could pick himself up and go and experience delight, freedom, beauty. I was happy then. For the very last time.

I don't believe in happiness. Or in freedom. Never did. I don't know why I was tempted that way: to be happy, to allow the child I loved above all things so much freedom... Why was I so stupid as to wish for happiness? So these boots here are only three years old. You'll have 'em forever an' ever amen, sir, 'cos you don't work in the fields...

She threw the boots down on the floor and left. She slammed the door so hard that a chip of paint flew off the frames. At first, I walked about in those felt-lined rubber boots outside in the yard, treading through mud and puddle, but something didn't quite fit, bothered me, it seemed as if it was harder for me to breathe, that I was losing my balance and was about to fall into some kind of chasm. And I felt the temptation... I felt the temptation, and I sliced them short right above the ankle, each at a different height, unevenly. That was wrong. Really stupid. After all, when they were whole, they slipped onto my feet easily enough, no sharp edges to chafe to blood. Why did I do it? I reckon I'm full stupid in the head. I wanted to make something better? But those short-cut fleece-lined rubber boots have now been serving me almost twenty-two years.

I'm not justifying myself, Rozmaryn, my dear sir. Never! I'm only telling you this so you wouldn't jump to any conclusions, get any ideas. I think that I'm stupid. Really. Stupid! Are you stupid too, sir? Who else is stupid? Let'm admit it; let'm stand up and say it loud: I'm dumb and proud. Nobody has anything wise to offer, anything wise to confess to.

Why did I cut short those felt-lined rubber boots? Maybe I was taking revenge for my lack of talent. If I'd had any talent, or if I believed in God, maybe I wouldn't have done it? But I do believe in God. With premeditation. It's just that the word 'God' is a mistake. And maybe that's why I cut short the boots. Because of that mistaken word. And maybe that's why I've oriented my life around Prodige, rather than any higher power. The great discovery of my life is a dog. My bitch Prodige, who is now in a black hole at the foot of a tree in my yard in Litental.

No, I don't taste any bitterness, any acidity. I'm quite satisfied with the coffee. Frequently, it's satisfaction that overtops all other experiences in me. Maybe if I'd lived in another town, slaving my way to an old-age pension in another place, maybe then I would taste it. But I love Litental. So I don't taste any bitterness.

And. I've ruminated on this often, if my life would be better if I had a lot of money. Of course, it would. But I don't know if I'd be eating anything else besides this cheesecake in this pastry shop in this city. There are so many people who can still buy me cheesecake. It seems to me that there's still a lot of such folk left here and there, hiding in odd corners and not yet revealing themselves. But they'll show up and treat me. O! Oooooo. And. And... and I've got a pain in the side. I went out to the dog in the evening in my trunks and a thin shirt. I didn't want to take the trouble of getting dressed.

Beginnings. Absorption. The painful hip, the tottering to this side and that, the stooping. The itch that comes from within the legs. The pain in the hips when sitting down and when getting up. Bloat and shortness of breath. Going out to the dog when it's cold and the wind is at your back. Dry dogfood on a plastic pizza plate. There was no bowl. It got lost in the darkness somewhere near the shed. Prodige would scatter that dry dogfood all over the yard,

RAFAŁ WOJASIŃSKI

the stairs, the environs of the shed, tugging around with her that plastic pizza plate. She didn't eat any of it, she just scattered it. And I'm watching her do that and I say: Stop it, stop that, stupid. What're you doing? It's so cold and here you are scattering, not eating; eat, don't scatter. And so on. And on. And so.

Rozmaryn finished his cheesecake. He even cleaned up the crumbs from his plate. Every now and then he wiped his lips with a napkin because it seemed to him that they were messy, and he didn't want to appear silly or inelegant. He liked that elegance of his, liked it a lot. He nourished it on English poetry. A little American poetry, too. With Russian poetry for balance. When he'd finished with his cheesecake, he took note of Tefil's hands. They were neither slender nor delicate, and that's the only kind of hands he liked. Tefil's hands had gone swollen and doughy with age and poor circulation. They had liver spots too, and were wrinkled. There was a scar on the index finger of his right hand where a rabid cat had scratched him. Tefil's stomach was distended, balloonish. It sank a little in the middle, but not so much as to cease being a big belly.

What job? asked Tefil. You mean my job as the porter in the veterinary clinic, or my job as the ticket-taker on the small-gauge railway? Nobody shouted at me there, spat on me, or humiliated me. And even if they did, I didn't notice it, so I came out in the black anyway. Although in the eyes of people that's not much to say. Laughingstock. Piece-of-trash. Rancid-beggar. Greasebag. Parasite. Weed. Tick. Roadkill. Drun. Kard. Toothless-fatass. Bal. Dy. Di. Ckhead. Roadkill. Dogsbody. Roa. Dkill. I was really happy as the subaltern of all subalterns. I knew only one side. And there are two. *Ya nachalnik – ty durak. Ty nachalnik – ya durak.* Two sides. During war and in peacetime. And I'm always the durak... I've been deprived of one side... Pardoned... Half-falsified... Half-fabricated. And so, the other half? Shakespeare posed a rather weak final question, there. Decidedly. It's my own I prefer, completely. Not any to be or not to be. But: what is this? What is all this? What does all this mean, my dear sir, Rozmaryn? You. Me. Your mother. Litental. Prodige. Tutberg. Garbarska. What is it?

Maybe we'll go for a walk after dinner?

It's only nine o'clock. We've not even been talking a whole hour, sir.

We're here for as long as I say. And no faces, please.

You can spend the night in the one little hotel here. Above the prewar cinema. A little hortello-bordello. My friend liked that rhyme, Rozmaryn, sir. Liked it better than Dante and Shakespeare, better than all phrases and descriptives known from literature, philosophy, and theology. He liked it, but he wasn't in awe of it. Maybe he liked petty things more than grand things. He liked the little flings of life? All that is grand is tiresome. And untrue to life.

What's that? asked Tefil.

Pardon? asked Tefil.

Come again? asked Tefil.

You mean? asked Tefil.

A profession? asked Tefil.

I have no profession such as one studies or trains for. Moving things from place to place, taking off my clothes, stuffing them into chests of drawers. Covering myself up to the chin with an eiderdown, putting on and taking off ill-cut, felt-lined boots. Opening and closing the door to the shed, letting the dog in and out, hitching up my pants. Notspeaking. Deadness of organs. Those organs. Of the throat. Of the vocal cords. Of the trachea. Of the tongue. Remaining silent unto eternity. In each of us... The silence absorbs all our words, every peep, stutter, challenge, call, prayer, cry, whimper, and song of joy... Beginnings. And so on. And on. And so.

The abyss of the elements, into which everything falls, the quick and the dead. After all, even a stone must cease being a stone someday. The mistake of becoming attached to what is living in us, to speaking... The silence of the dead is not mistaken. But a profession? A pro-fes-sion? Is.

Beginning. Getting lost in Litental, becoming ensnared in the darkness diluted by the moon, the thin light from windows and sparse electric lanterns, walking about aimlessly over the empty streets of an evening, when the inhabitants are searching for something in their houses, their little flats in the rental blocks, in front of the television, in the newspapers, bearing in silence those they once knew how to love. They're searching for something to reward their insatiability. Getting lost on foggy days on the broad streets near the market square in Litental or in the little park. Sitting on a bench in the evening as if humanity had already abandoned the earth, as if they'd gone extinct and everything had been forgotten, and so purified by the lack of memory. Then one might begin. Sitting without moving a muscle. Contemplating.

Love for the air, the aroma of pine, of the empty sky, of the earth parting beneath your feet from moisture. Walking about the fields and admiring the fields, delight at the wall of forest separated from the ploughed land by a sandy road with a green streak of grass down the middle. Delight at an abandoned forester's shack with a drainpipe hanging loose from the roof, delight at the tyre tracks on the road after a rain, the adoration of fields hidden beneath white snow, marked here and there with leafless trees, which watch over themselves as only life is able to do... I've never come to know anything and I've never been anywhere. I shall die underdeveloped.

Walls, roofs, windows, trees, pavements, three cemeteries, three houses of worship, shoes, overcoats, material that had been carted off for holocaust (would that be a sacrifice in the religious sense of the word?) Beginning. One foot, two foot.

Rozmaryn opened his mouth to say something, but he forgot what he wanted to say. He got up, took the cups, placed the plates one on top of the other, set the utensils on top of them, and carried it all over to the counter. The woman behind the counter didn't bother to get up from the stool she was covering with her great behind so that she seemed to be hovering in the air. When Rozmaryn returned to the table, Tefil had already arisen with his overcoat draped over his left arm. He was walking in place as if he couldn't decide which way to go. A loss of orientation.

Take me under the arm, sir, I'm feeling dizzy – he said to Rozmaryn. – It's cold outside after all. This cold reminds me of something from the distant past.

Man is a garbage dump. He'll remember all the things that mess him up with desires, hankerings, but which offer him no means of fulfilment. And then he has to carry that load of rubbish around with him for ages on end. As if those ages of his meant anything more than the ages of a dead fly. Now, in what way does memory differ from the lack of memory? There must be some interest at work here. Political? Religious?

Let's go over to the fountain and sit down on the bench. You don't have to support me any longer. I'll get there under my own power. Garbage dump. Rubbish bin. The spirit of history, providence, human history, the history of stones, trees, and leaves. History before and after us... What sort of history? What is history? Nobody knows what he himself thinks, nobody even knows entirely what he feels... A real jumble... Better? Who says better? I'm a little woozy. These turns of the head that come back from time to time... All the activities, which lead me to the bench by the fountain. One foot, two foot. Just a bit more, a little farther... The smell of the wet pavements on Garbarska. Humidity. Black mould in the corner of the ceiling of my flat in the garret. Mould will outlive us all... The history of humanity, of religion, of the nation, of our language, is nothing but clippings from the history of mould... Nations and religions are not immune... Nor is language... Mould is immune, even to the atomic bomb... Mould shall liberate us from being what we are... Can you sense it, sir? That aftertaste... The sky... The streets... The wondrous uselessness I...

But you can't just live and love. You've got to earn a living, too... Beginnings. Air mixed with the smoke of the first fires lit in the furnaces at the start of winter, which blows in through the cracked window frames of my flat with the icy breeze and the whistling on windy days. The mystery of the sill, of the unwashed pane, the crookedly hung curtain and the livid sky that's able to soothe one on the days of the greatest catastrophe. No names of any elements, no formulas or equations for that which calms me down, comforts me, and pleases me. There's a dead fly on my sill that I haven't cleared away though it's been years now. I've domesticated it. For myself. I'm in no condition to satisfy the needs of any others. That's why I'm sad... And glad. With a dead fly.

They walked on. Rozmaryin in his shirt unbuttoned at the neck. Tefil with his overcoat draped over his left arm. As was his custom, he set his feet down to the outside, which gave him a sense of belonging, of adaptation. He kept his right hand in the pocket of his loose, thirty-year-old trousers. His jacket barely covered his stomach. They arrived at the crossing, but no car was approaching at the moment, so they stepped boldly out onto the stripes. Tefil suddenly quickened the pace, noticeably – which made Rozmaryn take some funny skips from one little foot to the other. Then, walking alongside the little park, they slowed down. Tefil half-closed his eyes, probably because the sun was so strong.

When they arrived at the bench near the round fountain with its little blue tiles on the inside and the broken shards of glass on the outside, Tefil extracted a packet of cigarettes from his pocket and offered Rozmaryn a smoke. He declined with a wave of the hand, hitched up his trousers, and sat down. Tefil lit up. The fountain jets spurted to a height of two metres, and every now and then the wind, warm and from the west, wafted a drape of tiny droplets of water towards Rozmaryn and Tefil. Tefil sat down and inhaled the smoke into his lungs. He gazed at the cigarette, flicked off the ashy end, and tossed the fag into the fountain.

This is, all the same, an honour of a sort – said Tefil. – Yes, an honour all the same. This life. You can say something more. We've hidden ourselves on the bench near the fountain. No one will catch sight of us here, for the moment. But neither will they appreciate us (we are of a race of pushovers). Two studs near the fountain. An old one and a young one. How do you like that, sir?

Rozmaryn had thin hands with long fingers, which would like to find themselves on a piano keyboard or some naked body. They were very different from Tefil's hands. And yet with time, when there will be no more tissue, flesh, their hands will become similar. Maybe even in their shanks and bones one will uncover something like meaning. Nobody knows, when – to our misfortune – the sense of omnipresent meaning and truth will fall upon us.

Let's go to that famous restaurant, which you can see, sir, from the corner of your eye, if you twist your head to the right, just three centimetres, literally three centimetres – said Tefil. – You'll see the prewar doors with their heavy bars, of a light walnut colour, painted dozens of times. We have to wait because they won't open until twelve.

We have two hours.

RAFAŁ WOJASIŃSKI

I'll lay myself down on the bench, for comfort. When my left arm gets tired, I'll twist onto my right side. And vice versa. Coughing, spitting, snorting, moaning. And hee, hee, hee like when you're being tickled.

O! The last bits of my cheesecake have spilled out of my pocket. Last bits, remnants, that's one of my passions. In my pockets I have not only the remnants of today's cheesecake from the pastry shop, I have remnants that are months old, which dry up and become my relics, my derelicts, my museum pieces, even. Maybe they'll put our bones into glass cases someday for other people to look at, wondering – they're no longer here, but their bones are? Your remains won't be in any glass cases, Rozmaryn, sir. You've got too typically a shaped a skull. Now, my bean's another story! It's not beautiful, but it has its own character and I reckon that it might arouse great curiosity a few hundred years from now. Maybe I'll decide to hold back my head from cremation – burn the rest and save the head. That version seems interesting to me. A letter to future generations in the form of my untypical, empty skull.

Rozmaryn felt the warmth that arrived along with the tiny droplets of water wafted over from the fountain. He slipped his shoes off his feet, using the thumb of his right hand. Pushing and twisting until the given shoe came off.

You've taken off your shoes, sir. Excellent. It's pleasant to feel the wind blowing over one's feet – Tefil stated. – I'd also take off mine, but my feet are sweaty. And I have a problem with laundry. Turning on the washing machine, watching how my linen chunters in the suds, irritates me, greatly. The same as talented people do, geniuses. They also bore me, additionally. Abilities are a suspicious thing, especially in the presence of a dead man, who is silent, and who in his silence transcends every speech nobbled by a living mind.

Suddenly, Rozmaryn got up from the bench, but he sat back down after a few moments, as if someone else, inside his body, had been controlling its movements. Tefil looked on with that gentle expression of his on his face. Somebody might say that it was the mug of a glutton. Tefil looked nothing special. His thinning hair, combed back, lit up by the strong sun, took on the colour of pig bristles. Crookedly cut, they added asymmetry to his already asymmetrical head. His randomly scattered, rotting teeth. His nose, too large, crooked, potatoish. You could go on listing the defective parts of Tefil endlessly. Yep, he was no beauty.

Who worked it that some are beautiful, and others not? And why? So that we wouldn't know what to do with the ugly people? Or so that we would. And with cripples. And with those of a different skin colour. We can only pretend that the prettier sort are no insult to the uglier ones. They are! And how!

Tefil's legs were too short for him to sit comfortably on the bench. They either dangled in the air, or he had to slide down for his feet to touch the pavement. At such times he was almost lying down, which highlighted his stomach and caused his hips and buttocks to spill out the sides of his blazer.

I'll slide down a bit because I suffer from sciatica – said Tefil. – With my shortness, my fatness, my face, my hands. With my legs, with my knees, with my fat arse, with... With my mug... You know, sir...

Tefil leaned over comfortably on the bench. He was now beaming with satisfaction, but his laboured breathing and his head toppling over again and again made for a depressing spectacle. Tefil's hands were hanging at his sides below the edge of the bench. Hanging. The distance between them and the slab of well-worn earth measured forty-five centimetres. Gravity pulled (or, according to some physicists, pushed) them to the ground as if towards the grave. His blood kept pumping and filled his veins. At a distance of some one hundred forty-five astronomical units from Tefil, or in other words, about one hundred fifty million kilometres, an unmanned space probe was to be found. Beneath Tefil's legs, about two metres below, a human corpse was buried (next to many other, non-human bodies). Nameless entirely, unknown to all.

Tefil's chin fell onto his breastbone. And remained there. Tefil's eyes closed. With short breaths, his lungs began to shepherd that shapeless body into sleep. But that sleep lasted only three minutes, interrupted as it was by a strong, sudden snore, a choking cough, a splutter. Twenty seconds later, however, it all went quiet and ceased irritating Rozmaryn's organs of hearing.

And yet that smell – said Tefil, suddenly awake. – Arising to the nostrils from such a small distance. Until my stomach rouses me to life. Chicken flesh, fried chicken flesh. The aroma remained in my blazer. Or maybe it's a different odour? Maybe liver? Liver has such a strong smell... Aunt Marta's house. A wooden cottage, a clay stove in the kitchen... Everything from clay dug free in the fields... Houses, stoves... Burials for free... Where'd she get all that liver? Every time I entered that cottage of hers, it smelled of fried liver... Or liver in general...

Don't let anyone take you for a ride, sir... I'm telling you... Or... Cof. Fin.

You don't know anything, sir... you haven't heard anything, seen anything... Here, learn these few words, this ratiocination. They'll set you free... You feel it? Ah, inebriating ignorance. Camouflaged lack of deep thought. Thought has shallow roots. Very shallow ones. A fatty, smeary stain on the skin of the water... Beginning. Getting up, standing up, putting clothes into the cupboard, pulling on the trousers, plunging feet into sliced fleecy rubber boots...

I once had a genius of a teacher, an old cantor... He'd have tears in his eyes from time to time. For the slightest reason. Not from the wind. If not for him, my history might have been different. You know, this matter rankles me. The genius of the cantor, who when push comes to shove was an idiot. But if not for him and that unconscious genius of his encoded in his primitive mind, I'd never have discovered one thing: that mystery is eternal. Not a mathematical rebus, or a riddle from physics or chemistry or cosmology. Mystery, alone... Birth and death. Yes. And so on. And so.

To be stuck. Endlessly. Stuck. Shifting the cupboard. Trying on old rags, measuring socks, becoming inebriated by taking a walk in sliced fleecy rubber boots. Entering the city before noon, slowly conquering space. One foot, two foot, hitching up the pants, fixing the blazer, buttoning the buttons... Beginning. Lately, upon crawling out of my block of flats and still trailing behind me the odour of the stairwell, I have been enveloped in mist. Everything was less distinct, submerged, transformed, and delightful. Shorter distances, whole streets swallowed, buildings, stores, blocks of flats, and the famous restaurant invisible...

The real world. The charm of reality. To gaze with delight upon the clouds racing through the sky, on spruces bent by the wind, the sun poking through, throwing shadows... The wind's up a bit... A blast of breeze burls through the air around us. You hear it, sir?

Rozmaryn craned his head backwards, saw the crowns of the poplars spreading against the sky, the oaks, and, behind his back, craning his head even further backwards, he caught sight of the spruces. The park was a chaotic jumble of peacefully growing trees. Rozmaryn set his right hand down upon the back of the bench. His hand looked like a creature, a separate entity marked by existence, just like thinking beings, unthinking beings, making a go at their

RAFAŁ WOJASIŃSKI

fate in some none-too-spacious dimension, and those that don't make a go at practically anything at all. He pulled his penknife out of his pocket and unspooled and snipped a string that had been dangling from his cuff. Then he crossed his legs and took on a stiffer posture, more worthy of a human being who might mean something. Because suddenly in the face of Tefil and the fountain, and especially in the face of the passers-by on foot and in automobiles, on horse-drawn farm wagons, he wanted to mean something. People saw Rozmaryn, and what to sight is given, cannot be forgiven.

Sometimes I'm afraid to leave the house. This can last for weeks even. At such times it's hard to catch sight of me – said Tefil. – That's why my fridge is always full, just in case. I spend my pension on it all. On the tenth of the month, as soon as I get my money, I stock up for the month and blow all the rest. I'm struggling against inflation... Nobody realises how constantly and painfully I struggle against inflation... To what degree does inflation concern God? God and inflation... The rest I blow... What do I blow it on? After all, people are always treating me. What's going on with my miserable cash, what's going on with my starvation-level pension? As long as I can remember, my money has always been vanishing. I have to buy, I have to remember to buy things...

Money constantly vanishes. It vanishes in things that, later on, vanish too. The vanishing of money is a constant, nobody's capable of halting the process. Every single złoty vanishes, every hundred złoty that you've got to labour so hard or work so flawlessly even to get, vanishes. In the exhaust of your car, in books, in the roof above your head, in the basement, in ham, in smoked ham sausage. Have you noticed that, sir? Investment in education, in a sofa, in cubic metres, in a voyage to a paradisiacal island. Investment in life pedal-to-the-metal so as to have something to remember later. Have you noticed that, sir? Every last penny vanishes. Investment in a luxurious coffin. In a good plot in the cemetery – not somewhere off to the side by the fence. People are grand investors. To invest in something that'll pay dividends even a thousand years from now. To buy land, and sell it a thousand years later. So maybe those quarters at the cemetery after all... Yes, a good plot brings the best returns, I reckon... But those remote cemeteries, with no road leading to them, overgrown by the woods... A hundred years and no property at all, not even a sliver, not even a metre or two... That wouldn't be any sort of successful deal. Plots are risky because cemeteries fall no less than civilisations. Maybe you could buy some cliff... Or a portion of a road. Maybe wood... An old oak. Wire. Picket fence. Bottomless bucket. Cup with a broken-off handle. Broken fridge. Trousers. Trousers, socks, and sliced felt boots.

The sun was so hot now that Tefil's big head began to sweat. Just once, Rozmaryn took a quick glance at the drops of sweat on his brow. An ivory-coloured car pulled up at the pavement. A car-colour long forgotten. Tefil drew in his sluggish legs, bent forward, and extracted from his back trouser pocket a handkerchief of surprisingly large dimensions. He used it to wipe the sweat from his brow before replacing it in his back trouser pocket, but the one on his other cheek. The left one. All the while, bent forward, he massaged his belly, after which he straightened up. The buttons barely kept the two halves of his blazer fastened over his bulging stomach.

You coming? – asked Tefil. – There. Around. So we're off. Left. And... And straight ahead. And.

Tefil set off first, but Rozmaryn caught up with him after just a few paces. They turned left, entered among the conifers, pushed their way through them, and emerged onto a narrow path leading to the obelisk. This was a

RAFAŁ WOJASIŃSKI

monument honouring soldiers who fought in the Second World War. Up at its summit, in a little glass sphere, was some soil from Monte Cassino. Tefil unbuttoned his blazer and draped his overcoat over his shoulders. He was walking with a straight posture now, sucking in his stomach. A few dozen paces later, they found themselves on the path that circled the park. On the other side was a two-lane road, along which trucks were rumbling south. They kicked up dust. Rozmaryn felt little particles of it on his lips and tongue.

They walked on side by side, close to one another. Rozmaryn felt the warmth of Tefil's body. At a certain moment, they halted, as if on command.

'You have any smokes?' Tefil asked. 'Let's light up. How do you fight against despair, sir? Let's go! I just have to remember that I have something to buy. There's a hole in the roof of the shack, and a puddle's forming. It's not really a hole, but rather a crack, because the eternit's set badly, the seams abut at the wrong end, and water seeps in under the layers and drips into the shack. I've got to remember to buy a piece of some sort of roofing material to screw to the eternit 'cos I don't think any sort of adhesive would work. I've had this in mind for twenty years now. I've got to do something to stop the water from leaking in, seeping in under the eternit, and getting inside the shack. Next time I remember this, I won't be able to go. The more I think of it, the less strength I have to execute the movements that would lead to the liquidation of the leak. The liquidation of the leak is beyond my ability. You hear, sir? This is just one of the many thoughts with which I fall asleep and to which I awaken. And I can't execute a single motion. I can't just get up on the roof of the shack and plug the hole. And for Pete's sake it's such a simple thing. And safe. There's no risk whatsoever, and yet I won't do it. I know that I'm not capable of doing it. I'll die first. Good grief. Every time

I walk down the steps to show myself on the street again, to walk from one side of the park to the other, to feel that joy of walking, sitting down, buttoning the trousers, gaping in front of myself, sating my lungs with the gusts of air wafting around me, I know that I won't patch that hole. You see how the joy of life's muddled my noodle? Made me daft.

I couldn't sleep last night. Prodige kept coming over to me, Prodige buried so long in that black hole at the foot of the tree in the yard, reproaching me for that leak. Not directly, you understand, but she was whimpering and it was almost like she was speaking with a human voice. Kind of like a howling and a yawning together. Happens to you too, sir? You want to sleep and howl at the same time. All at once. Sometimes I want to weep too, there's such a despair inside here, which drains me of the strength to live. You stop giving a damn about anything. At such moments my body wants to die, but my self, you know my ego, I still want to live. My self doesn't agree with my body at such times, which has been wanting to die now for quite some time. Snafu. Scramble. Hash.

With pleasure, Rozmaryn gazed at the space between the thirteenth-century Catholic church and the bakery. In the distance he also beheld the outline of the rectory, the headquarters of the deanery. Rozmaryn was now walking behind Tefil. He placed his hands in his pockets and bent forward a bit. His own skinny limbs seemed somehow less interesting now in comparison with the bizarre, misshapen figure of Tefil. Yet Tefil was much uglier than he, so where did such a thought come from? Why should he feel worse than that miserable liar going nowhere, just straight ahead wherever his feet carried him? It was only when they came to a turning to the right, when they had the north-south highway behind them, that Rozmaryn came near Tefil. Whether he wanted to or not, he felt the power emanating from that man. Or maybe it was his stench that stunned and dizzied a person.

We're nearing the famous restaurant – said Tefil.

Rozmaryn felt hungry. When they'd arrived at the bus stop sunk in the vegetation on this side of the park, where they'd also built a petrol station, he smelt the aroma that the earth exhales at this spring season, which combines the energy of life and the energy of death. Those two elements without which existence cannot happen. The aroma was mixed of budding tulips, rhododendrons, and a cherry tree that somehow found itself here years ago.

There are already people in the restaurant. Time for us – said Tefil.

This time Rozmaryn took the lead. Tefil arranged the last remaining hair on his bald head, hitched up his trousers higher, tightened his loops and made fast his laces, pulled at his elastic bands.

Hold on, hold on – Tefil said. – And cash?

Rozmaryn pulled up suddenly and waited for Tefil to catch up. They stood face to face in silence. The warm sun shone down on their heads as if they were two planets that had fallen into each other's gravitational pull by co-incidence, orbiting now, governed by the laws of physics. Borne along by that mysterious energy from which there is no liberation, which brings all to birth and mercilessly summons all to death. We praise this energy, we give it the names of various gods, we subject ourselves to it and curse it.

I once rode right through Tutberg on my wagon in weather like this – said Tefil. – I fell asleep lying on the bare boards. Old Grey pulled me along, he knew where to go. The T-bar tapped against the drawbar. What a melody. At that moment I lost all my love for Mozart, Bach, and Tchaikovsky. It was a painless loss. And since then I've never fallen in love with any other melody. Love for the sound of the T-bar tapping the drawbar has depraved me once and for all. Just like my love for chicken soup, sour milk, pure vodka, boiled chicken, herrings, and red beets. What sort of meat did Christ like? What did he like to eat? He never said a word about music or pictures, masterpieces or geniuses. And he was right. What did he say? T-bar and drawbar. A wagon and drowsing on the boards of a wagon beneath the empty sky of Tutberg. A masterpiece is a bad idea, you know. Just like clothes that are too nice. And fashion. Those felt-lined rubber boots... That was a good idea after all, ruining them. When I slip them on and wend my way out into the yard for a stroll around the tree where Prodige is buried, some interesting thoughts come into my head. The first one is that I was right, for some unknown reason, to slice down my rubber boots and go about for thirty years in the same trousers...

For some unknown reason I'm right, Rozmaryn, sir, that even if you express the greatest wisdom in the world, you won't say anything at all. Beginning. For some unknown reason I'm right, pushing along my gams in those notoriously sliced down felt-lined boots and searching, searching, sniffing about. Searching about on an empty yard, around the tree, in the shack, under the stairs, sitting down on the wet board beneath the shack and looking up to see whether or not something is going to fall on my nut. I'm right in becoming an old bum, leaving youth behind me, and health, and success in life. I'm right to be constantly on the watch for a dead dog.

I'm right about those thirty-year-old trousers; the idea of those trousers surpasses communism, capitalism, liberalism, nationalism, free market, and free thought. The idea of these trousers surpasses even the idea of free will. The free will of the murderer of two women, who has an IQ of 62, and the free will of a bishop living on golden cushions. And the free will of a mother suffering depression, battered by her husband. And the free will of a child from the orphanage. And the free will of a forty year old with a brain tumour. And the free will of an old man with Alzheimer's. And the free will of an agent who made his pile by betraying his own people. And the free will of an intelligent fellow or dame who manipulates the weaker and the poorer with ease.

One foot, two foot. Beginning. Absorption. Draining. Encumbrance, shifting from corner to corner, from place to place, from Garbarska Street to Garbarska Street. Once upon a time in those slashed rubber felt boots of mine I stepped on something soft near the shack. I doffed my cap out of respect for my dog, out of respect for what is dead, and out of respect for the fact that the dead exist in the world just as the living do. And I sniffed that cap. I like the smell of my cap. I don't know who I got that cap from. Who it used to belong to. Somebody went about with it on his head. I've never laundered it. Maybe something from the earlier owner's come on down into me? Slid down, something from others, into me, entering me. Maybe I'm those people now? Maybe we're all of us just one, common, obscure person? I have a hundred souls! And a hundred souls have me. And if I want to think up something else, if I want to... Well then, if I want to do that again, to go down the steps and think, I have to forget about all the living, what they say to me, because they're destroying my brain. They cause problems for me in everything, changing the words round in my head. Leading me into mistakes. Counterfeiting death in me. Snuffing out. Stifling. Shh.

Beginning. Again. Again the same thing. I have to do the same thing a thousand times over in order to think, repeat, forge my own gait, creating, sitting down, getting up, pulling up the trousers, twisting the bands, tying the string at the belt loops. Once again I have to forge my gait, my burying of the dog, giving him food, setting out fresh straw for him in his corner of the shack, I have to forge my lack of life, which existed before I was born. I have to do the same thing to the end, the very same thing and all the time, constantly, for otherwise it won't work, otherwise it doesn't work... Each time I have to do the same thing, forge it, forge what I've already done, counterfeiting the earlier-forged lack of my life before my birth. Otherwise it won't work, it'll fail. I have to be dying constantly, but through doing the same thing, through repetition and a forging of the lack of my life before I was born. Round the clock. It's a very simple task, Rozmaryn, sir. To cease existing in the name of the lack of existence before birth. To become as forgotten as you were before you were born. A simple task. To forge the lack of life, which took place before birth. Simple, pure, a real vocation. Beginning. Absorption.

Tefil lifted his head and looked up at the sky, while at the same time at the level of his big stomach he was counting up something on his fingers, as if in the air. Rozmaryn pulled some money out of his pocket and showed it to Tefil, who pursed his lips as if to whistle, but whistled not.

You've got enough for two dinners, a bottle of vodka, and maybe four beers or so – Tefil said. – I reckon that this being the case, it's worth going in. I am constantly unsated. And add to this the drowsiness that sometimes pounces on me unexpectedly, without any reason. I've always had that, especially when I was working in the porter's office of the veterinary surgery. I just couldn't control that morbid drowsiness that engulfed me around ten o'clock, right after brunch, which usually consisted of two large sandwiches with goose lard and a pickle. My double chin would fall down upon my breastbone, and I'd struggle to stay awake with the last of my strength, even though the waking world seemed so oppressively unproductive to me. The waking world is a mental disorder. Drowsiness and weakness conducting me to thoughtlessness. Tranquillising, quenching, smothering.

Maybe it was then, in the porter's office of the veterinary surgery, that I lost my depth once and for all, lost my soul, once and for all time? My soul flew off somewhere without the least resistance, leaving behind my body and my self. Those two forms, those two merciless forms. That murder and eradicate one another, mutually. Contradiction. Life without a foundation. Death without a foundation. A vicious circle. Beginning.

My memories were born in the porter's office of the veterinary surgery, just as dreams are born, auguries, visions, flashes of enlightenment. Something uprose from the past like a newborn appearing for the first time. It was once. Certainly it was a long time ago. But it seems that pasts also touch upon births. The past is also born. The birth of a fact after the passage of a hundred years. One more time. From the top. The past is constantly being born. Do you understand, Rozmaryn, sir? Listen, please. Always listen. Images are born to me from memory. The rooms in two buildings with entrances one from Garbarska St and one from the courtyard. I remember doors painted white, with little panes in the top segment. Doors with two leaves, and when you opened them two rooms became one large salon. I see myself in that salon on all fours. I already knew how to walk about on two, but it still gave me pleasure to crawl about on all fours. Canvassing the area in search of toys and places where I could hide away from the adults, who spoke in full sentences and droned on their tales about ancestors or ghosts they'd never seen themselves, but, they asserted, there were others who communicated with spectres from the other side. That other side, which after all is on this side, on the only side of all sides. Small-house prophets being handed down from hand to hand, guardians of confabulation and myth. Somebody forced me to move into those houses. Maybe somebody from the family? There were other children there besides me. Two, three at most. Who also canvassed the area on all fours. Looking for something, sniffing out something, drawing into themselves smells, colours, sounds.

My memory restores a non-existent state of things, restoring something that really was. From the threshold of the house into which I entered straight from the sidewalk, I fell two steps down. I found myself underground, up to my knees. Then, to the left, there was a little room, where this grandmother drowsed on a chair near the hot stove. Then, somewhat to the right and in front, the kitchen, and, past the kitchen, a little room, and, behind this little room, a storeroom and a dark chamber, from which these little doors, as if made for a dwarf, led out into the yard. Almost the very same sort of yard as I have here, complete with a shed with a leaky roof. Then for the first time I went out into the yard, one of countless yards in our city. Thousands of such yards in heads like mine. They change each time they reemerge in memory. With a different smell, a different colour, occupying a different area. Right now I see the yard into which I emerged from the parlour on all fours, but it's a different one from the one I saw three minutes ago, when I told you about it, sir. The grass has a different colour, the smell reminds one more of the mustiness and rot of March than the freshness of summer.

To remember hundreds, thousands of times, that same spoon, that same table, divan, grass, face, shoe, parapet, threshold, door, yard, in order to see in one's head, each time, something different, to feel some different thing, a different world, a different love. I'm not here where I am because I'm not there where I was, and I'm not where I'll soon be. The falsification of the dead. The counterfeiting of the lack of life. The forging of the dead man. The dead as eternally present.

RAFAŁ WOJASIŃSKI

So when I take the decision to go down the stairs and once more lift my foot, and set it back down, when I take the decision to go down and be there one more time, to go out for a walk, and then to the pastry shop to which I return after each stroll, well, I'd already give it all up. Just as I give it all up at least once a day.

Beginning. Going down, going in, going across. Sitting, drinking coffee, eating the cheesecake. Drowsing. Burning down. Going silent. The cleansing wastes. Do you remember the road, sir, we took to get here? Waiting it out. Even if one's the president, department head, chief physician, genius, or latrine cleaner. Waiting it out. Nobody will confirm my existence, or yours, sir. Have you remembered the road? They'll wait us out. One waits out the other. Everybody waits everybody else out. The wealthy wait out the poor, the poor the wealthy. The beloved the lover and the lover the beloved. The genius waits out the lesser geniuses, and the lesser genius the greater. Consolation. The tyrant waits out his victim. And with reciprocity. One foot. Two foot. Movements. The repetitiveness of actions. One movement imitating another. The repetitiveness of reality. Of talent, of wisdom, and of God. I'm born. Well born. Almost in a sty. Chrum. Chrum. Chrum.

They arrived at the many-times-painted doors of the famous restaurant. Their interior, protective portion consisted of two wooden wings solidly screwed together. The hinges, forged from heavy steel, had been serving now for decades. On the right wing, some metre thirty centimetres above the floor, hung the bar, with which the doors were locked shut at night. Its end was fastened by a large padlock to a staple fixed in the stone wall just past the casing of the door. Inside, fixed to that same casing, was a delicate door with four square windows. Rozmaryn and Tefil entered through these. They were immediately pounced upon by the aroma of fried pork chops, mixed with the odour of tripe and chicken soup. It was market day, so you know. The transfiguration of life into eating, the miracle of trans-figuration. To the right side there was a wooden counter, a machine for the rinsing of beer mugs, a sink, and a silver beer-pull undecorated with the name of any brewery. Past the counter were the doors leading to the kitchen, through which the meals were delivered. On the walls, panelling in the colour of the outside door, in other words, light walnut. The paint shone brightly. To the left was set a row of none too large square tables. Four chairs around each table. Two out of five were free. Tefil chose the second table from the door. He removed his trench coat from his shoulders and draped it over the arm of the chair. In such a way he reserved the place.

There was a second room behind the first. There the tables were covered with linen, and the clients more rarely sloshed their beer or smeared the tabletops. A relief on the wall represented a peasant sitting on a stone and playing a flute – a folk motif familiar in the Kujawy region. No smok-ing was allowed there, but quite a bit of smoke seeped in anyway. There were more windows there – four, whereas there were only two in the first room. The sun poured in through the window near the door and illuminated the counter and the beer-pull. The other window was to be found between Tefil and Rozmaryn's table and the next table, at which two fiftyish women were sitting along with a man with a crop in his hand. Tefil sat down with his back to the door, Rozmaryn across the way, facing him. He could see who entered the famous restaurant and who exited. He could also see the people walking along the pavement and the horse-drawn wagons creaking by. This was a time when large trucks were already passing through the town, but there were also still people who came to market in such wagons, in which they transported pairs of piglets for sale. Rozmaryn was enchanted by what he saw through

RAFAŁ WOJASIŃSKI

the little panes of the door. Human figures appeared in them suddenly, and then vanished a moment later, heading somewhere further on. There's always somewhere further on (universes).

The colours of the rainbow appeared on the little panes of the windows on the door of the famous restaurant. Rozmaryn felt as if he were floating off somewhere. From the dark corners of his mind and memory some images came to him: a lake, a boat, and a forest on a hill past the lake. They penetrated the narrow veins and passageways of his brain. Recollections. Revelations of memory. And yet too weak to be grasped.

I know how it's done, beer first – said Tefil. – But we've come here to have a chat if I'm not mistaken. About your mother. You wanted to know, sir, what I know about your mother. Well then, first order us a bottle of vodka, some tea, and we'll wait for our dinner. We'll have a beer before we leave.

I've found no better place on earth than this famous restaurant. GS. *Gminna Spółdzielnia* – People's Cooperative. That's what brought this restaurant into existence. I hide out here sometimes when there's no place free in the pastry shop, and yet I must begin, I must abandon my garret apartment. They only open the famous restaurant in the afternoon, and that's why noon is the most important moment in the day for me.

Your mother. Something about your mother. Maybe God? Maybe he could tell you something about your mother, sir. There are so many gods. A whole mess of them. And more are on the way. Have you noticed, sir? They multiply. Have you noticed that? On all continents and in all social groups. They appear under different labels and they possess different skills, talents. Some of them are geniuses, others merely demagogues, but they feed off the same thing. Adoration. For my part, I'm no god. Not me... For my part. The word 'god' is mistaken. Well... Vodka and tea. A mortal set. Supposedly causes cancer... The chief cause of cancer is cancer. Or maybe life? GS. G–S. G.S. Ciphers.

Beginning. We'll sit here a long while and drink slowly, so that it will be pleasant, but we won't get drunk. Are you capable of ingesting alcoholic beverages in a normal manner, sir? Are you an alcoholic, sir? I know what you clever foxes are like. You only pay for the vodka, and the rest you gather in the fields... Potatoes, tomatoes, cucumbers, strawberries, apples, plums... You dog, you. You steal, don't you? Admit it. You pick up some potatoes, some carrots, here and there? Carrots are the gateway. You could follow a carrot to your death. Not only *Sidereus Nuncius*, *Istoria e dimostrazioni intorno alle macchie solari*, and *Il Saggiatore*.

It breaks out of me sometimes, gets weak, but breaks out, gets out of me. Word number one, word number two. Bearing what's fixed in every existence, the dead and the living pieces of the living whole. Bearing it along in the evening, along Garbarska, what's fixed like a bone between the teeth, the dead as proof of the existence of the living. A fatal proof. The proof of all proofs. Leading through the truth of the existence of the dead and the dead in the living... A well-known pattern, like the Pythagorean theorem, but incomprehensible. No one understands the pattern, but it's repeated anyway. One foot, two foot, one breath, two breath. Scratching oneself, putting on one's cap, buttoning one's jacket, slurping, listening to the silence, listening close, bearing the dead about in oneself, getting lost on Garbarska Street. One foot, two foot. The sky hanging firmly above your head, walls, roofs, elevations, cobblestones worn smooth by boots of different sizes and in different shapes. Bearing, bearing through, standing in place, wandering. It won't come out. The dead won't come out of the living. There's no exit from Garbarska. Standing, gaping, gripping a stick in one's hand. The tree by the street,

RAFAŁ WOJASIŃSKI

the smile on the extinguished face. The splendid evening walk, the comforting sky, colours, the floating clouds... It won't go out... Pork chop one, pork chop two. Tripe one, tripe two... *Gminna Spółdzielnia.* GS. G.S. Gee. Ess. Beginning. Inhaling the air, aroma.

Rozmaryn got up and went to the counter. The woman there turned around and stood before Rozmaryn in all her splendour. She was wearing a white apron and a little white cap. Her smile revealed some fairly white teeth (teeth live longer than mind and heart; are they of better quality?) The bosom of her dress was just as deeply unbuttoned as that of the woman in the pastry shop. Even that one breast, nearly naked, was illusively similar to that other one. Rozmaryn raised his eyes to look the woman in the face, and was struck dumb.

What is it? asked the woman. Are you looking at me, sir, or a little lower? That happens to everyone. The sober as well as the drunk. It's a law of nature, the woman added, leaning on the counter in such a way that Rozmaryn caught her scent – and it wasn't the scent of perfume. Young and good-looking fellows don't show up around here too often. Too bad you came in here with Tefil. He won't let you go, sir. He'll squeeze the last penny out of you, he'll suck you dry. And besides that, you know sir, they say that he takes boys up to his flat, but I don't give a damn. Well, what'll it be? Two beers? What else? Coming right up, young man. Laws of nature. Have you made the sign of the Cross today, sir? Have you lifted aloft any petitions? Can I be the answer to your prayers, sir? How does it go with you, as far as religion is concerned? And what about your loyalty? Are you faithful from time to time? And what about your ideological beliefs? Your roots? What sort of roots do you have, sir? Do you believe in anything at all? Do you hope, sir? Are you accompanied by such an ubiquitous, never-ending hope, such as is born from the nearness of bodies? Art thou fruitful, dost thou multiply, sir? Will you take up the question? What is it that you've lost? What are those losses? Let's hear them, sir, only, slowly, slowly because such things inebriate me. I have a sultry nature and fall immediately into inebriation, indeed, into a fever of passion. What is it that you've lost? Whom have you lost? What do you wish to reacquire in life, sir? You're devouring me with your eyes. You can't tear them away from me. How nice, how really very nice. That enchantment, that voracity in your eyes, sir, is something I dearly need! You make me so happy with those eyes of yours! I will long for your gaze. It's my bosom, right? How splendid. These needs of ours. Well, yes... We're not twins. The woman in the pastry shop is my older sister. I repeat: my older sister. There's two years difference, but as you can see, there's no difference at all, since such a young lad, who has young eyes, healthy eyes, got our bosoms mixed up, well, and faces too, by the way, although as we know, that's a secondary matter. Laws of nature.

Rozmaryn returned to the table with the bottle of vodka and two shot glasses. Tefil lit a cigarette and gazed through the window. Or maybe through a fragment of the window, rather. He had to crane his head to the left, twisting it unnaturally. His neck grew stiff, but he couldn't refuse himself that gazing upon the world through the fragment of the window of the famous restaurant.

Outside, life seemed a little bit lighter and cleaner. There was a hope, that if you kept on looking like that, there'd be more, more of something after all. A sliver, a millimetre, a second more. He was engulfed by a fragment of the area that could be seen only through the window. An image. Not the whole, but a clipping. A clipping. A piece of life, a piece of the world. Not a whole. Not everything. A tiny little part. The joy of existence. A scrap of what is true and irrefutable. You can't touch the

96   RAFAŁ WOJASIŃSKI

whole, you can only touch thighs, breasts, knees, elbows, cheeks, a belly, an eye, a mouth. You can touch a piece of bark, but not the whole tree; you can catch sight of several thousand stars, but not all of them. The whole cannot be sniffed nor tasted. Pork chop has a smell, as does a violet. Sweat has a taste; toast, cheesecake, and coffee. The whole falsifies, kills, terminates. The theory of everything. The theory of the whole. The Left. The Right. Ecology, Vegetarianism. Carnivorousness. God. The lack of God. God in the lack of God. In God the lack of God. One speech, two speech.

What was she gabbing with you about over there? She's the sister of that girl from the pastry shop. Did you notice, sir? – asked Tefil. – It's not important. The propaganda of nature. Are you sweating? No? Well then, pour us half a snort. My bones are poking up from my palms. As if they were leaving my body. I have lumpy hands, and the bones, look here. What are they up to? They're poking out of me. They're separating themselves from the rest. And probably saying something. Probably, every bone that pushes out of the body is saying something. Every mole, brown spot, distended vein, and the remains of hair on the fingers also say something. Look: bones in skin, even in old skin, don't look so very bad. That's still life, that's still thirty six and six, constantly still reality.

Everything is real, even when it talks rot. Protruding bones say: think what you like, but, all the same, reality will consume everything. Mozart, Bach, Gide, Miłosz, Pessoa, Wittgenstein, and Bernhard. The lawn mower, the chaff cutter, the harrow, the castra, and the rotavator. Reality will swallow Galileo, Newton, and Copernicus. The quern, the chimney on the roof, the warm stove lid in the kitchen, and the skillet unscraped of fried eggs. Beginning. My poking bones in my pale drying skin. Even schizophrenia won't liberate you from reality. Nothing will free one from it. No faith in any God, in any state, in any art, in any language and love.

Protruding bones. Beginning. Bones protruding beneath dry, bright skin. There weren't any such. I have so many strange symptoms. I can't wriggle out of these different symptoms. And you can, can you, sir? How do you deal with your symptoms? Some of them worry me, others I don't give a fig about, but they surround me, they transform me into something else. Again and again. I change into something else. I change into something I can't recognise. When my mug filled up with fat, that was the biggest shock. I can't see myself at all when I look in the mirror. I have to get a grip on myself so as to stop that picture of myself, to conquer in myself how I look.

Should I give myself a hand with plastic surgery? Is that the route to search for the real me? There are so many of them today... And that's what I'm afraid of, I admit it, sir... Maybe someday plastic surgery will be compulsory. So that we'll all have to look the part, all the more like purebreds... Pretty. After all, there is such a thing as development. The inevitable development of civilisation. A fashion for purebreds... For beauty. A little nose, cheeks, or what have you... Lower down, and higher up... I'm afraid, you know, sir, that someday somebody will get into power who will want the whole world of people to be beautiful so that beauty should triumph... A person can't deal with beauty... Ever... Beauty will destroy us... Just think, sir, imagine someone with such a huge need for beauty finding his or her way to power and – plastic surgery will now be obligatory. All of us will have to be pretty... That would be unbearable...

The fashion for beauty will kill us... Rozmaryn, sir, we must escape somehow, because otherwise fashion will kill us, will wipe us out... How are we to grapple with this?... The fashion for a race of pretty, intelligent geniuses; a race

RAFAŁ WOJASIŃSKI

of the rich, riding about in beautiful cars and living in large, beautiful homes untouched by mould; a race of travellers walking about in designer clothes... The fashion for capable people, for children with good careers, for children who are very smart, for children who marry well... The fashion for beauty, quality, and wealth... And finally, the fashion for liquidating the GS restaurant. That would kill me, for sure.

That trend already exists, doesn't it? I'm right... All we're lacking is the leader, but he's on his way, for sure... Or maybe that leader's already at it, in secret, from his secret bunker, his secret seat of power, and there's no way back now?... Jesus! No way back from the tyranny of fashion! No escape! We'll have to be prodded with needles, botoxed, stretched firm... Yes. We need to escape... To outer space... Launch ourselves out and up?

You know, sir, sometimes I don't leave this restaurant for hours on end. For many hours. I sit at my soup, at one dish of soup, because I'm afraid. This is my bunker... I emerge onto Garbarska thousands of times. And then I hide myself here. Because here's the bunker. You know, sir?

A thousand times I'm attracted by what's dead inside me, it attracts me, it consumes me. Rain or shine, or when Garbarska Steet is buried deep in snow, up to the window sashes. I go out onto Garbarska every day and begin. One foot after another. Whap, whap. Over the hard pavement. One, two. Stopping, Going. Gaping. One foot, two foot. Glaring about. Scratching. Fixing the cap on a cold day. Wiping the nose. Searching for an exit to another street. Beginning. One more time. Returning. Going up over the steps, going down. In the rental block that remembers eighteen seventy six. The same stairs. Dead stairs, in me, in a living being... Looking left, right. Choosing the road. Once more from the top.

For all this you need years, hundreds of years, thousands. I'm seventy years old? I'm eighty? What's seventy years? What's a hundred years? What's two hundred years? What's a thousand years? What's a billion years? What is four point six billion years? Extinction. Growing quiet. No phrase, no fleshy body, soft or hard, no alcohol, and no food. And no movement. Not even a millimetre. Don't anyone dare touch me, move me even a centimetre. Let my dust be used for the same thing as that of the children in the cemetery at Tutberg. Absorption. Beginning.

Rozmaryn twisted the cap off the neck of the bottle and began pouring the vodka. In even portions. He squinted one eye, first the left, then the right, because he had that ability, although not every human person has the ability to squint both the left eye and the right eye, leaving the other wide open. At last he placed both shot glasses next to each other. And it looked like he was successful, maybe a millimetre of a difference remained, not more (but sometimes a millimetre can be the difference between life and death). Then, between the millimetre of a difference and the rim of the shot glass Rozmaryn noticed a fingerprint. The print of a human being, some filth transferred, maybe, from the horse market. And that trace once more reconciled him with existence. Reality. Relief.

The white balls of light hanging from long wires created a reality which was becoming splendid. The existence of shot glasses, of schnitzel, of the little panes in the door to the famous restaurant, the existence of the odour of the piglets sold at the market, the existence of the breasts of the woman at the bar, of the shoes, trench coat, and blazer of Tefil, of the remains of the cheesecake in the pocket of his blazer, of the cigarette smoke swirling around those balls of light, of Tefil's hair, his fingernails, his protruding bones, of the fingerprint on the glass, of the transparent liquid in the little glasses, of the walnut panelling, the existence of the dozens of eyes fixed on the beer before them, of women's eyes feigning happiness, of eyes that say everything's

RAFAŁ WOJASIŃSKI

gonna be all right, even after death, of palms on the bar top, on little tables, on thighs, on someone else's shoulders, on someone else's waist, breasts, on someone else's cheeks, butt cheeks, on someone else's brow.

Rozmaryn kept the bottle in his right hand, the bottle which was now only a quarter full, and posed the following puzzling question to himself: which of the shot glasses was his, and which was Tefil's? Meanwhile, not waiting for Rozmaryn to make up his mind, Tefil took the one to the left in his hand, and the problem was solved.

Twenty-five minutes had passed since Tefil and Rozmaryn had entered the famous restaurant. There wasn't a single free place at any of the small tables. The murmurs grew loud. The men had to speak loudly to one another, and at certain times they didn't even know what they were saying because their voices were deformed by others seeping in from the first dining room of the famous restaurant. It was as if they were communicating by the movement of their lips. From this conversation, in which words became shapeless, an expectation of what was more real was born.

Neither tripe, nor schnitzel with a fried potato-and-sauerkraut mix, nor beer. Tefil rested both of his hands on the table before him, as if they were at rest. As if they had their own existence, something separately important. Expressed in unclear symbols. In his left hand, between his index and middle fingers, his third cigarette was fixed. A thin thread of smoke rose from it towards the ceiling. Tefil smoked it to the end and crushed out the fag in the ashtray.

Rozmaryn felt it getting muggy and warm in the room, and his view of the little windows in the entrance doors became ever more matt. He recalled a lake of that very colour, and himself sitting on a jetty staring at the tiny waves breaking on the small beach. Tirelessly, the waves broke that same water onto the sand, always the same water standing for age upon age in that lake. Or maybe the water from ages long ago had already evaporated? The waves were just similar to those of ancient times, and tempted one with the very same thing, that same beauty. The water wasn't the same, but the beauty somehow tore through the net of time, passing through the eyes of the net through which so many couldn't squirm their way through. He even remembered what he had eaten on the beach that day. It was a piece of cheesecake made by his aunt, his godmother. The warmth that emanated from the safe, because poor, house of his aunt, where she cooked dinner or baked cheesecake. And each time he began to eat it, he was gripped by terror at the thought that he'd have to finish it, he'd have to go away.

But don't worry – his aunt would say. – Don't worry. Life is good. Look: Grampa Władek passed away, Grampa Stasio, Grampa Czesio. Auntie Józia passed away. And Auntie Gienia, Auntie Hela. And yet: life is always good. Don't be afraid, life is always good. So many millions have passed away, little one – his aunt would say. – So many people murdered throughout the world. And so what? See: life is good all the time. Look: we don't even know who's passed away, they go off in such great masses. No last names, no first names, no house numbers, horses, tables, dinner plates, and life again is good, constantly. We sleep well in warm beds in places where crimes have been committed, on the ground of old cemeteries. And we feel secure. See how wise man is. See what he's able to do. You don't have to think anything up. All you gotta do is live. Unless maybe somebody don't even know how to live. But somebody else does. Life is good. Somebody always knows how to enjoy it. Even if millions can't and perish in the depths of crime. Always somebody can live when somebody else can't. It's pure goodness. See? Crime. But pure goodness.

O! Here comes the schnitzel – said Tefil, taking a drag on a fresh Zefir. He fixed his eyes on the unfinished smoke,

RAFAŁ WOJASIŃSKI

exhaled the smoke from his lungs, and crushed out the fag in the glass-brick ashtray. No, it's tripe. The schnitzel's not coming yet. Here, make some room. The tripe is coming! Tripe! Walking tripe.

The woman with the tray, on which there were two dishes of tripe and bread, neared the little table. She set the tray down on the corner so that the greater portion of it was hanging in the air. Then she took one dish in her right hand, the other in her left, and set them before the two gentlemen, gracefully.

You recognise me, sir? – she flirted with Rozmaryn. – There are two of us, but as our beauty has overcome you, maybe a third will suddenly appear in some dream or during an evening stroll. It's a simple recipe. You, sir, are the first normal-looking, above all the best-looking boy, well, no, man, actually, whom Tefil's ever pulled a dinner out of. And I just can't forget how it overcame you, that there are two of us. One and the other. Surfeit.

And the schnitzel? – asked Tefil.

Of course! – said the woman. – There shall be schnitzel! – And tucking the metal tray, scratched and rusted on the edges, under her arm, she threw one more glance at Rozmaryn. It was obvious that she was grappling with something inside. She stroked the young man's hair and turned, suddenly, returning to the bar. A whole line of those who'll have to drink their booze standing (since all the seats were taken) had formed there. You drink more quickly when you're standing, and more quickly cede your place to the next client. The market was winding down, so you might have expected that in a moment's time the famous restaurant would get crowded and they'd have to start selling bottled beer. And they'd have to call someone else to help at the bar as Amelia – that was the first name of the woman standing at the light-walnut-coloured bar – couldn't handle it all by herself.

Rozmaryn had a few spoonfuls of the tripe, chasing it down with a swallow of vodka. The sun pushed its way into the restaurant with broad shoulders now because somebody left the doors open so as to air the place out. Tefil looked on calmly while his companion ate, and waited. Even in childhood he didn't like hot dishes. He lit up another cigarette. He took a drag and observed how the smoke wafted before his face. It seemed as if he found the moment inebriating. Rozmaryn ate his tripe. Every now and then he shot a glance at Tefil, the way you shoot a glance at a child or a dog, unsure as to what it might do – watching its movements with unease. Tefil smoked his cigarette to the end and set himself to eat. He ate slowly. He sniffed the bread before putting the spoon with the tripe into his mouth, and sniffed the tripe itself every second spoonful. When he'd scooped up the penultimate spoonful, his hand trembled and several drops of the broth from the tripe dripped onto his shirt, leaving two smallish stains. Suddenly, Tefil wiped his lips with the napkin and chucked the spoon onto the table next to the dish. There was such wrath in his face that Rozmaryn wiped the table with the other napkin and placed his spoon in his empty dish.

Perhaps you're witty, sir? – Tefil asked.

Facial expression, comb of the hair. Hand, foot, eye, ear. You're at the witty stage, but who knows...

Better forget about it, sir.

Forget about it. You need to constantly forget. That's the way it is. There are so many paths of forgetfulness. And I'll go along each of them with you, gladly. Don't be cross. Don't turn away with disgust. You're looking at my cheek? My left cheek? That soft tissue has been tormenting me for years. Between my left middle tooth and the cheek. That's why I stick my finger into my mouth and check it out. It's constantly soft and swollen. A sponge, kind of. And how am I to deal with that piece of life, which is that part,

RAFAŁ WOJASIŃSKI

exactly that part? It's like my tooth isn't really hurting bad, but the inflammation endures. It dies down for a while, for a month, for example, a year, but then, without any rhyme or reason, because of the slightest change in the weather, because of an open window, an open door, it returns and starts to irk me. It's been like that since my earliest youth. All I had to do was have it taken care of and stop going in the predetermined direction. The development of that state of inflammation is inevitable and the results entirely foreseeable. But, you know, sir, I'm not in a proper state for a cure. I'm not in the proper state to cross that boundary, beyond which I might find myself in a better world, a world of people cared for, healthier people, people of better promise, and, God forbid, talented people, dressed up in new trousers. New trousers would be the death of me, I know that for sure. Nobody is more mortally threatened with quality than I. Especially trousers. I had to launder those old trousers, you know, sir, for many years, because all it took was for me to go outside, which I often put off for hours on end, all it took was for me to take myself in hand and go out to buy bread, milk and butter, and kefir, and herrings, all it took was for me to go outside and Prodige would already make me filthy. That is, my trousers. First she'd come up from behind and scratch me with her paws, as if she wanted to restrain me so that I shouldn't get to the tree next to which I'd bury her later, or to the shack, where sometimes I'd sit with her. And then, completely out of control, she'd jump all over me and mercilessly mess up those trousers, all over, waist to ankles, front and back. And she'd leave these blurry paw prints all over me. Those at the height of the calves were especially so large that it'd be hard to find a clean space there. And the more emphatically I'd tell her not to do that, the more stridently she'd soil me, jumping around. Don't jump! – I'd say. – No! Down! Stop it! But she'd just keep on doing it all the more, jumping, pushing her nose into the pockets of my cotton-lined jacket or my trousers. She'd lick me, she'd make these soft eyes, she'd take my hand gently between her teeth, but all the time she'd be jumping, all the time making me filthy.

What were you dreaming of, sir, when you were pouring out the vodka? I noticed the expression on your face... Of little waves breaking on a beach, right? And that...

That, that, that... What kind of a word is that? Tell me: That, that, that... I think that it's raining outside. You see those drops on the windowpane, sir? They're running down it.

I ought to be sitting under that little roof with Prodige right now, making sure that it's not raining on us.

I'd waited so many years to get interested in something. And out I come with taking care of Prodige. I shall free myself of this sense of obligation that oppresses me, this unending sense of obligation towards Prodige. This constant worrying if it's dry for the dog, warm enough, has remained so deeply ingrained in me that the dog's death changed nothing. It doesn't pass. Even dying doesn't nullify the obligation which was born in me during the life of my dog. That obligation has so tormented me, depraved me, that only with difficulty can I start every day, unable to find the strength to move my hand, my leg, my head. Responsibility causes me to assume a dead position. I wait an hour in that position, pretending to be dead. Pretending to be dead is also one of my joys. I lie there like that and wait until an affection for something, anything, of this world should occur to me, an affection for some business, for some activity to give my life what we call sense, an idea... And so I wait until there awakens in me that great strength that creates works, civilisations. I wait until something really interests me. And nothing. Nothing but waiting... Each day the only thing that remains to me: a senseless love of life. A love of breathing, looking... And that ever-returning waiting...

RAFAŁ WOJASIŃSKI

That I'll get some passion in the end, some hobby, religion, ideology. And nothing.

Can a dog be that interesting thing? Is Prodige my great interest? My passion? Is the ceaseless care for a dog, so it's not cold for him, or wet, so that he's not hungry – is that a hobby? Is staring up at the sky an interest? Is schlepping about aimlessly a passion? A type of religion? Is stuffing your face and drinking a hobby? Is praying in a foxhole a passion? Is the constant terror that you're a stupid and an evil person a hobby? Is scratching your armpit a passion? Scratching your back? Licking clean your dish and your spoon – a passion or interest? Is the desire to pretend you're dead a passion? Is stupidity a hobby or a passion? Is the lack of intelligence a hobby? Just to have one passion, one, just one hobby. And nothing… No message from the cosmos… The stars don't speak to me, nor do the planetary movements, the seasons of the year… Is getting lost at all seasons of the year, day and night, on Garbarska a passion? An interest? A hobby?

So nothing's left me, Rozmaryn, sir, but Prodige (not a hobby, not a passion, not an interest, not a religion, not a culture, not manners). We sort of found one another, took one another in. We'd snuggle on the cold days under the roof in the shack you can see from the other side. There, where the window of my flat gives out onto the yard, down to the left there's that ramshackle outbuilding. The doors don't close, and nobody's gonna fix them. There's a little heap of old things inside… But me and Prodige felt best in that shack. It was so nice there. Like nowhere else. Sometimes I slept out there with her. I brought out her food and my food and beer. That food was always the same: bread and sausage. And the same beer. Prodige loved beer. That was paradise. I don't give a fig for any other. And because that was paradise, I ought to be with Prodige now. I should be. Was there anything else in my life like Prodige? Anything so important? Oh! Nothing. There was nothing. Now I can see it as plain as the palm of my hand, that there was nothing.

You think, sir, I'm a little, you-know? You don't think anything. You have to take care of a dog. And I do. From pure love. How can you protect that dog's body? How can I pour her water? Well, I suppose I could. From top to bottom. Plum, plum, plum... But how can she drink and eat and defecate since she died so long ago? I need an answer to that question. I need an answer to that question! Or, how can you embrace cremated ashes? Because these days they cremate dogs. Just like people. Did you know, sir? I buried dogs, but today they burn them. So then, how can you cuddle ashes? And Prodige was a person, you know? Real. In truth. Only now there's no trace of her. I can't find anything that would be that dog that got me filthy, that sometimes took away my desire to leave my flat in the garret so effectively, that I'd be camped out there for a whole week and only tossed out the window the scraps of my food to her.

I don't even find clumps of Prodige's fur anymore. But I find socks. You know, sir? I find quite a few socks. I collect them. People toss out an enormous amount of socks. I don't darn them if they have holes, I just put them on like that, with holes, and walk about in them. They wash them, and then they throw them out. Isn't that strange? Or at least it seems to me that they're washed... Have you seen the holes in my socks, sir? Not yet? No matter. That's my way. These socks are the best way to keep calm. They're material for free will and freedom. It's an excellent, pure thing. Cleanliness and hygiene. The hygiene of vanishing. The hygiene of collecting someone's old socks. Not transforming, burning, recycling, grinding into dust in hand mills. The hygiene of collection. So that in the end you can't find a single trace. Especially the trace of a dog who never had a doghouse and

RAFAŁ WOJASIŃSKI

whose picture was never taken. There's no doctor, no house-wife, no ambulance driver, and no postman. There's just a sock with a hole in it. I hope that this is sufficiently clear to you. The sock remains. But the owner must be removed. That is, the owner of the sock. Just like Prodige was the owner, let's say, of her clumps of fur. Beginning.

Cleanliness. Cleanliness in houses, in beds, hospitals, night-shelters, autopsy rooms. And cleanliness of the tongue, obviously. Purity of expression, purity of faith, religion, ideology, purity in confessing crime and love. And finally – the cleanliness and purity of God Himself. My mother always said that it's got to be clean, that it's got to be cleaned up. Just like you've got to wash a corpse, which has to be cleaned up, but, above all, taken away. But you don't wash a dead dog. Dirty he goes into the dirty earth. Although the earth isn't dirty, it's the font of life. Birth, sprouting, the bulb grows, the root lengthens, carrot, pars-ley, swede, potato, onion, radish. So the earth doesn't soil anything. And so on. And on. And so.

Instead of sitting here with you, sir, – Tefil also said. – I ought to be with Prodige. It's really windy out, and it seems to me that it's gonna start raining even harder in a bit. Prodige would eat something (she hasn't eaten in a long while) and she'd stare in one place, just like she used to (she hasn't seen anything in a long time). She'd freeze like that with her eyes glued to one place. X-raying it with her motionless stare. Looking, breathing, odour. She'd take a few canine steps and then she'd lay herself down beneath the little roof of the shack. Then suddenly she'd get up and start searching for some place to leak and make a pile, because a man'll go any-where at all, but a dog, no. Then she'd sniff at what she'd done and then lie down again beneath the little roof. And so on. And on. And so.

How many times with my toothache have I sat near her on a stool in my yard that I inherited from the chemistry teacher, which she inherited from some forgotten person (millions of forgotten children, grandmas, daddies, mamas, sisters, brothers, sons, daughters, beginning). I sat like that. And so on. And on. And so. I add my forgetfulness to forgetfulness, people, animals, things, and images. Forgetting is memory at the outset, and with time, with death and the births of further people and dogs, hens, rabbits, it stops being memory. Inexorably it heads towards falsification, to the forgery of reality, and at last it becomes what it was before, when memory had not yet been born. And so on. And on. And so.

I have added nothing to forgetfulness except forgetfulness. Slipping on slippers, washing plates, changing a child's diaper, the cutting of hair, the kindling of fire, the drawing of water. Beginning. I admit that I've done everything that has been forgotten: I fed the dog, I let her out of the shack and into the yard. I admit that the dog (a bitch) shed her fur, lay down, chased a ball, and hid from the rain along with me under the roof. She displayed a great love of life by living. I admit that the bitch was Prodige. I confess that I ate and drank. I confess that I slept, that I looked up at the sky and sat on a stool during her life. I admit that for many years I traipsed that same road every day, in search of the path destined to me, and that that search did not differ at all from the search for slippers lost a day before. Going out into the streets, going out, strolling, breathing the air, gazing up at the sky during the day or at night.

I confess that I can't be with my dog because my dog cannot be. Every day. And so on. And on. And so. The dog cannot be. If I can't be present by my dog and if I can't protect her… If I can't… So then, if not… Yes. In that case it can only be that… And nothing more… That's how it stays? That? And now? And so on? And on? And so?

As you know or don't know, sir, the yard belongs to that little flat in the garret. To my flat now. From the chemistry

RAFAŁ WOJASIŃSKI

teacher. You know that. The yard is five by ten metres. Or fifteen by thirteen. You enter my flat from the yard by climbing up steep wooden steps, just like you would to reach such a little cubbyhole set up high. Maybe it was a little cubbyhole and that's why there were so many treasures in the cupboard? But probably not a cubbyhole because there's windows, a door, because there's a floor and a ceiling. And that niche for the cupboard. The yard has a fence with a gate. To the left of the yard stands that shack I told you about, and that's where Prodige slept at night. In the evening, before going to sleep, I'd block the door to my flat in the garret with a felt plate with a hole for the handle and I'd push the garden bench up against it. I'd set a huge, twenty kilo pumpkin on the bench. When the pumpkin rotted, I'd use two heavy pine logs. I placed a thick staff diagonally behind the handle so as to block the plate. Because Prodige had this custom of scratching at the door all night long, and I just couldn't listen to that scratching and whining, so I blocked the door.

I can draw it for you, sir. It's simple. 1,1,1,1 – these are the four corners of the door. 2 x 2 are the legs of the bench. 1 is the seat. 5 is the seat and the backrest. 0,0,0 is the pumpkin – – – – – – – are the pine logs. / means the staff set up at an angle against the handle. See it now, sir? Have the clouds parted? Do you see it now with the eyes of the imagination? More or less?

When I'd already set up the felt plate with the hole for the handle and pushed close the bench, pressing the plate tight to the door, and when I'd set the pumpkin on the bench, I'd go back down into the yard and then, through the gate, onto Garbarska, and then left, another left, and I'd enter the building from the other side and go up over the stairs to my little flat in the garret. I'd lock the door from within. For a while I could still smell the scent of the wooden stairs, the odour of humidity and the darkness of the stairwell. And I'd do this every day. And so on. And on. And so.

Tunnel. In the tunnel there are births, in the tunnel is the life and death of father, grandfather, great grandmother, mother, aunt, uncle, happiness, and salvation... You never exit the tunnel. You never get out anywhere. You remain. You can't see any fur; Prodige doesn't eat or bark or scrape; she doesn't hide under the little roof of the shack in wind and rain, but remains where she is. All the time.

There's no exit from the tunnel. That's where all the little carts are collected, the boots, fingernails, scarves, dog dishes, sleep, cuffs, spoons, forks, the grumble of the engine, the song of the skylark, the mooing of the cow, and the grunting of the pigs. Taken away are washing of the face, the singing of a young girl, and the closeness of two bodies. Taken away is beauty, ugliness, and the gap between the teeth; at last, love, vows, faith, peace, hope, salvation, and the all-embracing, incontrovertible joy of life... There's nothing like it, nestling in one's arms whatever's lost its name, the colour of hair, the size of the foot, the girth of the waist, the colour of eyes, and the temperature of the body. There is however some hope because somebody remains here, always. Always and again somebody's here. Really. Looking into a dish of tripe and lifting it to the mouth, then a swallow and into the gut. And that's where hope and the joy of life is made. There, in that dark stomach, it's made. That's all. The God who speaks, and the dumb God. The ideal God. God, before the word 'God' came about. It all takes place in the dark stomach. Give a dog food and it takes place in the dark stomach of the dog. It comes about by itself, of itself, or alone with existence. Because nothing exists besides existence in the entire endless area of the cosmos, galaxies, and tiny corners. In doghouses, in shacks, and underneath the benches in the park. Alive or dead. Comes to be and comes to be. And it is.

RAFAŁ WOJASIŃSKI

Absorption. Beginning. I know, Rozmaryn, sir, forgive me. And pour. And forgive. And a spoon of soup. And forgive, and forgive, because it all goes on in the dark stomach. Beginning.

There was nothing in the beginning! That's the whole mystery. It was a little at a time. First something like a leg, something like a hand, something like walking on twos, something like a head, like ears, a knee, something like a nose, something like speech, something like a tongue, like a song. There was nothing first, at the beginning. Let's stop talking about that beginning already. That thinking about first beginnings has messed us up in the head so that even the first secretary came about, the first bishop, the first man on the Moon, the first murderer, the first adulterer, the first...In the beginning, beginning, beginning. Bluff. Rub. Bish.

That mother again. Rozmaryn, dear sir! You are constantly interrupting me with that mother, sir. You're jamming the airwaves. Mother, mother, mother. Mother above all. The question of all questions. About your mother. I also had a mother. I remember her, not like you... She could gripe like nobody's business. She had such a talent for griping that she could go on for hours. And how! I get that from her... That's the only trait of mine I like. Maybe it's only griping that I find likeable in me. Liberational griping, griping that bestows beauty upon the worthless breaths of wind, the fluffy white clouds that sail the heavens... Her griping went more or less like this:

Cheese, no. Pâté, no. Eggs, no. I ate the ground cutlets. Two and one and a half. The cat got the other half. Why did I eat so much? I'm worried that if somebody dies on me, I'll eat myself to death with longing and mourning. I eat too much because such was my life that I never went anywhere. I never experienced anything. I shall die undeveloped. I didn't even read my schoolbooks. They talked at me, and

I didn't even glance at them once. I didn't have any free time to. I didn't develop and I didn't visit any place. I don't know the name of any composer or scientist, any writer, any genius... The Germans knew a lot of names like that... Whole biographies of the great and the wise... Just a snatch of a melody to identify the whole... I never developed... I was always in the field. Or in the woods. For mushrooms. Or at a dance at the fire hall. What bad luck. I'm undeveloped. An undeveloped old cow. What did I do with my life? If at least I'd developed religiously. But not even that. Chickens, pigs, and cows. And one technique. Slicing, frying, cooking. One technique. Walking from place to place, squatting, sitting, getting up, milking, carrying pails, plates, rakes. The same technique in all of that. Giving birth, feeding. Making beds, lying down, getting up, looking for the cat because there are mice, looking for the dog because he got out at night through a hole in the fence... Sandwiches for school, sandwiches for breakfast, scrambled eggs for breakfast. On Saturday bathing one after the other in the same water, drying everyone with one towel. Washing the floor, carting the manure, sowing, making furrows. Day, night. Freezing cold, sweltering heat. One and the same technique... Digging potatoes, burying the dead, making holes, putting in, covering up, money on the plate, money given in bribes. Our Father... Hail Mary... One technique.

To deceive, to delude, to poison, and to give antidotes in proof of goodness. It's best to go stupid and make others stupid... And to take a beautiful park alley amidst the songs of skylarks beneath a blue sky, in the aroma of flowers and perfumes... One technique.

Getting attached to walls, a piece of grass, a door. I always knew there was something not right, especially at those times when I felt beauty... I didn't develop, and that's how I'll die. I'm an example unto myself, a lesson, and a warning. I won't eat and I won't drink. Maybe an egg? I

RAFAŁ WOJASIŃSKI

don't like to eat anything. So why am I growing bigger and bigger around the waist? Why?

That's the way it might go, Rozmaryn, sir, more or less. To put it gently, switching things around, changing their order, falsifying, counterfeiting. Beginning. My mother gave birth to me. As yours did you, Rozmaryn, sir. Two mothers from one and the same world. One and the same material. Shared material. One body encoded in millions of bodies gives birth to us. And takes us away, not letting us out of the tunnel, shining deceptive lights our way. A brightness which can engender nothing because it is in the tunnel. And the tunnel is only one element of itself, its existence, the existence of a tunnel. The tunnel has no exterior. Everyone and everything is inside it. The outside does not exist. The poles are in the tunnel, north and south. Hope. Faith. And love. It's impossible to exit, to get up and go and escape. Beginning...

It sucks us in. Can you feel it, sir? I certainly can. It engages me. Even those little windows in the entrance door. And the panelling. The colour of the panelling, which changes as the sky goes overcast. The sight of your shoes, Rozmaryn, sir... The sight of the table legs in this restaurant... The same thing with the dish after the tripe has been eaten, the woman at the bar, the voices of the people from the market, of whom there are so many here. Grey reality, as those who are uninitiated in it all say. But how to initiate them? Let's have another toot, sir – half a glass each.

And so, as if to begin once again, that a man has a dog, and the dog dies, well, then, as the dog dies leaving nary a tuft of fur behind him, well, it's like to begin once more that the dog's here again and is eating, that the man is giving the dog food, the dog eats it, and then it takes place in its black belly, you understand me, sir, what takes place in the belly of dog and man... The joy of life... Love for another existence... So as if to start again... As if to start. Just think now, sir. So to begin again another dog and another man, who gives him food, to begin it all again...

Dog begun and man begun. And thought. The thoughts of a dog. The thoughts of a man.

Rozmaryn noticed that the cuffs of Tefil's shirt had been stained with the fatty broth of the tripe. There were also some old stains on the cuffs, the fattiness of which seeped into the bun-like hands of Tefil.

I can't pass out – Tefil said. – Not before the bottle's finished. People condemn the little and the poor for the dirt under their nails. They praise the toff for the very worst things. Three, seven, twelve, eight, five, zero, two, thirteen. I'm counting. How much is left us. Booze in the bottle.

And what business is it of yours, Rozmaryn, sir, how I count? You concentrate, sir, on that which penetrates you because the rest won't penetrate at all. Although even that which does get through, that is quite familiar to us, is nothing but a head-fake... Was there a funeral today, too? Did the funeral bells toll? It's so dry. Probably not... But one, maybe. If there had been a funeral procession, we'd have noticed it. The songs and all the rest. Funerals are good for a person's mental health. Especially strangers. When a person isn't moving, but something penetrates his noggin. Nothing special but something. They carry off the corpse, and here a six-year-old's looking on, and it tastes good to him. A little miss passes by and the driver of the hearse ogles her as she passes. This or that one, maybe every other one, is hungry for the chicken soup at the funeral brunch. And the music plays. Fantastic plastic. Perpetuum mobile. Well then, down the hatch! No one can resist the love of life... Bewildered... One foot. Two foot. May we... – Tefil said. – Oof! And onward. Rum, tum, tum. Marvellous. Even more...

You see, sir? Left, right. From the door and from the bar. Such good luck. And inexpensive too. Ever more inex-

RAFAŁ WOJASIŃSKI

pensive, it seems to me. Each one cheaper than the last. The cost... Imaginations in the image and likeness. The heart fairly sings. All you need do is throw a glance at those mugs by the bar. They are what they are... But it sings. It's worth coughing it up. It's worth wasting it. The abyss. Even if you feel kind of stupid later on. Wretched. And the weeping. And the grinding. And the penance. And Ash Wednesday. And Ash Thursday. And maybe Ash Friday. And Saturday. And even Sunday. And. There are eyes, but they see not. Because it's better not to see. Or hear. Because it can't be seen, heard, caught sight of. That it's all different than you reckon. That's the foundation. And that you can... You can anything at all... But only theoretically. So then, bottoms up. So that. We might rave a bit. Touch wood. And... And... And... Staring at a bone. Kicking the pebbles along the country road, skipping stones across the water, thrashing the burdock leaves with a stick, digging in the sand, making holes, drawing lines in the dirt (signs, signs, signs). Now we're talking rubbish... And that's why we're sticking it out together... Patterns, patterns, patterns... Estimating, overestimating, descriptions of nature, of love... Descriptions of the fates of entire families, villages, and nations... We recount stories, anecdotes... We search out boobies... To listen to us... All we can do is chunter and babble... In search of wonder... Shh! Hush now! All you gotta do is wait, nobody'll give a toss about the stains. Nothing will remain of people that'll be worth anyone's notice. Not a single sentence! Everything discovered turns out to be mistakes and glitter! All you gotta do is wait.

I feel a draught about my legs. They keep opening and closing the doors. Why're you looking at like that, sir? You feel unwell? Was it the tripe or the alcohol? What's up, sir? You just go slack like that? Without rhyme or reason? Is it a sickness? What is it? Maybe you're astounded? Or ravished? Or maybe you're dreaming of lakes and rowboats?

No, no!

I begin and begin again. And I know so many jokes, after all. So many good jokes about drinking, sex, food, power. The church. And nothing. Good for nothing when you're here. Like a dungeon. A mystery of reason that I can't even get a bit of traction with you. Just keep spinning the wheels. My best jokes are about the dead... Standing, sitting, lying down, of dead people in a crouch. Man has become fussy about his dying. Everybody wants to lie off to the side, alone, nobody wants to be together in a group, even for a few years before the headstone gets chiselled with other names. Just think: all they have to do is dig one pit, really. But no! No! No question of that! Everybody wants his own monument. And even monuments break down, sink, and over the dead they set a new person and a new monument. It's driving us to ruin, not only mental ruin, but economic ruin. That square metre of graveyard is probably the most expensive square metre in the whole city. I follow the parish price tables. That's the best, most sensitive economic indicator. The graveyard square metre. When you tot that up along with the marble, even terrazzo, let's say, and the priest's fees, the doctor's fees, and all, it comes out to be more expensive than a square metre in a new apartment, in a new building of flats. Can you make sense of that, sir? Because I can't.

Maybe we should be buried standing? So many things we've thought up... Inventions. One more, one less...

So then, I don't remember, I don't know, it doesn't get through to me... No written truth, proven... Pictures, memoirs, notes... Perfect descriptions of the process of... Escapes... And the return, which must be followed by the next escape... Faith... That it'll all turn out well... Nothing gets through but propaganda... One foot, two foot... Going down the steps, holding onto the banister... Sniffing the must and the cold fixed into existence like a fingerprint on

RAFAŁ WOJASIŃSKI

the banister... One foot, two foot... Passing from one side of Garbarska Street to the other. Walking, stunned by the view of the sky, seeking joy and delight in the consciousness of the endless regions above our heads... So there is no end to it... How splendid, that no end exists of what you see with your naked eye in the blue of heaven... Space without end... As if evidence of eternity... The rest is ritual devotion. Or deviation. As you wish.

I should gather my thoughts... But when I try to, this beginning worms its way into my head and swallows everything I want to think up. Sucking, beginning. The least little motion brings me ruin, a left turn and a right turn, prayer and the fact that sometimes I can't recall a single word. All that remains to me is aaa, ooo, huhuhuh, or something like that. And it so happens that sometimes I don't even have so much at hand. The second, after which the letter of the law no longer applies to a man, nourishment in groups and individually, chronic illnesses and those that are curable, taxes and honoraria. Then just one dog. Winter or summer, rain or shine. Night or day. War and peace. Unease and ease. Just one dog then, already.

I once went along Garbarska for the umpteenth time thinking about this, after about an hour or two sitting in the famous restaurant, only at a different table than that we're sitting at now. I was going to Kolska Steet and returning to the hydrant on the pavement right next to the crossroads that leads to the Catholic cemetery. I remember that it was bitterly cold and every now and then I started worrying about Prodige, who was still alive at the time, wondering whether I left the door to her shack open. I was close enough to my yard, but I was in such a state, in such a situation, that I couldn't leave Garbarska Street. So I went along the street, arousing the hostility of passers-by and those who noticed me through the windows of the low Jewish houses. I would go there and back, there and back.

I would glance down each free space between the houses, into the entranceways of the blocks of flats and the low houses behind which there stretched yards similar to mine, yards with sheds and cellars for coal and privies... And... And... Aaaaa stuu... stuu... stuuu ...u... uuu... uuttering. Stu...u...u...tuh...tuh...tuh... Stut... That's the vanishing of speech. O! There we are. Stopped of itself.

My hands and feet were frozen, I felt my bladder beginning to pain me, but I couldn't leave that place, because I'd discovered there the ideal discardedness, the stunning worthlessness, a straying which isn't getting lost, but had become already a sort of happiness, the lack of belonging. The ideal of life on Garbarska, in old trousers, thinking about a dog, wanting to drink a beer or a shot of vodka and the feeling of all-embracing beginning, all-embracing reality. Absorption. The ideal of life. Emptiness in the head. Wind. Cold. Livid clouds in the sky. The beating of the heart, breathing, warming the hands in one's pockets. God. And the word 'God'. The soul and the certainty that the soul is unnecessary. Beginning absorption and that. Second after second, minute after minute. Days, weeks, years. The beginning of time. The end of time. The lack of time and orbits around the Sun. The lack of a beginning after the end. Beginning absorption and that.

Amelia then approached Rozmaryn and Tefil's table with a tray from which she took two white plates ringed in blue with schnitzel and cabbage and potatoes and set them before them. She then set the empty bowls of tripe and dirty napkins on the tray. She said nothing, but her face was sad and tired. Rozmaryn poured out the rest of the vodka into the little glasses, upon which Tefil took the empty bottle from the table and placed it near the table leg, on the inside so that no passer-by should stumble against it. Such was his custom. Rozmaryn understood the allusion and went off for two mugs of beer.

RAFAŁ WOJASIŃSKI

I apologise for talking with my mouth full, but you must know, sir, that you may stay the night with me. I have one little corner of which you are unaware, as the time you've spent so far in my marvellous flat inherited from the schoolteacher was too short to notice it. So I also have a place for guests. In a certain sense, guests are an essential matter in my life – said Tefil. – The arrival of others is not only a disturbance. Coming over, sitting, talking, and crossing legs. Like a church ritual… And one pontificates thus and thus… Speaking.

Tefil glanced at the watch he wore a bit too high on the wrist of his left arm. He also took the opportunity of making sure that the coarsely weft grey band was well fastened, and fixed one of the loops. He'd bought that band a couple dozen years before on the same market square where they sell porkers. The day once more became un-expectedly warm and bright. It was getting close to noon.

Rozmaryn's thoughts suddenly began to rattle and scratch. Khr, khr, khr, and then shshshshshshshsh, and at the end plum, plum, plum. There was no end to this, as the thoughts were jostling against one another to manifest themselves in Rozmaryn's head. They hissed and whistled. At last they grew a bit silent, only to once again make themselves known: iiiiiiiiiiii, uuuuuuuuuu, ooooooooo, eeeeeee, aaaaaaaa. There was a look of concentration on Rozmaryn's face. His brow was furrowed, his eyes fixed somewhere in the distance, where the door of the famous restaurant was found, and a little beyond it – through those little windows set therein and held in place with some putty, which bore the distinct prints of someone's fingers.

Rozmaryn glanced at Tefil. Tefil made a sign to Rozmaryn. A delicate, actually barely noticeable signal: a nod of the head to the left accompanied by a simultaneous motion of his index finger, also pointing left. Rozmaryn got up as quickly as he could. He was polite by nature. He was himself surprised at the way he'd sometimes take three steps forward in life, and immediately four or five to the rear. Tefil was already standing by the door of the famous restaurant. He went out first, and Rozmaryn followed. He'd hardly set his foot on the sidewalk, warmed by the strong sun, when right behind his back Amelia appeared.

Money! she screamed.

Does this often occur with you? – Tefil asked Rozmaryn. – Not paying, I mean. How could you forget that, sir? You are young; compared to me, very, very young. If you live to my age, you'll be completely off the rails by then.

Rozmaryn pulled out his wallet and counted out the sum of the bill, handing the money over to Amelia. Then, he stuffed a tenner in the pocket of her apron. The smallest value printed. Amelia folded the money in her hand and placed it in the left pocket of her apron (the tenner was in the right pocket), after which she stroked Rozmaryn on the head with the same hand, mussing his hair.

Good lad – she said. – Please come again. Maybe without Tefil next time.

Rozmaryn felt a pleasure flow all throughout his body. As Amelia turned to leave, as she was opening the door to the famous restaurant, he stared at her from behind, he was unable not to. He wanted to drink in as long as he could the motion of her cheeks as they rocked beneath her dress (beginning and end). Amelia vanished through the doors, and Tefil grabbed Rozmaryn by the left arm, right above the elbow, and, holding on tightly, led him onto the zebra crossing. A moment later they found themselves among the trees of the only park in town. They stood there next to each other. Oriented for a moment, as they knew where everything was to be found, where the bread is baked, where it's sold, where you can buy shoes, trousers, or a hand meat-grinder. They knew where people wash the

RAFAŁ WOJASIŃSKI

corpses and where they plant them, where the city director lives, and where the parish priest.

So look over there – Tefil said. – between those two trees. You see? Look! That's the fat old lady that was screaming at you when you went for my glasses. Standing there. That's her. Her. Until the day she dies. Inevitable. In this case, the algorithm is unerring. Something is born, becomes a screamer, a real pain in the arse, a martyr, a good man by choice or by nature, because that's determined by the algorithm. And so it goes until you die and cease to exist. You can't get out of it, you can't grow out of it. From evil or from good.

Here. Always here. We always end up here, even the way we picture God ended up here, ghosts end up here. Everything ends up here. Even the space aliens we dream about are supposed to end up here. This is the limit of our imagination. The province. Our imagination cannot be greater than the imagination of a dog. It's only different. His life solves the riddle of existence in the same way as ours. The difference is only that we can pound a couple of shots and babble, babble, babble. Even when the world ceases to be, there will be no changes in the offing because you must know, sir, the algorithm is the same and works the same, constantly, whatever the birth or the death. Tunnel. Beginning. It won't give an inch. Tunnel, Beginning. One structure. One technique. Whether something is or something is very lacking. Even at the birth of some new world. Here is the end of our knowledge. A province, a shabby province, no larger than Mars or Venus, of course. Rozmaryn, sir, the knowledge of a dog cannot differ from our own. Impossible. Understanding does not exist. Beginning exists. The algorithm. The only technique. And. Damn it, concentrate, sir! You dullard, you! Concentrate? Well, and? Well, and? Well, what? Nothing? What do you mean? And that image? Look, sir. Look well. Look.

Between the decorative apple in bloom and that old poplar there is this little path – Tefil added. – Now, set your head almost in the very centre of that hole and look. Not at the window. Lower. On the wall. The image of a human figure. But if you go right or left, the figure disappears. What is that?

A damp stain? A verdict of destiny? A prophecy? An unexplained phenomenon? Hope? Sense? Peace of soul?

Do you think, Rozmaryn, sir, that God might manifest Himself in this way?

That I don't believe?

There you have it. Right on the money.

That I don't pray?

But what has that to do with anything? I'm constantly praying. I'm unable to do otherwise. I mix up the words, I think up my own aves, but I pray... I pray because sometimes I just can't handle it. Especially when I exceed the limit with alcohol, although that boundary is well known to me. I fall into such horrid terrors, so I pray, I become humble, meek. I pray my rosary for hours on end. Because I'm terrified, Rozmaryn, sir. Terror is my good counsel if we're speaking of theology. If it weren't for terror, I'd have no theological depth. My soul would become terribly shallow and frivolous. Without terror both soul and intelligence can disappear. Just like in the absence of authority. If one stood not in terror of the mighty... That'd be the end... How did you know, sir, that I don't pray?

When I'm falling asleep after something sweet, I actually kind of purr, and in that kind of purring you can make out the words of a prayer.

You. Take. Give. Go. Come. Have. Kill. Humble. O yes and some dirty words as well.

Dirty words. Dirty words never change – same old, so they needn't be repeated.

RAFAŁ WOJASIŃSKI

Tefil buttoned his blazer on the button that was hanging desperately from its thread, and lifted up the collar of his trench coat. The wind was up. Quickly, it dried his head of sweat and Tefil felt more comfortable. Rozmaryn took a couple steps forward. He peered at the figure on the wall of the corner block of flats with its oval summit. Slowly, Tefil moved on ahead. Rozmaryn was walking to his right.

Two minutes later, without rushing, even slowing their pace, they passed through the park and pulled up at the zebra crossing that ran across the road on which the trucks rumbled from north to south. There were maybe ten of them every day. The road was clear, but the dust was still floating in the air above it. They entered that cloud of dust, Tefil and Rozmaryn, two wanderers, who had, after all, only a moment, this short life, which seems to be such an extraordinary coincidence. Eyes, moving hands, the sense of taste, smell, touch. And the coincidence that they might unite their existences in this walkabout, together. An extraordinary coincidence. That is, concrete data: place, time of day, degree of rotation of the planet, the age of the persons, their height, names, the state of their heart, liver, pancreas, the magpie who was just outscreaming the sound of the cars, the half-shut gate to the garden near the rental block on the other side of the zebra stripes before which they were standing just then. Coincidence. Indispensable pieces of a puzzle. The certainty of the pieces and of the algorithm.

To the right, some hundred metres away, the Catholic church stood on its hill, the oldest part of which dated from the thirteenth century. Coincidence. Proof of the great superiority of existence over the lack thereof and the nonexistence of those who once existed, and had the advantage over those who at the time existed no more. The dubious superiority of the living over the dead. The real superiority.

We've got to turn round – Tefil said. – I took a wrong turn. We should've gone to the place where the old German gendarmerie used to be. We have to turn round. Let's go. Now. We'll go past the famous restaurant, the pre-war hotel, and the cinema that was on the ground floor there. What's with you, sir? Maybe we'll stop in at the restaurant and have a beer. You still got some cash? You'd like to have another eyeful of Amelia, wouldn't you? That is, Amelia's tits. Right? What else in this world could be righter? That's the only thing that's right. And if it's wrong to anyone, well, he's wasting his life in sadness and regret.

They crossed the stripes again quickly. A moment later they were at the fountain in the park, but on the other side of where the bench stood, on which they'd rested after eating their cake and drinking their coffee in the pastry shop.

Who taught you to swear, sir? – Tefil asked.

From whom did you most often hear 'f' and 'c' and 's' and 'd'?

You don't know?

I learned from a certain lady, so to speak, when I was six years old. She lived with us, that is, with my family, next-door neighbour. She had a lot of chickens and ducks. And she cursed a blue streak at them all. She might not have known any other words except those beginning with 'd' and 'c' and 'f' and 'mf'. Whenever she said 'f', the hens would walk calmly to the coop and make no mistake about it, as if suddenly a lightbulb had been lit above their heads. But in the depths of my soul I was certain that they didn't understand that word beginning with 'f', but just went there of their own will (the will of hens). I stood by the fence and listened to the splendid melody of swearwords swirling amidst the buildings, the trees, the henhouses, the barns, and the doghouses, which later floated upwards into the heavens like a litany. I couldn't get enough of those words. I stood rooted to the spot with my little hands on the fence.

RAFAŁ WOJASIŃSKI

If the chickens and ducks understood nothing of all that, just went along knowing what they were supposed to do upon hearing them, that meant that I might not understand them either, but decipher them, too. Then I cursed a blue streak myself for three days without pause. I used no other words. I did that when I was alone, in the barn or in the garden. And suddenly... I lost the power of speech. I stood there in front of the apple tree, dumb, and just stared out in front of me. No mistake. Not a single error. And then everything returned. Complete sentences. Grammatical clarity. The eternal, intractable, overwhelming, and pitiless forging of the truth. Rubbish. Rub. Bish.

That fountain water's nice. You can freshen your hands. Go ahead, sir. I will. I'll wash mine. And I shall become cleaner.

Zero. Reckoning. I must reckon something up. Cash. In recollection. Lying there amongst the old socks in the drawer. I count it up sometimes in order to know how much I have. Long-distance counting. And zero again. Minus seventeen. Plus seven. Minus three. It doesn't add up. In any language. Null. Nope... Nothing. There are no numbers. Digits... There's no addition... And there was... Once upon a time there was plus, minus, times... And it worked. It don't work now... Has anyone discovered this before me? I'm the one who discovered it? Me? That there's no more addition in the world? Me? I was smart enough to?

Tefil submerged his hands in the fountain at the height of his knees. Rozmaryn stood to the side, on the right, and watched his companion bend over and rise again, straightening his back with a moan. Tefil took off his trench coat, his blazer too, and lay them down on the bench, a few steps away from the place where he washed his hands. Then he unbuttoned his shirt half-way and inserted his hand with some water scooped from the fountain. He washed his belly, then the back of his neck and his face. He didn't dry himself, he just sat down on the bench next to his trench coat and blazer. He breathed evenly. The satisfaction in his eyes, the relief, was plain to see. Rozmaryn went over and stood in front of Tefil, blocking out a portion of the sun. He had his hands in his pockets. He smiled.

What are you making such a face for, sir? – asked Tefil. – What is it? You're smiling? Body language says a lot. Wash yourself. The water's a little dirty. But I wash myself in that fountain from spring to late fall and do you see any scabs on my skin, sir? It's dirt, quite simply. Benevolently, ordinarily. Graciously dirty. Some specks are floating about in it, leaves, hair, a stick, and, it seems to me, the remains of some little animal.

Do you still have a bit of money, sir? A good bit?

Are you afraid of ghosts, sir?

No?

But you're afraid of specks in the water?

Ah, people have got out of hand – said Tefil, changing his tone. He grew serious. – A mug of beer and the sight of a stain on the wall, and the sun that blinds a person sitting in the park on a bench with his legs stretched out, that's no longer enough to satisfy them. There has to be propaganda. Or a win. A win in the lottery. And propaganda. And these days twenty million in the lottery is death itself. Sudden death. You can die without rhyme or reason or realising it... I think that the synonym for every word is 'money'. It's easier that way. Money, with money to monetise monetarily, money monetisable. 'Cos look: funeral, and in your head: money. Schnitzel, and in your head: money. Car, and in your head: money. Greece, and in your head: money. An acre, and in your mind: money. But don't play, sir. Don't play the lotto. Any game. Because twenty million can kill... There's no help for it... I know what I'm talking about. That's why I'm alive, wearing thin the trousers of others. And socks...

RAFAŁ WOJASIŃSKI

Rozmaryn was now standing before the fountain. The sun was shining so brightly in his eyes that he had to close them. He felt a pain in the frontal regions of his head, just above his eyebrows. He bent down and then he knelt. The edge of the fountain reached to his armpits. He leaned against the edge and looked into the water. He couldn't see his reflection there. He sank his hands in the water and kept them there for two minutes. He felt the cold penetrate his flesh, and with that cold came cleansing. Cleansing from what? He couldn't say, but he felt better, as if life could still mean something, although no additional 'still' would introduce to existence anything more than more existence. No additional activity, no additional birth could be anything more than what it was. Otherwise, everything would just have to halt.

The cold of the water penetrated deeper and deeper into Rozmaryn's body. It helped him to come into contact with himself. With that unclear mixture in which he searched out his soul and the extraordinariness of the phenomenon of what was supposed to be his mind. Fiasco. Counterfeiting. The falsification of sausage, of thought, of activity, and the values of real estate. Fi. As. Co. And yet the coolness cleansed him. Cleansing, eliminating, burning down. Beginning.

You just gonna hang like that, sir, on that little wall? – Tefil asked.

You gonna just hang like that, or have done with it at last?

You look like a pile of misfortune, sir.

Man is a sum. Not a pile. Pardon me. Maybe, after all… A pile. Of…

But with an immortal soul.

Have a look to the right, sir – Tefil explained. – You only have to raise your head a bit and turn it a bit to the right and you'll see something: the entrance to the food store, the stairs. At one time that was the door to a regular house. To the right of that door is a corner villa shaped like a block. Two floors and two balconies with short balustrades. And when you turn behind it to the left, sir, and continue on down the left side of the street, well, just past that villa, you'll see a butcher's shop, sir. The butcher's name is Jaszun, just like his father's and his grandfather's. They sell splendid meat there, for as long as I can remember. I don't fix up anything for myself, after all, anymore, because I just don't want to. I take my meals in the famous restaurant.

Recently, when I went to the butcher's to get some pork-and-beef sausage, that woman started screaming, the one who bothered you on the stairs when you went up to my flat for my eyeglasses, sir. She told Jaszun that the meat's not the way it's supposed to be, that the meat's mistaken, a mistake. The butcher explained that meat can't be mistaken, that there is no such thing as a mistake in meat, because meat is life. A doctor can be mistaken, but life, no. It can be cruel, stupid, devoid of sense or marked with crime, but it's never mistaken for it has no reason. And so on, and so on. And on. And so.

If it's to begin, it begins. Reason is no help at all, because if it's to begin, it'll begin. Even cannibalism: if it's supposed to begin, it'll begin. And so on and on. And so. And it begins. And there is no other possibility. And so on, on. And so. Everything that is supposed to have reason, proves the lack of reason. That which has no reason, cannot be mistaken. A paramecium, an embryo, a jellyfish, and so on, on. And on. And so. So it's better that one, the third, the seventh, the twelfth, the hundred and third, the eighth, should say nothing, just go along, strut, look, make faces so it should seem that he's a huge brain, so that people shouldn't lose faith and hope, and love. Just don't let him say anything... And.

RAFAŁ WOJASIŃSKI

Rozmaryn arose from his knees, and water began dripping from his hands. He went over to Tefil, wiped his hands on his trouser legs, and plunged his hands into his trouser pockets. The wind suddenly puffed his blond hair, which was a little too long but elegantly cut, the wind that was winding around the trees, and it even brought a few drops of water with it, which cooled the balding pate of Tefil. Tefil arose from the bench and set off in the direction of the famous restaurant on the other side of the park. The expression on his face resembled none of those that Rozmaryn had so far seen that day on his companion's face. He went along the left side of the pathway, nearer to the road, and Rozmaryn was a pace behind him, on the right side. He could see only a portion of the profile and the right side of the balding pate of Tefil. They were going along at a rather sprightly pace. They crossed the zebra stripes, the same ones they'd crossed earlier entering the park after their dinner in the famous restaurant. Just before the doors of the famous restaurant, Tefil, passing by two carters coming out with whips in their hands, suddenly turned left, took seven steps, and then turned right. Ten steps later he stopped. Rozmaryn caught up with him a few, maybe nine, seconds later. Tefil took a pack of cigarettes out of the right pocket of his blazer, lit one, and with the hand that held the lit cigarette pointed at some wooden doors with little panes in their upper regions.

That's the famous cinema, established before the war. Above it was a hotel – said Tefil. – Supposedly, a real prostitute was there once. Just passing through, of course, but she was. A real, professional prostitute, who was long remembered here. And behind me is that small block of flats. You see that airy porch, sir? They used to call it the 'sukkah'. I liked to hide there, even when I was already grown. I'd sit there for a few hours thinking that here I am sitting, hidden. All sorts of creatures squirm in under roofs and in holes. And obtain satisfaction from that indubitably unusual state, being in a hole. A hole in the tunnel. Beginning. It was then I knew that I'd go my own way. To the hole. Whose path were they treading who have no way back now? Their own too?

There's only one sign of life on that ploughed field – the wood. A tiny square of wood. The trees still leafless, a few acacias among them. All around is space and freshly ploughed, bright earth. A square of trees that hides beneath it a cemetery. From the hundred-and-twenty-year-old wall there remain only some stones and bricks, still held together with mortar. To the east there stand three pillars of red brick, the remnants of the entry gate, but these days they're no taller than a metre and a half. The top has vanished. Around here a lot of doghouses were built of red brick. At that cemetery you can count twenty three graves of children, year of death 1923, 1926, 1934, 1941, 1943, 1943, 1917, 1928, 1931, 1933, 1936, 1936, 1938, 1938, 1939, 1929, 1940, 1940, 1916, 1912, 1908, 1912, 1914. The graves are akilter, almost fully sunk in the earth. The headstones are tossed about, broken. Besides the graves with headstones there are only cement borders, as if for the production of large cinder blocks. I didn't count those. And anyway I get mixed up in my reckonings, the dates from the headstones and the encyclopaedia. I'm completely untrustworthy. Just like the whole of human history, the history of the world. And that's why I believe in love, although the word 'love' is a mistaken term.

When I was nine years old and went to school, I'd linger around that cemetery often. The graves dug up, skeletons laid out on the slabs, skulls at the foot of the trees, telltale signs in jaws of gold teeth having been prised out. Gold is stronger than death. The Germans knew that. Once there was this tin coffin. The tin was nothing worth: a chisel does the trick and the lid is bent back. I had a peek into the

RAFAŁ WOJASIŃSKI

coffin. It's hard not to look into a coffin. That was my one encounter with the universe, for I'm not going to fly off to the Moon or to Mars, after all. A stranger's skeleton, the remains of a skeleton, a shoe...

Nothing tempts me as much as a coffin. Really, it's hard for me to think of anything more interesting. Perhaps if nature had better developed my sexual inclinations, I'd have a different point of view, but in this situation, the only one that is available to me... Well, the coffin, especially the coffin pried open a crack, is the most interesting fragment of reality.

Come on over here. Between the cinema and the community centre there are two benches, a few trees, and a neglected playground. Do you hear that, sir? That bell – Tefil said. – My feet are swelling a bit, but you, sir, you've got a sort of ripeness about you. You've been sweating since our visit in the famous restaurant. Demon Rum is squeezing out of your pores. You're steaming. And I'm swelling. You hear that bell, sir? That little bell? Something's always ringing in my head.

Tutberg, my village. One ploughed field, and beyond it, another. The road that goes on so that I've never seen the end of it. But roads never end; they just join up with others or with the trackless waste. Door after door, scratches upon them, knobs burnished and tired with use, cracks in the slats vertical and horizontal. Made by those who will never return. I count windows, window after window, those badly painted, with loose paint and those just refreshed with the next coat of white enamel. Entrance after entrance. Gate after gate. Balk after balk. Birch after birch, willow after willow, pine after pine in the woods at the end of the village. I count, I count up...

They arrived at the bench that Tefil had been pointing out. A few drops of rain fell from the sky; Rozmaryn and Tefil felt them at the same time. They sat down side by side. Not a single person was walking along the pavement, not a single car was rolling along the road. Everything had gone quiet. Ever more deeply the buildings, trees, traffic signs, and the sparrow, which had alighted across from them on the low rubbish bin, fell into the silence, along with the swing-sets and the slides behind the two men's backs. The sparrow was motionless. It didn't open its little beak, it didn't give off the slightest sound. The wonder of the world, the silence and the beauty, when nothing's left us except the beauty of the world, awe in the face of existence, and the great will to live…

Tefil closed his eyes. A cooler breeze wafted over his face and his feet in black socks liberated from his shoes. He didn't feel the breeze so pronouncedly on the other parts of his body. His hands were locked and resting on his stomach. It'd become less visible in the position he'd assumed. Rozmaryn sat on the bench to his right.

Do you remember when we sat down on the bench? – Tefil asked.

You don't remember how that happened? – Tefil asked.

I mean the moment when we sat down on the bench. Did we approach it from the right or from the left? Did we wipe down the slats of the seat? – Tefil asked.

Well, tell me, sir, how is it? Do you remember that moment, that scrap of time, that second, those three, four seconds, those five, ten seconds in which it all happened? Do you remember, sir, in which pocket your hand was resting? How your trousers creased? How the wrinkles bulged on the back of your blazer, which always forms a kind of hunchback shape when you sit down, sir? Are you able, sir, to recreate the number of strides that led you, sir, from the street to the bench? Are you able to recall the degree to which your shoes were soiled? Do you remember, sir, how the light fell on the wall of the community centre?

Let's go, right now, tell me – do you remember, sir!

RAFAŁ WOJASIŃSKI

Please, calm down, sir. Rozmaryn, my dear sir, please...

I'm supposed to calm down? Do you know? Do you know what I could do to you? You are completely helpless in regard to me! – Tefil screamed. – You calm down, sir, cut it out! Calming down is your one hope of rescue. Sit down, you cretin! O! You're already sitting, sir. I forgot. So, down, boy! and cut it out already!

I've seen you through and through, sir. I now know everything about you. You thought, sir, that we're going to hide like that forever without any consequences. But unfortunately, that's not going to happen. What were you counting on, sir? What was it you'd imagined? You're constantly asking about your mother... I know what you're after here... You're leading me on, sir, you're trying to beguile me with the mother lode of your reality...

Don't try to frighten me, no frightening, or you'll soon be shite-ing your pants...

And what am I supposed to do with you, sir? Mother, mother, mother.

What am I supposed to do with you, sir?

It somehow seems to me, my dear sir, Rozmaryn, that you don't feel well. Quite simply. That something's not quite right in your head.

Do you remember, sir?

Do you remember, sir, how we came to find ourselves on this bench?

No? No?! No???!!!

Rozmaryn laid his hands on his bosom. He stared in front of him. On the cuffs of his shirt he felt the dampness that was cooling his wrists. That dampness travelled farther up his arms and set the skin on his chest shivering. A coolness, he thought, but a pleasurable coolness. The world is full of pleasurable things, he thought, additionally, even a walk like this is pleasurable. Once more he saw on the canvas in his head that little boat on the shore of the lake. That was the lake of his life, eternally the same, remembered from the times when he was a little child. It seemed to him that he could hear the lapping of the wavelets and smell the scent of the water, which soothed all that ailed him. A sanatorium. Something like a sanatorium deep inside his head. The surface of the lake stretching out, especially on a late autumn afternoon when all you can see are the livid clouds in the sky – it overpowers a man, deprives him of the destructive force of understanding. Rozmaryn held onto that vista, gazing at the lightly wrinkled, somewhat metallic surface. There was no way of returning there. He knew that there was no return.

And again you've got that lake in your head. It's getting tiresome – said Tefil. – I can tell from the expression on your face. Constantly the sound of those waves (I hear it too), tensing. And that smell of water that invades the lungs. There's some hidden violence in all that. Just like in beauty and charm, especially in the beauty of women compared to women deprived of beauty. We're haunted by that sound of the tiny waves of the lake and the breeze wandering over the surface of the water. When I catch sight of the miracle of that lake, the pier and the little boat that rocks there, tied up, well, I just die away, gaping in front of myself, thoughtlessly overwhelmed with the beauty. And all the knowledge I have in my head of the ancient Greeks, the conquests of powerful kingdoms, of gods, bards, and messiah vanishes. And. I've got it just like you, sir. Nothing else. I see the same thing in my head. Enough! Enough already! Cut it out, sir! Are you incapable, sir, of cutting it out? You're disrupting! You're disrupting, sir! Stop disrupting, sir! Enough already! I say enough! Cut it out with that beautiful lake of yours!

Maybe somebody will pound out a closing speech? A speech at the end of the world... – Tefil said. – Maybe some politician? They don't read much, but for all that they've got a lot to say. Or not... Maybe the woman behind the counter at the butcher's shop ought to pronounce something at the end. The last word should belong to her. Maybe she'll toss in some real meat? As long as it's not human flesh. Or simian. Or any other that recalls the image of man (in other words God). Have you ever practised such a speech, Rozmaryn, sir? You ought to. Otherwise it'll be up to the lady from the butcher's shop... You hear them, Rozmaryn, sir, those words of hers? You hear? Do you hear her speech, sir?!

Bones five seventy. Pork chops sixteen ninety nine. Shoulder eleven seventy. Chicken drumsticks six ninety. Chicken fingers five. Apiece. What a splendid pattern, an equation explaining the complexity of the world, the mind, and the sad face of an old man falling asleep on a cot in the kitchen. So that the youngsters might have a little space to themselves in the room (youngsters over fifty). Pig's feet three fifty (not on sale). For meat jelly. You'll be able to have a little party on Saturday night. Mama, Dad, Unkie from your Mama's side, Unkie from your Dad's. My sister'll be there as well with her husband; we'll turn the lights down, fill up the shot glasses with vodka, and we'll feel alive in our flat. Splendidly alive. Splendidly, because individually, each for him- or herself. Each alone with the meat jelly and his or her own shot glass. The savour of feeling individually happiness comes from the individual, only from there. It's true that the living has to kill the living and consume it in order to sense a certain savour. That's no extraordinary discovery. Nothing extraordinary tells us that.

Fortunately, we don't understand anything, although reason goes off the rails, seething – in forest and field, on battlefields, in offices, in schools, in nurseries, in three-room flats and one-room flats, on empty parade grounds, on streets, and in churches. Reason goes off the rails in queues for Toruń kielbasa, at political meetings, at feast-day bazaars, at village meetings and at the sittings of Parliament, next to newspaper kiosks and beer stands, in old folks' homes and in insane asylums. Regular kielbasa twenty one. Motive power. Headcheese eighteen thirty.

My grandmother likes headcheese. There was a time she'd eat nothing but headcheese for a whole month. In the evening she liked to lie in the kitchen on the couch that her husband, who died thirty years before, had dragged in there. She never washed her face or her hands after eating the headcheese, and the fat stains above and below her lips gave her a shine. There were also stains left on her hands (polished to a bright shine). I love the sight and smell of fat, especially the fat of headcheese. All evening long Grandma would smell of headcheese, sometimes all through the night. Until one day she stopped eating headcheese and never took to it again. Her period of mourning her husband had run its course. She had the couch taken out and thrown away and said that she's no longer jealous of her sister, who was a widow for forty years before she died herself. She used to say that that other one always had it better but now she knows how to have it better. It was then that I came to believe in happiness. I saw it with my own eyes. Boiled ham twenty seven ninety. Black pudding sixteen fifty.

My father made black pudding in the tin, zinc-plated bathtub in which earlier Mama, Father, brother, sister, and finally I had bathed, after which he poured in the groats, the blood, and mixed it all with his hands. It was three-quarters full of the black mass. Everything was done in the hallway, poorly-lit, as midnight approached. My father was hunchbacked. I remembered that bulge with my fingers. What should I remember of life? The sight of the ruins left behind by the ancient Greeks. The Eiiflas Tower... or what have you... Or a spaceflight... Or a cathedral, a work of art... Ooooo! Those things bore me... Just like testimonies to morality and testimonies of all other ilk... And diplomas, the television news, and all sorts of awards. And cloth of gold, and monuments. And the lives of the saints... And various stories with a moral... Especially those with moral and message.

The species! I'd initiate a new species. A better one. Ours. But I've no one to initiate it with. Smoked ham sausage. Price reduced. Twenty seven. Who cares that the end is nigh? Or any beginning? Any middle? What does it matter? Ham sausage twenty five. Frankfurters fifteen. Pluck one seventy five. Price's gone down. The people were going to Mass. Kraków kiełbasa twenty four. The funeral began at eleven. At eleven? Funeral? Funerals don't start at eleven, not usually. I should have been eating my cheesecake already. If a funeral, then noon. So I'm eating. I feel bad for the person. They cart here the dead from the whole region round. I feel bad. One after the other packed into a wooden crate, as Tefil would say. He'd say something, or he'd sit down by the fountain with the next young lad or some lady who's extracted the fox from the closet and put it on, little mug facing downward. I don't know if there's any fox left in Litental. My mother had one, she got it from her sister who had three and gave her the one that was most flattened, with a crooked snout. A fox around the neck would soothe the women. Warmth, comfort. The comfort of riches. Unless maybe... Unless maybe what? There's no way out. None. And so on and on. And so. That's how Tefil would repeat it. And Tefil would also say: Everything gets narrower. Gets narrower and closes, like two lines that become a corner. A sharp point.

I've laid out the meats according to price, from left to right. The cold cuts too. The counter is positioned so that when I'm standing behind it I have the window to my right. The light falls on the glass doors of the refrigerator and patterns arise. Turkey necks five seventy. Wings four thirty. Today. Goose paté seventeen ninety. Jellied turkey seventeen fifty. Beef shank sixteen twenty. Fatback. No price. I forgot to pin it on. I don't know what it's supposed to be. I'll call and ask. Call who? My father's no longer alive. Who's in charge of the butcher's shop? Mother. Not mother. Mother's alive, but no. Who's in charge? Me? I don't feel in charge. I just sell things. O Jesus! My mother's the boss, but she's not in charge. The bookkeeper keeps the books. There's no one else. It's getting narrower. And without Tefil, well, you know. You know.

I am a different woman. My mother is a different woman. My father was a different man, before he died. Everyone has to be different before he dies. Schnitzel with bone sixteen fifty. You can see the bone more and more. With each delivery. Meat and bone are uncovered to our eyes. Like faith and reason, which are stages on the road to the lack of comprehension, to anger, to hatred, to quartering, to pricing, and to eating. Reciprocal consumption is the summit of incomprehension. Or comprehension. As you wish. Horseflesh pastrami sixty three fifty. My grandfather had a horse and he'd lead me about on him around the tree, which grew in the centre of our yard. Around the oak. One. Two. Three. Four. I felt like I was beautiful. But stupid.

Our minds must be very shallow, Tefil would say when buying black pudding or Podwawelska kiełbasa, if we must believe in miracles and fairy stories. We're not growing up. We're childish and we make excuses for everything. For every crime. At confession the priest asked me if I had pictures of the saints at home, if my parents were good examples. A childish priest, so a real one? What's he getting at? Nothing? That it's good as it is? So good? That it's best this way? All good children go to heaven. All the childlike go to heaven, so he blabs on like a child into his advanced age. Do you love the Little Jesus? I mean, really, do you love Him really? Do you love yourself the same way? Ask yourself the question who are you? Who? If you love your-

RAFAŁ WOJASIŃSKI

self but not entirely? So who are you? Nobody? You're so beloved, but you love not. You have to love entirely, to the end. Childishly, for otherwise you won't squeeze through the strait gate. The Little Jesus knows everything, he knows what you're thinking, he knows how you love.

What're you asking me for, then, Father, if the Little Jesus knows everything? Why do you interrogate me at confession if the Little Jesus knows it all? What're you tormenting me for? If the Little Jesus knows everything, then what for? The Little Jesus hears my thoughts and knows everything. And what's the Little Jesus want to know all of my thoughts for? He gave me free will, so why should He know all my thoughts, especially those dirty ones about the boys? Is this a bug in the wall? Has He installed a bug in our brains?! Have I been notoriously listened to? From love? From care? For the good of society and humanity? A bug out of respect for man created from love? Ah! I get it! He has to check whether the overheard material agrees with the confession. That's logical! But then why confess at all? In order to snare you? In order to break you down in repentance? But the Little Jesus knows I break down. I break down in the corner of my shop when there's no clients. I break down in the cellar when I go down for coal, and in the shack when I'm alone in order to choose a carrot from the pail. I'm constantly breaking down. Without respite. For God's sake the Little Jesus knows all of that. He knows every word, thought, even the thought that hasn't arisen yet but is sure to. Snares then? That's childish. But children can be cruel. Not only naive and pure.

Please. Please, close the door behind you. Please close the door because it's cold. There's no more mortadella. Black headcheese sixteen. Yes. Sixteen even. Toruń thirteen seventy. Regular twelve.

It's the feet that are most in danger – said Tefil, sitting there on the bench, still shoeless. – Sickness, rheumatism, starts there the easiest. So you see, sir, but I don't think of such things. Illnesses. Lately, I think rarely of illnesses.

I prefer different things.

You know, different ones. You want me to list them?

But that'd take hours.

As you wish, sir, but I warn you, Rozmaryn, sir.

You want me to list them?

List them?

Tell you?

Normally, my conversations with people don't hold together. Everyone turns out better. In every field… As soon as I begin, it's cast aside, pushed away. It don't hold together at all… Even amongst my closest family… We didn't have anything to talk about. With me there's nothing to talk about. And I felt that very early on, that with me you can't… That with me there's nothing you can… Completely… When I began about the socks, about the holes in the socks, about wearing dead people's clothes, about the speech at the end of the world, which I drew up for the woman from the butcher's shop, it turned out immediately that there's nothing to talk about with me. So I changed the topic to the cemetery in Tutberg, and then right away to my thirty-year-old trousers… But, no, it didn't work out… Each word of mine about Prodige, about the shack, about beginning or again about collecting socks from the rubbish heap cast aside, and I felt that being cast aside…

As soon as I took up one of my topics, immediately it turned out that none of them could be a topic in common… That there exists no possibility for the topic of socks, trousers, or Prodige to become a topic in common… No possibility. Then, with the last of my strength, I tried to move the topic of felt-lined boots sliced low. To prove that I was right in slicing low those felt-lined boots… And nothing.

So then, speak?

Speak?

RAFAŁ WOJASIŃSKI

I like to think about the scent of lilac blowing about towards the end of April in front of the entrance to the cantor's house, that genius who couldn't teach me to count to twenty. My mother and father occupied the cantor's house when I was a few years old. That house fascinated me extraordinarily, as extraordinarily as the cantor, that absent-minded genius.

Well, I also like to think for whole hours, what am I saying, whole days: about the curtain I've been intending to put up for a year now, about the unwashed bucket, the dripping sink – I need to change the washer, and yet I'm not changing it, perhaps for some unusually important reason, as if on account of eternity, so that nothing should evade me, because you know everything evades one and evades one so that a person remains eternally stupid like that. I like to ponder whether it wouldn't be better after all to visit other places, planets, cities, but then I arrive at the conclusion, by way of this pondering, which I like so much, that it's better to sit in one place and experience the dripping sink and get pissed off at any little thing, like any other self-respecting person, citizen, and believer. I like to think about the fact that I'll go off for a pastry, that I'll eat it, that I'll be shaven and fragrant, that I'll rise to such heights of culture as are normally unattainable to man.

You know, sir, I adore pondering whether to go up the hill where the pine remembers the Jewish cemetery, of which only the faintest traces remain underground, or to go to the Catholic cemetery and visit the graves of my two splendid friends who committed suicide, or to go to the Lutheran cemetery and stand on one of those little mounds that signify that there are corpses beneath it, and to feel like a corpse upon corpses, living upon the dead – such an exchange of generations. Standing like that, you can gaze at the hill on which the Jewish cemetery was and still is, only now without a single matzevah. The grass grows on the hill more or less evenly, betraying nothing of the lives of those who beneath the soil have already lost their eyes, thoughts, fingernails, hips, mouths, and hearts. They've lost their facial expressions, their smile, and their characteristic gait or motion of the hand. Motion has no particular religion. Eyes, backs, mouths, hips, ears, fingernails have no particular religion. Crime can have a religion. Love has no religion (I don't know where love comes from, but I do know that evil comes from a lack of love). Creation has no religion. God has no religion. Otherwise he's no God of mine.

In the end I don't go anywhere. I grab a book and read. Though I don't understand a thing, because the letters mix around for me. You know, sir, 'e' mixes up with 'a', 'p' with 'b', 't' with 'l', and even 'k' with 'r', 'u' with 'a', 'p' with 'o', 's' with 'w', 'a' with 'x', 't' with 'l'. And so on. But while I'm reading, I adore to think about my teacher – the cantor, that self-proclaimed master, genius, who lived before the war in our house, in the house of my mother, of my father, in my house. And he was a genius, undeniably. He lived in Tutberg, in the room next to the kitchen in which I later lived before I became grown up enough to leave and become the porter in a veterinary surgery. He occupied two rooms in this old Lutheran school. He was the son of the cantor before him, born in the big room near the white stove, the same one I used to warm myself by in the cold winter nights, where I experienced enlightenments. One after the other: because of a fly buzzing by, or the creak of a floorboard on a lonely, grey, autumn evening, or a stain in the corner of the ceiling, which kept appearing over the space of a few dozen years despite the fact that the roof was constantly being sealed. My enlightenments arose from any old cause. It was enough for me to keep my lungs pumping and my eyes open, but I had to be there by the white stove, there, where the genius had been born, the Lutheran cantor, who taught me neither how to count

RAFAŁ WOJASIŃSKI

nor to read (maybe he didn't on purpose, maybe he loved me and wanted to rescue me).

The smokehouse that we inherited from him and which continues to serve whoever now owns the house was a source of happiness to me. When the hams and sausages had already been hung up to be cured in the smoke of the firepit, I would sit on a little stump in front of the fire, where I experienced a cleansing so profound that I no longer had any need of truth, wisdom, or religion. No need of multiplication or speech. I lost the need for any sort of confirmation or proof. The illusion of my continued existence as I gazed upon a photograph of myself from years before, vanished. I never see myself; even when I look in the mirror, it's another person I see. I see beginning. I no longer am, and I still have not become. I see beginning. Descent, entrance, the pulling on of linen, trousers, cap. Beginning. Of every day, every moment, every second the beginning, which absorbs every civilisation, every evil, every darkness, every crime. Only to begin again, only so that beginning should never end. And it never shall end. In no cosmic space, on no square centimetre of soil around the smokehouse. I've already passed away, and yet I've not become. There is only beginning. The present moment does not exist… All of my activities are the past, all my life, the development of civilisation, evolution…it's the past… Something is born. Dies. And is born. Has ceased to be… And then is born.

In building that smokehouse, that genius constructed the only temple that ever spoke to me. It created no illusions that there can be any greater accomplishment than beginning. Repetitive, quickly passing, unconscious in the face of the unconscious, eternal existence of all matter. In building the smokehouse, the genius made it so that I should become like unto the smoke emerging therefrom, like the lilac branch that hangs there near the fence. I became a part of all being and eternity for I lost the consciousness of being myself. An exit from humanity through a smokehouse built by a man. Unconscious of his own work. His great work of genius, which elevated me for a moment above the prison I carry about within me, wherever I go or wherever I am herded. I'm always sitting in a slammer. A more or less pleasant one. A tunnel… Life sentence… Eternity… No journeys west or east. Beginning… The discovery of the fascinating, overpowering mystery of space. Mystery…

The smokehouse was a metre forty high and a metre and a half square. It rose like a chimney. On the outside it was red-brick, while the interior walls were of non-fired brick. Only at the smokehouse could I safely be no one because the greatest and most difficult thing to accomplish in life is to be no one, safely. Sitting there in front of the smokehouse on my little stump, I experienced the ephemerality of all chaos, all power, all authority, all art, religion, and science. And that is the very core of my core. Without the genius of that Lutheran cantor who was unable to teach me to count or read, I'd never feel that and I'd never be expressing it. The genius, who didn't know how to count to twenty, was cut to my measure. Made to order. You understand, Rozmaryn, sir? He hit the nail on the head. My head. Neither Plato nor Descartes was able to do that. They weren't up to the task. He was. And that's why, sometimes, I feel happiness and joy, my dear sir, Rozmaryn.

I like to think that almost all human thought is boring, but we can't tear ourselves away from it. Or maybe that it's just a sort of demimonde, or quatremonde, or something even smaller? Maybe it's a micromonde, like the tiny world of a beetle? Have you ever considered that, sir? I love to meditate on this: that, I don't know, it doesn't matter what our capabilities are, how big our army, how magnificent our discoveries and accomplishments, it's still just a mi-

RAFAŁ WOJASIŃSKI

cromonde like that of the larva of a silk moth, which eats and eats. And eats, and later wraps itself up in an egg-like cocoon, closing itself up like that to change into a mono-chromatic moth devoid of all beauty. And lays eggs so that there should be more larvae that'll eat and eat until they weave their own white cocoons and change into a moth. Monochromatic and devoid of beauty, to lay eggs the size of grains of flour, from which larvae will hatch, becoming a part of beginning.

Tefil started to put on his shoes, using only his feet. Rozmaryn cast a sidewise glance at that activity with an expression of disapproval on his face. And yet a moment later that activity began to intrigue him. To usher him into a state of happiness. He completely forgot about the lake; it even occurred to him that the beauty of that lake is mean-ingless. That here and now, something essential is happen-ing. Right here, exactly now, that which is decisive, passing away, unaesthetic and yet decisive, is happening. A person becoming shod. Why, thought Rozmaryn, am I more at-tracted by the orbits of the planets, the invention of a new engine, a musical work, a painting, or even English poetry? This attracts me. Disinterestedly and passionately. It nei-ther disappoints by its greatness or its pettiness. Rozmaryn couldn't tear himself away from those rickety actions of Tefil's. It even seemed to him that this was the most essen-tial observation of his entire life. A signpost. It took Tefil at least four whole minutes to execute the act of putting on his shoes without resorting to the use of his hands. When the process had stretched to six minutes, Rozmaryn arose, and spat behind him with impatience, after which he sat down, calmed down somewhat, but once more he couldn't tear his eyes away from Tefil's feet. At last, contempt ap-peared once more in Rozmaryn's eyes, a contempt that was indubitable, easy to decipher and decisive. Tefil noticed it. He looked into Rozmaryn's eyes as if he wanted to communicate something to him without words but felt that it might be like talking to the wall. He waited. For a moment, Rozmaryn closed his eyes and brushed his hair backward with his left hand. Then he opened his eyes and gazed to the front, but his expression now changed from contempt to one of boredom and vapidity.

Tefil breathed deeply. He puffed his cheeks and then expelled the air. He repeated that several times. Idiot, thought Rozmaryn. Stupid idiot.

Thus, Rozmaryn, sir, my will – Tefil said. – You happened by. I have no one else to express it to. My last will and testament: I want to be buried in the cemetery in Tutberg to lie there until my grave mound begins to lean and sink, to lie there until it becomes unrecognisable, or spread my ashes. Burn me and spread me. No touching, no prettying up, no bringing near candles or flowers. No caring. Leave me alone. Only Tutberg. Our great, our oldest TRADITION. Death. Burial.

Tefil leaned down over his shoes and set himself to tying the laces. Immediately and automatically, Rozmaryn began observing that activity, like it or not. He froze. The bulky, large hands of Tefil with their short fingers squirming about to tie the laces; the gasping that proceeded from Tefil's mouth for his stomach was pressing up against his interior organs, making breathing and circulation difficult. At last, Tefil tied his laces and rose once more to the vertical, to button his overcoat for the umpteenth time that day. To Tefil's left was a building lit up by the afternoon sun on which hung the sign: 'H.P. Maciejewski Funeral Parlour'. The words were inscribed upon a heavy sign, which might have been an unused portion of a gravestone, and glittered like gold.

Let's turn to the right now, then we'll go along the pavement and behind the community centre we'll turn right again – Tefil said, setting off along the road he'd indicated.

A minute later they were behind the community centre. On the left, Rozmaryn noticed a two-storey corner building painted beige but with a small admixture of indescribable yellow. This was the former station of the German gendarmerie. There was a corner balcony on the topmost floor. Tefil walked straight ahead. Rozmaryn walked behind him. He was wearing a discouraged look on his face, expressive of a lack of hope and joy.

Tefil approached the news kiosk and leaned his elbow on the sill outside the window. Rozmaryn was standing near Tefil. His smelled his odour and his breath. He also leaned upon the sill. The halves of Tefil's blazer were set flapping by the coldish wind. Rozmaryn glanced to his right and noticed the cinderblocks piled there, where the balcony window had been bricked up. The grout was broad and unevenly spread. The rusty gutter was hanging loose; it had been sagging like that for years, just like stomach, breasts, butt cheeks sag. And on the hedge near the wall of the building – sparrows.

I need to rest – said Tefil. – We have to pause here a space. I told you I'm old, and age will have its way. I like to move about sometimes. Left, right, straight ahead. But not right now. Here, sir. Stand with your back to the kiosk and look left. That's the road that leads to the railroad, the choo-choo. Have a good look, sir, absorb that landscape with the shining heavens and the little trees that bend in the wind. We'll go off to the watchmaker's daughter. Her name is Magdalena. I want very much for you to get to know her. She'll offer us some pierogi, because that's what she does in that kitchen of hers all cluttered with books – she makes pierogi. Often.

They went along for a while, now more slowly, now more quickly, until finally, four minutes into the walk, they evened out the pace and steadily, like horses, they walked side by side with strolling steps, slowly. Despite the wind and the cool that was blowing in, Tefil took off his overcoat and carried it henceforth draped over his right forearm.

The greenish colour of the old food store near the tracks where they enter the city never bores me – said Tefil. – Paling, ruined by frost, sun, and autumn winds, the paint is peeling. Near that green store I once saw this drone, I beg your pardon, that tongue of mine!... this drunk. Drunk to his armpits, drunk to his ears. He lived between the scrap-metal pile and the store. He'd come by my vegetable patch because I have this vegetable patch, three hundred square metres, with a little wooden shack... I got it from a certain veterinarian who made his pile and ran off with his lover. He wasn't married. He just had a lover, who was married, and he ran off with her. And one night he signed that little shack over to me because he didn't want anyone else to get it. And that drunk, whenever he'd see me on my vegetable patch, he'd come over and begin. He was constantly beginning. It could drive you nuts. He'd begin and never let up.

He never came along the path worn in the grass by people. Most often, he would suddenly emerge from the mist that spread wide about the fields in the morning, cutting the forest off from your view. Cutting the world off from your view. Each and every time he came along as if he were trying to get to know the terrain, as if he'd forgotten all that he'd seen hundreds of times already. That drone – sorry, there's my tongue for you again – that drunk, of course, never approached, he just materialised and began. I didn't want to tell you, he'd begin, I didn't want to tell you, but when they, those workers, were fixing that piece of roof for you, well, look how they did it. There's this hole there and it's gonna cause a draught for you, and one strong wind'll get in there and tear the whole roof off. I know that maybe I shouldn't be telling you, but I'll tell you something about their work because you don't know anything about work yourself. I didn't want to tell you, but you ought to tell them so that they'll fix it. You paid them, after all, you paid them, I know you paid them a bunch, I reckon you paid them too much and they ought to fix that for you.

But they're dead, I'd tell him: one after another, the one died and then the other, I'd explain to the four-eyed drunk, I was at the funeral of the one and the other. And he keeps on going with his version of events: What does it matter if they're dead? I'll find them. The one and the other. One by one, I'll find them. and then you… You… You have to convince them, he explains to me. If you want, I'll go with you. I'm not afraid of them. I've known them for twenty years. And he stood there waiting for me to say something, but I hadn't the strength. There was nothing in me that I could possibly say. In his presence this very profound silence always swelled in me. How he would sit there and stare, and as he could stare like that at a dead mouse on the verandah, a broken broomstick, a rotten tomato that still hangs on the vine, I had nothing to say, my grey matter stopped working. His staring put paid to any and all familiar sense. That drone, sorry, drunk, who, with what brains and eyes remained to him, would stare at a bone, a stick, a dead mouse, manifested a vacuum in my head. The same vacuum in each and every head. There's only one head. And it's in every head. So let's not say anything, let's not orate. For God's sake!

And. And I stopped going over to my vegetable patch. Keep away from that one, I told myself. Only when he starts pushing up the flowers, feeding the birches and begonias, only then will you love him for love needn't be fulfilled, all you have to do is wait in expectation for the form that can be loved unconditionally. The form that says nothing, stares not, hears not, and breathes not. The sort that's already in paradise. Long-distance love to paradise. But he's still not sitting there. He wanders around the city, and I have to be careful when I go along this street, especially when I get near the tracks. He sometimes pretends to go through the gate from his yard and goes back in, that he collects something from the yard, as if he's cleaning up. He pretends to be cleaning the metal parts of his fence with sandpaper, trimming the arborvitae. But he's on the lookout, with one eye at least, the left one usually, looking to see whether I happen by in order to spring upon me. And then it begins. He starts again about that repair, that they should fix it because I paid them after all. He won't let go of it. He lurks about and every now and then pounces upon me. It's usually a piercing cold winter afternoon in late fall that he chooses. That time of the year activates his aggressive nature towards me. I have to really watch out then because I submit myself to his pouncing and lose the possibility of autonomous existence. Every thought of his is expressed with more intensity, and louder.

At last one day he confessed: I'm about to perish, I'm taking myself off to extinction, I'll kill myself, and then I'll convince you that they need to fix that roof for you. I won't allow it to remain as it is. I won't allow it. Neither prison nor mortal illness will get in the way of me bringing the matter to a proper conclusion. I've never accomplished anything in my life, but this I'll do. This is my vocation, the one and only vocation that remains me. You can mock me, you can eliminate me, you can wipe me out, but I won't let this go. I'll bring it to a proper conclusion!

Concentration was etched on Rozmaryn's face. They paused by the railroad tracks, and Tefil pointed at a two-storey building in front of them. They passed over the tracks and stood in front of a green building, the old store of the community cooperative. Tefil froze and began breathing heavily. His mouth seemed larger.

It's like I was a child again, walking through the village with my mates – Tefil said. – Between the fields sown with

RAFAŁ WOJASIŃSKI

rye we'd go, after school, to the cemetery in Tutberg to have a gander at the naked skulls of the Lutherans who once lived in our houses. None of us knew which of these dead people had lived in which house or in which grave he'd been laid. You couldn't fix skull or shank to gravestone with first name and last name and date of death. The skulls were shining on the surface, dug up by a well-known neighbour of ours, who along with his band had been digging up the Lutheran, Calvinist, and Protestant graves in the area. Thanks to them, we could pore over those skulls and skeletons disassembled, lying around in the grass or on the tilted gravestones. There were no skeletons of children. They didn't last, or they weren't dug up. Those naked skulls made us into a group of initiates. I don't know in what, but initiates all the same. And it remained with us forever. The empty skulls of the Lutheran cemetery filled up our empty skulls. Even after the passage of forty years I'd meet one of my childhood mates, and he'd ask from the get-go about the skulls. Remember those skulls?

Your mother, sir. I don't know if we have the same woman in mind. Can it be the same woman? Can it be that your mother and that woman, whom I knew and with whom I am on that photograph, is the same person, so to speak? The same being? And one more thing: is it important that she be that same being? Is it meaningful that you, sir, should obtain information from me about that being who was indeed your mother? And is that, which is the truth, believable? You're not very convincing, sir.

Well, tough. If we can't arrive at any certainty that your mother is your mother, sir, let's try another way. Let's see whether your mother, sir, whether that woman is that woman who used to receive pornographic letters from me? In my day I wrote quite a lot of pornographic letters to women, but you must know, sir, that I touched none of them. It was not in my interest; I didn't peek into those women's knickers. To speak the truth, I never even saw some of them with my own eyes, but those that I did see, I only saw. And, of course, I wrote pornographic letters to them. We must be clear about this. And so on. And on. And so.

Beginning. I just recalled the story of this neighbour of mine. When his daughter was sixteen, he couldn't tear his eyes away from her eyes, her brow, her eyebrows, her forehead. There was something there that wasn't right, something beguiling in those eyes of his daughter. Something's just not right, he'd say to me sometimes when he ran across me on the road between the store and my grandparents' house. You see, he said, I don't know what it is attracts me to those eyes. Is it normal to stare like that at one's own daughter? Until it all came out. One summer day it came out. He was standing in a queue for bread in our village kiosk, and he glanced at Broniek, who was standing in front of him in the queue. He had those same eyes, those same eyebrows and the same forehead as his daughter. He returned home and jumped into the well. And from that time on he never worked, his left leg was crippled. He went about in a suit, always a little tipsy. His wife died soon after that. And then he saw me again on the road between home and the kiosk. You see, he said. So you see. I can't understand how I could be so stupid. Jumping into the well was complete idiocy. How can you be so stupid? Who cares who has whom with whom?

I don't remember any concrete women. The only woman I really remember is this one old woman – said Tefil, scratching the back of his head and then behind his ears. – I just can't get rid of this impression. So, one fall day I was raking leaves in front of the entrance to the veterinary surgery. The rustle of leaves domesticates the world for me, just like the sky reflected from a puddle. The rustle of raked leaves is for me a more perfect sound than the music of any

RAFAŁ WOJASIŃSKI

hit you care to name. Hits and bestsellers are the death of me (do you think, perhaps, that there might be some sort of fascism in them, just as there is in fashion?). So I was raking leaves, uncovering the concrete that had been poured so many years before. I was making this narrow pathway. And suddenly I caught sight of the old woman. She came around the corner of the building in which the store was located. She stood at the beginning of the path, waiting. I had no idea what the old girl was waiting for. She didn't smile, she didn't make any sort of sign in my direction, she didn't even move her hand. Her standing and my standing and looking at her grew longer and longer. Three dry oak leaves were lying on the path. I approached the first of these, picked it up, and put it in my pocket. The old lady didn't even tremble. I took the second and did the same. When the third leaf finally landed in my pocket, the old woman went on her way. She didn't even glance at me. Well, and that's how it all began. Everything that begins begins in its own way. Emerging from the depths of beginning, in which there might be a breath, the beating of a heart, scratching after being bitten, blinking and euphoria at the sight of something that ignites our emotions, which might be the lifting of a leaf, the fastening of one's belt at one's trousers, or leaning the spade against the wall after the work is done.

I followed the old woman. A moment later I wanted to turn back, leave her where she was, return to raking leaves, but she began to skip, and with this skipping she attracted me all the more. I wanted to scope her out. Disinterestedly. I was hardly able to keep pace. Once she even looked back at me. And at a certain moment she began to run. She vanished from my eyes when she turned left just past this wooden house, but a moment later I saw her again. And once more she vanished through the gate leading into the courtyard of a small apartment building. I ran into that courtyard, stopped, and pricked my ears at the sounds coming from behind the door. It was the sound of running up stairs. I followed those echoes and found myself standing before apartment number seven. Come in, come in, sir, I heard. Don't be afraid, sir; come on in and make yourself some tea. I didn't make any soup 'cos what for? I don't know what I'd be supposed to do with it. If I knew that you were coming, sir, it would be a completely different situation. But I didn't know. Do you eat, sir? Do you drink? Do you breathe?

I entered the foyer and passed from the foyer to the kitchen. There was a door on the left leading to the only room in the flat. It was bright – a lot of light entered through the one great window. The old woman was lying on a bed near the window, covered with a blanket. I came near her. I only wanted to see where you lived, ma'am, I said. I don't want any tea. I don't want anything. My presence here is entirely disinterested, I added. I leaned down closer. She was dead, cold.

Every day I go over to the surgery or the veterinarian or the shopping centre, sometimes to the restaurant, but no one ever notices me – says the cold old woman. – No one listens to me, no one sees me. You're the only one, sir, who noticed that I exist. Because I no longer figure on any list, my data does not exist. I don't remember what my name is. I can't be employed, raped, robbed, gassed, burnt. I am useless. You can't do anything with me. Because it's already been done. I'm free? I come here to rest because I don't know what to set my hand to. What's a free person to do when she can no longer be annihilated? I can't think up anything beyond lying down and just lying around.

Can you help me at all, sir? – asks the little woman on the bed. But how? – I ask. I don't know – she says. – Help me somehow, some sort of first aid. Are you familiar with mouth-to-mouth, sir? Artificial respiration? Natural

RAFAŁ WOJASIŃSKI

respiration is out of the question, so I prefer artificial. In general I don't like anything that's natural. Naturalness is suspicious, naturalness can cause harm, can kill. It's got some bad connotations for me. Nature itself has some bad connotations, just like normality, familiarity, authenticity, and communication. So, if you'd be pleased, sir, to perform artificial respiration on me, through that plastic doohickey that they make these days, it's not out of the question that I'd feel joy, even bliss from breathing again. I haven't breathed like that for some time now. I've forgotten what it feels like, but it seems to me that I should start breathing again; that I always ought to be breathing, that I ought never to stop breathing. You know, sir, that I've already forgotten how to smell things, how to taste? You know, sir, it's a lack of documentation. It's unaccountability. The impossibility of counting and noting. No three millions. No two hundred thousands. Five thousands. One hundred. Two. One. Female or Male. How many are not? More? Nothing. Completely nothing. There are no personal data (today the world's fascinated with personal data). And yet I had a first and a last name, a birthdate, maybe I even slept with some fellow, maybe he pawed me all over. Maybe I ate, drank, had a good time, maybe I worked hard. Maybe I adored these things, maybe I even most adored those very things (is it even possible to adore anything, really?).

But you know, sir, my skull is empty. You want to see? Is your skull empty too, sir? What's in your skull, sir? What do you have there, sir? Well, come on, tell me, what do you have in your skull. Please don't be shy, sir. Tell me. It might be a sort of therapy. Come on, please, be sincere. Don't hide anything, sir, not from me. What do you have there? Well, you're just deaf to all appeals, aren't you? Come on, tell me what you've got in your skull, sir. And again. Again the same old thing. There remains this one most tormenting thing, that something still exists, that everything exists – in other words, everything once was. And shall be. I have nothing in my head, so what else can I want? What do I want? That's just it, what? To move about? Nope. To believe in something? To hear some irrefutable truth? To come to know the deepest mystery of the world? Another person? Not at all. I was only teasing you, sir, with that mouth-to-mouth. What am I after? I'm not stupid. I don't want anything. Nothing, nothing at all. Nothing.

And the others? – I asked. What others? – the old woman asked. – There are no others. Knowledge kept so many things hidden: beloved places, favourite shoes, the beloved scent of flowers. Knowledge kept the others hidden. Knowledge of one's own existence. Your knowledge of your own existence. I also was hidden. I don't even know if I had sex, if I had time to. Maybe I even slept around? That'd be something. That's always something. In every era. Did I pray? My empty skull and yours. The consciousness of a corpse. A living corpse? I walk about the streets, have a peek into the rectory, the shopping centre, and I know that I won't find a single trace. On any street, in any workshop, any block of flats, on any stairs, in front of any tree in the park or on any bench which, after all, was frotted by me, by my body. On no shop counter, in no corner of any store, on no block of pavement. There is no trace of me. I can't find my fox-fur, my dresses, pots, overcoat. Someone's taken my things? Or thrown them away? Those were good pots. Table. Overcoat. That I remember. Overcoat in the closet in the attic. Where'd you get that overcoat, sir? And that blazer? So something wasn't wasted after all. Something always remains.

I'm not afraid because I don't know my sins. What was sin? What was it? Is it the same with you, sir? Is it like this with you? These holes in the memory? This sort of vacuum following the very worst moments or even those usual ones when you bought ice cream, ate a pastry, soup, paid for a

RAFAŁ WOJASIŃSKI

beer? Do you remember that, sir? Would you be able to describe that moment when you were walking along the pavement holding your mother's hand? Do you know, sir, how to reclaim time? In my skull there's no knowledge of what evil I've done, what evil someone else once did. I don't know what happened. I don't know. Now, when I have nothing anymore, because I'm dead, I'm not even moved by dying. I have been saved, as people say. Only, what is salvation? Having been saved, still I don't know what it is. A lot of questions arise in an empty head. Questions from an empty skull. What are dogs? What is a chair? A mouse? A fly? What is a priest? What is a president? What is a million? What is zero? One? What is a poplar? What is it? This, that, and that over there? That is the question. And not: to be or not to be? That's a cheap question. The cheapest. Shallow.

I can get up. The autumn grass is still fragrant, and the birds are singing their song of life (life is most praised by songs about nothing, and only birds are able to do that because they sing without words), a dog will still race at the wheels of a truck rumbling past, barking, because he knows how to enjoy existence, chasing what eludes him and never returns. Sometimes the wind still gusts a bit more strongly. The empty, splendid gust. How salvific is a lack of content.

Would you like that, sir? I can get up and take four steps in each direction. To the four, five, six, or seven corners of the world. I can get up and walk about. O, yes. Take a few joyful steps. But you don't want that, sir. Nobody wants that. You're at some nasty business here, like those who blabber about love and buy Mercedes and build, build, build cold, huge palaces in praise of gods and governors. Those cold temples, palaces, office blocks will always be more important than the hungry. And you shuffle there on your knees, to those cold palaces and office blocks so that someone might sell you some hope (not for those dying of hunger, only hope for you, who lack nothing except an elevation over others).

I am shallow. I feel completely shallow. Unutterably shallow... I have no more soul, liver, spleen, or any other things that pass through my... What don't they pass through? After all, I don't have a throat anymore. I'm shallow, so saved. The banality of depth... Of mind, of soul, and of mystery. No archaeologist will dig down to my skull. I have no skull. Ash after cremation. And thus it is perfectly obvious that we haven't stumbled on any further than our cremation of one another. We haven't accomplished anything. Gas. Cremation. The summit of our accomplishments. I'm supposed to get up? Me? I won't. I prefer being the way I am now. Dead.

You don't know any truth. And you'll never come to know any. You know only the division between the truth of the strong and that of the weak, the truth of the sick and that of the healthy, the truth of the hobbling and that of those that walk evenly, the truth of the young and that of the old. I won't get up anymore. I won't get up. Humanly speaking. I won't even lift a finger. And no one will lift a finger anymore on my behalf. No one knows anything about me. No one will say a thing about me. I am pure. Saved. Because no one has heard of me and no one will ever learn my name, no one will evaluate. No one will ever hear of me... Salvation. The lack of a trace.

I sat down on a chair upholstered in green. The back of the chair was bent in such a way that it pressed uncomfortably against my back beneath my shoulder blades. The table, the floor, and the carafe on the table covered in dust had been saved. The flowerpot on the windowsill. The plates in the cupboard. The tail of the fox poking out of the chest of drawers (and she had been searching for it for so long). Slippers. Candles, which remained on the table. Gloves and stockings thrown to the side in haste.

RAFAŁ WOJASIŃSKI

Tiny grey shoes in the corner not far from the window. A sugar bowl with a crust of sugar. A shrivelled fly on the windowsill. Two piles left by a dog, resting on the floor-slat nearest the door, had been saved. The remains of a shrivelled mouse beneath the bed had been saved. The overcoat on the hanger hooked high on the door of the armoire. Forks and knives in the drawer. Rubbish, which no one had taken out now. A wet stain on the ceiling which had now grown to the size of seven large watermelons. A wedding portrait on the wall. Photographs of two little girls in white dresses had been saved, tucked in the chest of drawers beneath some bedclothes gone mouldy. Banknotes in a roll beneath the floorboards under the door. Bills of exchange, notes, receipts, and debts entered in a small notebook. A wedding ring, an engagement ring in the lower drawer of the chest of drawers. The view of the street through the window. And silence. Quiet. Looking. Voices and sounds. Empty spaces. Both hope and hopelessness had been saved.

I don't remember how I returned to the porter's office at the veterinary surgery. Fortunately, no one had noticed my absence.

I have a stain on my blazer – Tefil said suddenly. – Where'd that stain come from? From the famous restaurant. From the soup. It splashed from the spoon. I only noticed it now.

From one spoon? Such a large stain?

You'd like to learn something about your mother. Too bad you don't want to know anything about your great great great great great great great great great great great great great great great great great great-grandmother. The one that still was a bit monkeyish. Such knowledge… Do you believe in spellcasting, sir? In charmed circles, magic sequences, sympathetic magic, numerology, automatic writing? In the never-ending threads that bind us all to our ancient origins in all of the species? In genetic memory, weldings, secret bonds? In such enchantment? Rozmaryn, my dear sir, I've explored the depths and found nothing deep therein. It's the same thing there as here. Same old, same old. Beginning. Either you begin to drink, sir, or you begin to stop. Either you begin the hour, sir, or a minute or a second. Either you begin to eat or to stop eating. Either you begin to live, sir, or to die. And so on and on. And so. Eternally. Eternity exists, Rozmaryn, sir. Perhaps indeed only that.

Tefil moved on. His pace was slow but not sluggish. Some sort of digestive transformations must have been taking place in Tefil's stomach because his bloat was getting worse and you could hear some growling going on inside there. Rozmaryn immediately set off at his side. He kept to the tempo set by Tefil, whose arms were hanging limply at his side as if he didn't need them for now. Tefil's blazer was unbuttoned, which gave free rein to the upper parts of his body. Rozmaryn was walking to his left. A minute later they turned to the right, between two buildings with gambrel roofs covered with tarpaper. Then, forty-seven paces later, they pulled up in front of the entrance to the staircase of No. 1. They entered through the wooden door, warped by humidity.

Inside it was cool. Tefil held on to the red plastic handrail with his right hand. It was thin; you could wrap your hand around it. He ascended very slowly, conquering each step by first lifting his right leg and then bringing up his left to the same step before he moved on. Rozmaryn was walking next to him, supporting his left elbow. The terrazzo stairs bore traces of long use. The beige panelling received the light falling in through the windows on each landing. The uneven surfaces of the walls resembled another world – of rolling hills, desiccated arroyos, valleys, but without a single living creature. As if everything had already happened.

RAFAŁ WOJASIŃSKI

Tefil paused on a landing, squatted, after which he sat down on the first step from the top. He straightened his legs so as not to cut off the flow of blood in the bends beneath his knees. That's what a certain acquaintance of his taught him. He'd had his leg amputated on account of necrosis and was convinced that this had arisen from his sedentary lifestyle. You can't keep your legs bent for too many hours, all the more so if you curl them beneath the seat of your chair. Because if you do, they'll need to be amputated later. And the amputated limb is just cast aside to lie somewhere and wait until they toss it in the furnace. Before it perishes in the flames, it just lies there somewhere among the medical rubbish. And rots, poor thing, alone, abandoned. And after all, what is it but a portion of one's body detached from one's consciousness? Unless it be a relic. A relic of a shard of bone, relic blood, relic gristle, relic skin, relic finger, relic ear, relic nose, relic fingernail, relic hair from the leg, eyelid, liver, heart, hip as well as relic leg overtaken by necrosis on account of poor circulation.

Rozmaryn felt tired too and sat down to the right of Tefil. A bond had been born between them. Who knows by what channels the silent presence of one man penetrated the presence of the other so that each of them was losing the familiar peculiarity of his own person to become instead one part of a whole. Tefil rested his hands on his legs. Rozmaryn rested his head on his left fist and lay his right hand on his left knee. In his mind tattered fragments of words, sounds, rustles, and disconnected memories collided. A minute later and he stretched out his legs in front of himself too. The sun was high in the sky. It warmed and brightened the landing more and more through the window, falling upon the figures of the two sitting on the stairs. Tefil's stomach seemed to be even larger than before when the two gentlemen had been sitting at the fountain in the town's one park. Tefil waggled his fingers, as if he wanted to kill time that way. His eyes clouded over, and his back hunched. Suddenly, the waggling of the fingers stopped. Three minutes later a loud snoring resounded, a snoring that began and fell away somewhere deep in Tefil's big stomach. At last it seemed as if Tefil was suffocating. Rozmaryn got up and started to tug at Tefil's arm. The latter then straightened up, and his breathing became more even. He blinked his eyes, stunned. Nothing could be read from those eyes.

What's up with you, pulling at my arm like that, sir? – Tefil squawked. – What is it you're about? Have you lost your mind entirely? Have you been deprived of your reason? Your presence...

Following these words, they got up and moved on, higher, in silence. At the next landing, where the window was blocked by a balustrade to a height of nearly two metres, the noon sunlight lit up Tefil's sweaty bald spot and the long face of Rozmaryn. On the landing stood a metal chair with a pasteboard seat, upon which rested a ficus about half a metre tall. Tefil set this on the floor and sat down on the chair. Standing next to Tefil, Rozmaryn smelled the scent which he first discovered in the little garret flat. Automatically he glanced at the window but soon realised that it didn't open. Again he glanced at Tefil and his bald spot drenched in sweat. He noticed that the odour didn't bother him. On the contrary, it put him in a good mood.

Co. Py. Rozmaryn, sir – said Tefil. – It's really a difficult task. Yours. And mine. The task. Coming to terms. Guarantee. Heresy! He – re – sy! Life. Mediocrity denuded.

I can confess to you, sir. Would you like that? You will absolve me. So I begin. Well then, it was like this...

Well then... – said Tefil. – My greatest sin is...

Well then...

Your movements. Your voice. The shaking of your head. The raising of your hand. The scratching of your smooth

RAFAŁ WOJASIŃSKI

cheek with the fingers of your right hand. The care you take with your good looks. It's obvious.

It's a vocation. I see the priest in you.

So then, my sins: one divided by one and two; 3241, 0987, a + d + c = hroc*2; o − s + p; Helenka + Władek; Helenka − Władek; Władek − Helenka; 0 + 0, k + k; eeee, rooooooo; pooooooo, suuuuu, noooooo, leeeee, lyyyyy, liiiiiiii, luuuuuu, laaaaaaa, loooooo…

From the top.

So then, my sins…

So then, it's like this…

Like this.

So then, my sins. I have sinned as follows; Mmmmmmm. Chrum, chrum, chrum (well born). Hau, hau. Pipipi. Sssssss. Kokokokokokoko. Miau, miau, miau.

Well, yes.

Just like that, yes.

I can tell from your movements.

It's as plain as day. That way that you bend at the waist, how you sit on the bench, and that pace of yours with your hands behind your back. And then the way you smooth your hair, preening yourself like a cat; that false politeness of yours, the voracity of your eyes and the way that you're constantly checking the smoothness of your cheeks − is there any five o'clock shadow poking out? Is your skin still perfect? You fix your clothes, you smooth out every last wrinkle. It's as plain as the hand before my face. You can't disguise it, sir, no chance − Tefil finished, growing more silent. Then he began scratching at the back of his head, where he still had quite a lot of hair.

Rozmaryn noticed that Tefil's eyes were brimming with tears. Not the first time that day, either, it seemed to him − when they were sitting in the pastry shop eating cheesecake, sipping espresso. He didn't want to be looking all the while at Tefil's tears, so he averted his eyes but still he couldn't restrain himself from glancing over from time to time. The sight of those tears attracted him as if it were a supernatural phenomenon.

Beauty. And gossip – said Tefil. – Gossip above all! And. What's new? The wind is rattling the windowpane. My mother would say: Look there, son. See how pretty the world is? How much light. Have a look at the light down there by the sugar refinery. Look and see how much electric light. Gaze your fill. Perhaps you won't see that anymore after death, so gaze your fill now. You have to live your life to the full because maybe later it won't be like this. Maybe someday people will live in just such light; maybe they'll electrify every village someday and it'll be bright everywhere, paradise. There'll be radiators in every house, bright light, comfortable furniture, and a person will no longer have any reason to complain or to hate. He'll be able to be more human. There'll be fewer wars and hatred, more love. For that's why the world's developing after all, the discoveries like those of Skłodowska, vaccines, you read about that in the paper, didn't you?

I don't know how to read, mama, I say. But you read it anyway, after all. But I don't know how to read or to count, I say. But you know, after all, that that's the way it is, you had to have read something about it all somewhere. I don't know how to read, I say. But you saw it on the pictures, she says. But I didn't, the pictures are black and white, and they have so many strange spots, you can't see anything, I say. Stop it, she says. Stop what? I say. Stop it, she says. Shut your mouth, she says. You don't respect me, she says. Why are you screaming? I say. You're still being bold, she says. Shut your mouth, she says. I can tell you and tell you a hundred times, and nothing, she says. And... And... And... Well there, see what you've done? she says. I can't say anything at all now. And... And... And... I started stuttering with And, she says. And. Ooooonly

RAFAŁ WOJASIŃSKI

And remains. From the whole language. I've become a stutterer. And stuttering on... And.

O God, because of you, because of your boldness, I've become a stutterer. What'll become of me now that I'm a stutterer who can't get past And? You see? And... And... And... Stuttering on And. On And. On And! I can't handle your stupidity any longer, she says. You're horrid, she says. Idiot, she says. Retard, she says. A sort of idiot, she says. You cretin, she says. I gotta repeat everything a hundred times, she says. Motherfucker, she says. I just can't handle it. Can it really be that you're a retard? she says. A retard, yep, a retarded retard, she says. You can't even dress normally, she says. You can't even clean up like a normal person, she says. You don't know how to be compassionate, she says. You don't know how to help your own mother or people like Skłodowska, she says. You don't give a fuck about anything, she says. You look disgusting, she says. I want to puke, she says. Keep your gob shut, she says. Go off to the well and wash yourself, she says. Your ears are as dirty as shit, she says. Your hands look like they've been digging around in shit, she says. Go and wash yourself, she says. You're disgusting, she says. Shame, she says. I can't even look at you, she says. Shame, she says. Disgusting, she says. I love you, she says.

Rozmaryn placed his hands in his pockets and went a couple of steps higher. He stood still on the fourth. A moment later he came back down just as Tefil was getting up from the chair. Gasping, he bent over, lifted the potted ficus from the floor and set it back down upon the chair. He took his hanky out of his left-hand trouser pocket and wiped the sweat from his brow. It was a coloured hanky. Each time that Tefil balled it up or spread it out there was that odour that Rozmaryn remembered from Tefil's flat. And once more it seemed to Rozmaryn that it was the scent of violets.

Let's go up higher – Tefil said. – Of course, we shall – he added, and set his foot on the first step, leaning on the red banister with his right hand. The sweat broke out on his forehead once more, but now there was a new expression on his face. It was a smile. With his left hand he smoothed back his hair, the hairline of which was high above his balding brow. No, no, thought Rozmaryn. What sort of hair is that? Disgusting, so thin and strawy.

That's the road to Magdalena, higher and higher and ever more difficult – said Tefil, breaking the silence again. – But when I see Magdalena, well, immediately I desire the joy of life to pierce me through in a simply unbelievable matter, just as sense pierces through nonsense. So even though the ascent will be the death of me, entirely sapping me of the strength that I eke out with such difficulty in the little garret flat, still I go on, so as to feel that joy. When that joy arrives, without the slightest agency on my part except for trudging up the stairs to the very last floor, the need to think vanishes. All that spinning of words on all sides in order to dig down to some hope. My opinion on any subject vanishes. I become deprived of independent thinking, which never suggested anything to me anyway because all it is is a manifestation of beginning, one of many such manifestations. My opinion is a counterfeit opinion. I don't believe in any autonomous statement of my own.

Personality. Repetition. Counterfeiting. The omnipresent and omnipotent beginning. Mockery. I, you know, sir, Rozmaryn, sir, am just as much of a believer, just as immortal, in the same state of grace as my dog Prodige. In the same way I am just as much of an unbeliever and just as mortal as my dog Prodige. Do you think, sir, that you, sir, or I am capable of believing anything more or disbelieving anything more than Prodige? You know my dog, sir, correct? Well, sure. You never met her. Protige is in a black hole at the foot of the tree in the yard. You don't know what I'm talking about, sir. The famous dog Prodige. Everything began with her, and I can begin nothing without her.

Although every morning I say to myself, This is the last time, no – still I go downstairs to the pastry shop just like the day before, for cheesecake and coffee. I set myself to it one more time, to begin... And I go down the steps one more time, once more lifting leg after leg downstairs, down the stairs worn down by those whose family names and first names are sunk in oblivion. Once more I begin.

Do you understand, sir? Can you see, sir, before your very eyes, Prodige? Do you know what it means to begin from her? Do you know what morning is, sir? Descending the stairs? Ascending the stairs? I begin each morning descent sitting motionless in the chair near the window in my little garret flat. And. Feeding Prodige, protecting her from the rain, talking with her as if she were a human being. And again I wash out her bowl, pour some macaroni and fatback into it, open the door to the shack a little crack so that she might escape from the rain. And I go down, halting on every landing so as to gaze out through the little windows onto the square, onto the only park in town, onto the fountain and the people who are just passing by along the street. And I make a sign with my hand, as if I were making a sign of remembrance, of blessing, providing myself with range. Rub. Bish.

And every day as I descend the stairs I tell myself that I'll write up a will: that I wish to be reduced to ash and scattered in the Tutberg cemetery, on all the forgotten graves, so that my ashes should mix in with the ashes of the forgotten children, women, and men in the cemetery in Tutberg and be blurred across the leaning tombstones bereft of script and the concrete blocks of the children's graves. Let the wind puff the rest of my ashes against what remains of the cemetery walls and the fields around the cemetery fragrant with freshly ploughed earth or stubble. Let them fall on the feathers of the crows crouching on the balk; let them fall, carried by the wind, onto the fur of the fieldmice, the stray dogs, the foxes out in search of conquest. And on the caps of the women returning exhausted from the fields trying to remember if they have flour at home, milk and eggs so as to make at least griddlecakes for supper. And let my ashes fall upon the hair of laughing children, the third generation already to visit the cemetery in Tutberg in search of what neither I, nor my mates, ever found, an explanation (for nothing falsifies, subjugates, and seduces, nothing beguiles quite like an explanation). As long as I'm not burnt alive in the name of any idea, truth, or religion. I don't want to be burnt in the name of truth, idea, or religion. I want to be burnt in the name of forgetting. And so on, on. And so.

When you catch sight of Magdalena, Rozmaryn, sir, you will be shot through by an incredible feeling. I'm certain of it. Although, on the other hand, sometimes you have such a mug, sir, such an ideological, confessional, racial puss that I just want to break away, to leave you here and escape, for anywhere at all. Where did you get such a puss, sir? How'd you come across it? Through a lack of reason. Because of a deck not quite full. And such a thing leads to tragedy in life.

I have to tell you, sir, that before I came to know Magdalena, I knew Magdalena's father. He came to my flat. As you know, hardly anyone ever comes to my flat, but he came, and not for the first time, because having screwed up the courage to come once, he became convinced that no courage was needed for that at all and came again. His name was Wincenty. Now this was a Saturday, and he came by and wanted some money for fixing this little radio. Along with him his gasping entered the flat, which he acquired on his way upstairs. And that gasping of his derailed me totally. Everybody who comes into my flat derails me totally. Especially when they gasp. I still haven't got used to it. Happens every time.

So then Wincenty comes over to me and demands what he always demands – money. These demands for money! Everybody's owed money. I handed over as much as he demanded, opening my mouth and creating those strange things – words, through the agency of which we can't come to an understanding. When somebody approaches me too closely (especially through the agency of words), even for a payout, I know that nothing good is going to come of it. Bitterness, wake, ignominy, and the vanishing of the last bits of one's freedom. Nothing takes away my freedom as does another person who comes over for money, for what's due him. You get it, sir? Rozmaryn, my dear sir. Do you get it? Do you read Pascal by any chance? At least every other word, every other letter, like I do? So then, Wincenty's standing here in front of me and wants money for the radio. I sit down at the table to slice a bit of yesterday's bread, which I haven't even wrapped up in foil, so it's got hard, but fortunately I had some acacia honey and a little wet, soured cheese. A real feast. The mouth waters.

I began slicing, and this Wincenty won't leave the flat, just keeps droning on and on. I'm not reproaching you, I'm not coming over pouncing on you all the time like others about money because you know others pound at the door, knock, rap, come around again and again whining, accosting, just to get what's coming to them. I know that you won't let them in, you pretend that you're not home, you pretend that you're abed, you pretend that you're dead. You once even papered the town with obituaries in your own last name because you owed somebody (and I know who) two hundred złoty. You kicked the bucket so as not to cough up the dough. You hung those obituaries around everywhere, but there wasn't any funeral, no wake, no vodka, no cutlets, and so it was a washout, from the very start, but you, as always, squirmed your way out of it, you waited him out, the one you owed those two hundred złoty to, until he died and there was nobody to pay back anymore. You even went to the funeral and the wake and you ate your fill and you drank until you were reeling, you went home and the whole town saw you drunk and satisfied with your drunkenness. But I don't want to end that way, I don't want to die without the money you owe me for fixing your radio and for you to come around and drink and eat at my wake and go away satisfied through the whole town.

I can't permit such an insult to my honour, all the more so since I have no honour, as you well know. You have to be born with honour, and here I, I was born without that particular thing, maybe fortunately, but all the same without that item, so I don't want to tell you that I didn't take as much as my labour was worth to fix that radio for you. But for the last six months I kept thinking about the whole deal and I couldn't sleep on account of it, and I'm certain that I demanded two hundred złoty too little for that labour. I want this evened up now, I want to be recompensed, I want justice, and so I'm coming here for justice or, rather, in the name of justice. I don't want you eating and drinking at my wake with those two hundred złoty in your pocket.

It's got around that I fix radios and take too little for it. And it makes me suffer, suffer. And I'm supposed to suffer because of you? I've been suffering on account of so many people already, and now I'm supposed to suffer on account of you? No, that's one too many. You, exactly you, are one too many. The time has come, and I can no wait no longer. You've known me for so many years. So many times I've fixed your radio and I've always looked at that bald spot of yours, that belly, those arms and legs, at that ugliness of yours, and I've always taken too little, I had to take less out of pity, and then I couldn't forgive myself for it for many months on end. I'd look at my wife and feel guilty, I'd look at my mother and I'd feel guilty, I'd look at my sister and I'd feel guilty, I'd look at my mother-in-law and I'd feel guilty, I'd look at my father-in-law and I'd feel guilty. I'd look at my father and I'd feel guilty. I went to church to pray, and I felt guilty for having a wife and children and in-laws, a sister, parents, and taking too little. It's all right for you because you don't have a wife and children on your head, you can even... I won't say what. You've bought yourself freedom, you shyster, you, you need to know that hatred will not pass you by. And punishment. I beg your pardon, I really do beg your pardon, but hatred and karma have their laws.

Here Wincenty stopped talking. I'd taken the first bite of my sandwich and had to tell him, with my mouth nearly full, but there was nothing for it: it wasn't for this that I gave up a life of sex so as to listen to anything like that in my own flat. I'm not in need of any advice, any wisdom, or confessions. I'm not developmental, so knock it off. I don't need to listen to the advice of fathers, mothers, fathers-in-law, sisters-in-law, brothers-in-law, brothers, sisters, neighbours, doctors, sellers of ham, aunties, uncles, wives, husbands, directors, assistant directors, department heads, contractors, butchers, accountants, surveyors, division heads, gaffers, automobile mechanics, politicians, priests. Educators of all stripes. It wasn't for this that I sacrificed sex so as to bear human toxins in my close environment, listen to sermons. Not for this, damn it, have I foregone emotional bonds so that somebody could stand here and nag at me. Any sort of life, please, except one where I have to listen to sermons. Wisdom. Cruelty camouflaged. And that modesty. Humility. Falsification. Counterfeiting. Get out! I told him. Get out! Out!

Fortunately, Wincenty's been dead for six years and I have relative peace as far as the debt for fixing the radio is concerned. I ate my fill and drank to the gills at his wake. That was one of the best wakes I've ever been to. A whole bunch of people were in orbit after only an hour, and I became lighter and lighter, ever more soaked through with my own existence. After I've eaten well and had some vodka, I regain my best traits. It sometimes happens that I regain my faith. Wincenty left behind Magdalena, whom I've liked to ogle ever since she turned seventeen. Now she's nearly thirty, but all the time I like to look at her. Singular acceptance. Individual adoration. One on one. One concentrating on one. Self-reliant adoration. Mass adoration means the cult of the individual. Camouflaged hatred. Dregs in the head. The mass is wretched. The mass hangs everyone out to dry. Abandons. In wretchedness. And a black hole. To adore in mass is to hate. Mass adoration. Recompensation. Crime committed on oneself. And on one's children.

One more landing and we'll be there – Tefil said. – Because after all there's no higher floor in this building, dating from before 1939.

It's the brown door to the right.

Tefil looked upward and began counting the remaining steps in his head. He counted without numbers, as usual. Tefil's counting: this one, and that one, and this one, and that one, and here, and here, and there, and another slat, then another slat, and a grave, and a grave, and then a grave, and one more grave after that, and one more, and a shack, and a dog, and a bed, and a part of a bed, and a shoe, and a sock, and a sock, and a sock, and a trench coat, and a sleeve, and a sleeve, and eyeglasses, and a comb, and a gold tooth, and a wedding ring, and an earring, and a fingernail, and a rag doll, and a hair, and hair, and millions of hairs, and billions of hairs, and a girl, and a boy, and a girl and a boy, and a girl, and a boy, and a girl, and a boy, and… and, and, and, and, and, and…, and Dad, and Mama, and Auntie, and Grandma, and Uncle, and the doggie, and the kitty, and

Mama, and Dad, and Auntie, and Uncle, and Grampa, and Grandma, and, and, and, and, and, and, and, and, and, and, and, and, and, and, and, and... And.

In just such a way Tefil was able to count everyone and everything he ever came across. You couldn't fool Tefil with numbers. He didn't give a fig for mathematical formulas. Tefil was unfoolable.

Tefil repeated his counting many times. Images from his childhood, especially the cemetery in Tutburg, mixed up with the image of the little bits of glass on the fountain's base, and additionally there shouldered its way into his head the image of the panelling from the famous restaurant. Every thing, every object, every memory filled with objects blocked off his route to counting. Feeling about in the dark with his hands. Touching who knows what. Or whom. The digestion of light. Existence. The digestion of light, air, rays of sunlight, of the dust billowing up in the air which you can see so well when the afternoon sun penetrates the stairwell. The digestion of the handrail, the stairs, the hairs, the windowpanes, the fingernails, the eyeglasses, the gold teeth, the gold rings, the bills of exchange, the jottings-down of debts. Digested: every smallest crumb of bread, every grain of the ash of the cremated soul.

When Tefil arrived at the halfway point in his counting of the stairwell, something got in the way and broke it off, so he returned to the lowest step. He gazed at the panelling patterns lit up by the afternoon sun. The brightness reflected from the area over which people descend and ascend. Tefil was breathing heavily, but once again he couldn't move. He tried to arrange that peculiar manner of counting of his in his head and return to the moment in which he began counting the stairs for the first time. But his memory weakened with each passing minute. That's how his mind worked when he counted too intensely. He repeated his sums until he arrived at the uncountability of the stairs. Then there appeared that something that got in the way of his counting of those common stairs, those pickets in the fence, those forks in the drawer, those screws in the cabinet, or those spokes in the bicycle wheels.

It was something that messed up his sums. Evoking something that Tefil didn't have in front of his eyes. Evoking something that hasn't existed for some time now. Evoking his grandfather who died thirty years ago (that he might add him to that which is). Evoking his mother, who is lying now in the wet, cold grave (so that she might be counted). Evoking the rickety house of the Lutheran cantor (so as to be accounted for). Evoking the smokehouse, that work of genius of the cantor. Evoking the sugar refinery, the woman behind the butcher's shop counter. Evoking the cow that swallowed a nail and died of it. Evoking Prodige. Evoking his worry that the dog won't be warm and dry enough in the old shack, that she'll be hungry.

Once more Tefil was deprived of his counting and had the strange feeling that he had been deprived of it forever. He didn't expect that his strength would flag like that. If only he could have two shots of vodka, immediately his youth would return to him, his strength and his authentic hope. Tefil knew no other hope than what he felt after two or three shots of vodka. That state set him most in motion, and at such times he most clearly saw his life. And love was born in him, love for everything, taking the place of his anger and hostility.

Six steps yet remained to him. He lifted his right leg, then pulled up his left alongside it. When he was standing on the very top, he took his hankie out of his pocket and wiped his sweaty brow. And suddenly he felt fantastic. He raised his hand to knock at the door. He knocked several times. Silence, no response, no sound from the other side of the door. Tefil stepped away from the door and sat down on the uppermost step. Tefil's head shone in the af-

RAFAŁ WOJASIŃSKI

ternoon sun against the background of the billowing dust. It seemed as if the rays of sunlight were lifting the specks of this sign of all time and all history and bearing them away. Rozmaryn sat down to Tefil's right and leaned himself against the wall. He felt the cool of the panelling. A sign. The quiet, stubborn, return of hope.

No, Rozmaryn, no, sir! – Tefil said with a smile. – Lift up that mug of yours, sir. We must go. Rozmaryn, sir, you first, please. You have one minute. Hop to it. Don't drag your feet, sir. It looks bad when you drag your feet.

They found themselves out on the pavement quickly and turned right. Just next door was a large public school. Tefil pulled up at the main doors. He was looking for something in his pockets. At last, from his left trouser pocket, he pulled out a half-broken cigarette. He set it on his lips and lit it with matches that he'd extracted from the right pocket of his blazer. He took a puff and set off again. Rozmaryn was walking to his right, just at Tefil's shoulder. For a moment they went on like horses. As if they were pulling some cart that was fully laden, but none too heavily.

If we cross the street now that leads to the Catholic cemetery – you can see it there, sir, if you turn your head a bit to the left – we'll come out onto Garbarska Street – said Tefil. – We'll take a nice, calm, slow stroll all the way to Kolska. That's the street along which those trucks barrel down from north to south. We've got quite a way in front of us.

And now, quite parenthetically, do you take care of your personal hygiene, sir? – Tefil asked in a softened voice.

You don't know what that means, sir, hygiene? Hygiene is important. I, sir, you know, am lazy. I go at it lazily, the wiping, the wiping clean, the washing clean, the washing away, the washing up, the scouring. There are some motions I am no longer able to execute. You know, sir, I must execute some strange contortions with my entire body, with my stomach, so as to arrive at those places I need to wipe clean. And it's ever more difficult for me, so I get all wet. I pour warm water into a tub and soak. You know, sir, all I do these days is to soak until the water goes cold. Sometimes I get warm water ready in this thermal pot that I bought from the Russkies at the bazaar, and add warm water to the tub from it. Then I can soak for two hours, even. It's a luxury item. I can recommend it to you, sir, with a clean conscience. It's worse with my head. Fortunately, I don't have too much hair. It's quite impossible for me to bend my head down. I get the spins and want to vomit when I do. At such times I've got to knock back a shot of vodka and lie down on my back. And dream. Yes, don't look at me like that, sir, I must dream. When I dream, the nausea passes. Only, I have to achieve a certain degree of happiness, not overmuch, but still and all. But it's more elevated than sexual pleasure, I reckon, because it can last even a couple of hours before sleep overtakes me – and disappointment, and breathing troubles, and a headache.

Soaking. I most recommend soaking. I reckon it's the most splendid thing I've ever invented all my life long. Well, perhaps at certain fleeting moments I've had better ones, but for the long haul, if someone has the intention of living a bit longer, nothing remains but soaking. Soaking has led me to some elevated thoughts. I'll certainly bring forth something living unto the world. Did you know, sir, that the mushrooms you've digested and evacuated from your body are still able to live? You also heard that, sir? Is it true or no? As they travel along the sewers, somewhere they are born again, and on and on, endlessly. Mould, sir, you know, can live even two thousand years, eight thousand years. It can transform every poison into healthy nourishment for itself. It's cleverer to be a mushroom than a man. Mould lives upon us, it eats us. Mould absorbs us, Rozmaryn, sir. Our intelligence is no help at all here. Reason constantly deprives us of reason. A mushroom never loses its reason. You know, sir, what I'm getting at.

So I soak in the evenings. I sit with my hind parts in a tin tub, my legs are sticking out in front, my arms are hanging at the sides, and my thoughts carry me away. Only when I'm soaking am I one hundred percent someone. I have no need of common topics.

At this moment Rozmaryn was first to set his foot on Garbarska Street. He had sad eyes, a sad mouth, and his head was slightly bent forward. Tefil, on the other hand, had the shoelace of his right shoe untied. They went along at a slow pace. A scraping noise arose from the shuffling of their heels along the powdery dust of the berm. They weren't walking along the pavement. It would have been easy to trip against the unevenly set paving stones. Wretched weeds of various heights were growing in the cracks between the stones. They had their own beauty and might even have given a person the joy felt by one life contemplating another life.

Tefil was slightly hunched over as he began to feel a pain between his shoulder blades. He got this from sitting in the porter's office at the veterinary surgery on the edge of town, on the road to Waldau. This condition had got worse from him sitting at home and reading for hours on end, squeezed into an old easy chair. It was a tough row to hoe for him, reading. Sometimes he could only make out five of seven letters in a given word, so in order for him to read anything through, carefully, he needed a lot of time, certainly more than one life might afford him.

The road that Tefil and Rozmaryn were taking was short, but it took them a long while. They had already been going like that some few dozen minutes, and still they hadn't gone farther than the public pump placed some hundred metres from the crossroads. They pulled up alongside it. Tefil looked the wearier of the two. He pressed down on the handle with his right hand, which sent some water pouring out of the spigot located at the height of Rozmaryn's thighs. With difficulty, Tefil bent over and set his face under the stream of water. After a moment or two of wetting his face in this way, he began to gulp the water. Rozmaryn heard five or six gulping sounds. That made him thirsty too. Tefil's gulping seemed unusual to him. Five or six mouthfuls and the bending of his head: he repeated that sequence some ten times at least. Rozmaryn couldn't tear himself away from the sound of that gulping and the repetitive image. Gulping. Bending. Bald head. Remains of hair. Hanging stomach. Lunacy. As soon as Tefil straightened up and wiped his lips with the sleeve of his trench coat, Rozmaryn himself bent over and repeated Tefil's motions, pressing down on the handle with his left hand. Tefil, sated with the water, sat down on the high kerb a few metres from the pump with a look of relief on his face. After a moment or two, Rozmaryn sat down to his right.

It's nice – Tefil stated. – That cooled air, sun-filled but already cool afternoon air... You ask about the evening, sir? Why? Is it late? No. It's spot on as it should be. It should be darker already? But it's bright. The sun is high. Are you blind, sir? It's just gone noon. You say, sir, that we've been walking a very long time, eating, and noon hasn't passed yet? How'd you get that into your head, sir? What are you getting at, sir? That it's constantly noon? What are you saying? Perhaps you've got heatstroke, sir. How can it be impossible since it is as it is? You, sir, are quite simply befuddled somehow. The time has been accounted for, Rozmaryn, sir. Accounted for. To the last second. Even to the lesser intervals. Each time, every hour, minute, second, and lesser, as you say, sir, interval of time. It begins of itself. That which is recognised as having been finished is set in motion. Without you, sir, without us, without anyone.

We, one might say, Rozmaryn, sir, have been sentenced. Sentenced to beginning. Even without us, even without the memory of us, even without the slightest trace of us. It's noon. Just as it should be.

Tefil pushed the shoes off his feet, executing the same motions as before on the little square in front of the community offices.

They're swelling on me – he said. – I've got to rest a bit. Nothing's better for the feet and the lower legs than a fresh breeze.

What's left to me? What do I still have? I've counted it up. Three loaves of bread, nearly a kilogram of bacon, a sack of potatoes – maybe ten kilos. A whole smoked ham. And those two hundred złoty...

It's harder for me to leave the town. I can't find a place that leads outside my beloved Litental. I can't get myself out of it, but the more I find myself on its crooked streets, its squares, in the one park in town, at the fountain and the clothing store or the butcher's shop, I claw my way more and more out of words I don't know how to read because for me 'r' mixes up with 't', 'b' with 'e', 'd' with 'a', 's' with 'o', 'j' with 'q', 'x' with 'l'.

If I could find just one sentence with which I was satisfied! – said Tefil, gazing at his feet. – But it's so hard. So difficult. Impossible. I'm not satisfied with any sentence. No poet, dramatist, prose writer, no philosopher or theologian ever created a sentence which satisfies me. There is no such sentence, and I know that no such sentence will ever come about. Not a single sentence worth remembering will be left behind after humanity's gone. Mediocrity denuded. And yet the more these streets, blocks of flats, cemeteries, and the pastry shop in Litental hold on to me, the more certain I am that I shall finally emerge from all words. Each day, the walls of the buildings reconcile me to existence. The cup in the pastry shop, the oaken counter in the clothing store which remembers the hands of those that no one will ever recall by name anymore – all of this liberates me from language, from counterfeiting. From this it's easy to see that everything beyond Lithental is a squalid hole.

Tefil gazed at his feet, from which the swelling was beginning to ebb. He grabbed at his head with his right hand, then stuck the index finger of his left hand into his nostril and moved it around for quite some time. It seemed as if he would pull the nose right off his face. He did this with such force that his nose went shapeless for a moment, becoming the nose of some new species, as if it were intended for some different sort of animal, a new, as yet unknown species.

They got up and went off. The time began to move more quickly.

Go on ahead, sir, – said Tefil. – You must go, sir. And be not afraid, sir.

Don't permit yourself to be fooled, sir. In our books, symphonies, inventions, words, holy scriptures, there really isn't anything at all. Nothing. They might as well not be at all. And once they were not. For quite a long time. And when some new humanity makes its appearance, out of sheer pride they will once again create that product for which there are no interested clients, and which must be forced upon them. Beginning absorption and that.

Life is the transient form of the dead. A sickness of sorts. What is dead never falls ill, though it is real nonetheless.

Look here, sir. I once had a dog with a real look to her, real behaviour, and real barking. When she died, I buried her at the foot of the acacia. Five years later I dug up her remains. There was no colour, no barking, she didn't move, she didn't breathe. I buried her again. Beginning.

They arrived at Kolska Street and turned left in the direction of the narrow-gauge railway station. Rozmaryn felt sweat pouring down his back beneath his shirt. It was noon again, and the sun was sending down a merciless swelter.

RAFAŁ WOJASIŃSKI

Down there, just before the next crossroads, is this new restaurant, a pizzeria really – said Tefil. – We can get something to drink there, but I didn't bring any money, on purpose, so you'll have to pay, sir. I have those two hundred złoty cleverly hidden away in my apartment. I move them from place to place, take them in hand, constantly checking to make sure they still exist. Two hundred złoty for the black hour. And every hour is black, even when lit up with the flash of love and health. And every hour depends on money, my money or the money of others (who, actually, does money belong to? Nobody, like the universe?). So I'm constantly checking.

Money is my most beloved human creation. Truth does not exist without money. It becomes lunacy, illness, nonsensical babble. Only money and the power it brings, make the truth the truth. Money has power, Rozmaryn, sir.

And where is your money, sir? Do you also check on it every now and then, to see that it's in its place? What else gives a person such a feeling of justice as does checking to see whether his money's in its place? The profundity of thought and the life of the spirit in comparison with the profundity that is found in money is nothing at all. The spiritual life of man is money. Money is more to the point than the word. Well then, where do you stash your cash, sir? Do you carry it about in your pockets? How much do you have in your pockets, sir? Sometimes I'm afraid that I'll forget where I've hidden my money, and I'm overcome with a great sadness.

In other words, you're paying again, sir.

When words come out of me, phrases, sayings, commas and full stops inaudible, this sort of melody is born within me, and it seems to me that I should tell you something about your mother. I'd like to say something about love. Love is, for me, the only road to nontalking, to sitting, gazing at the television, and enjoying a sandwich with black pudding. Just sitting at the table. That's how I imagine love. Sitting at the table with the television on, peace, calm, evening, a clean house, tea on the table, sandwiches, maybe herring in oil, cheese, honey, and a tablecloth beneath it all. A little tiredness after a long day at work, sleepiness, but not an overwhelming exhaustion, just a delicate sleepiness, one that's lined still with strength and the great hope that everything is marvellous. And that it'll be the same on the next day at supper too. And again. And on into infinity, forever. That evenings and suppers like that are never-ending, that they'll last for ages. That's love. Love is like that.

I'm in love with life with just such a love, and I'd be very grateful if you, sir, could confirm this somewhat. Or whatever.

Pardon me, Rozmaryn, sir – added Tefil. – Really, I do apologise. You have to understand me, sir. I'm helpless when faced with that, which allows me the only possibility of continuation, which allows me to discover a tiny area of happiness and the joy of life, which affords me the possibility of nourishing fully my own organism, and Prodige as well. It's my only prescription for fate. I am what precedes humanity, not quite human yet. That's also a weakness of mine.

Everyone is counterfeit, only the great majority are counterfeited in such a way that they are unable to see their counterfeiting, that is, their falsification. Just like one doesn't see the world which is right next to one, and yet it exists with a never-ending and very real strength. Just as real as our walk to the butcher's shop and the famous restaurant.

You live parallel to me, Rozmaryn, sir, and the woman who works in the famous restaurant lives parallel to you, and parallel to her lives the woman behind the counter at the butcher's shop. Just as parallel as you, sir, and the dead children in the Lutheran cemetery in Tutberg. Nothing exists but parallel beings.

That's why I return. I return, despite the fact that… I remain in place. And I return. I pass from one side of the street to the other, I change directions, turning suddenly, stopping, and going on further, after a certain time returning to that same place – only that place no longer exists. Walls, rain gutters, porches, stairs, broken fragments of kerb. The hour, the second, sucks dry the roofs, streets, doors, doorknobs. Flotsam of things, words, thoughts.

Language. The word 'stone' does not name the stone. The word 'roof' does not name the roof. The word 'Marynia' does not name Marynia. The word 'Prodige' does not name my dog. Counterfeiting. Falsification. Falsehood. The names of streets on the walls of buildings, convex tin signs with white script on a blue background. The names of abandoned streets, left to their own destiny. Rust-eaten, with holes from nails and screws.

There isn't a single good name. That's why I'm not satisfied with one single thought of this world, why language has never satisfied me. The barking of a dog satisfied me, the chirping of a sparrow, the snorting of pigs, the rustle of the wind and the little waves on the lake.

We'll turn to the right when we get past the synagogue. Right away. Where are we going? To Słubicki Street, Rozmaryn, sir.

An impediment – Tefil added. – The path to the toilets down the corridor. An impediment right at the bedside. I woke up in the middle of the night last night. Swung my legs down onto the floor. Right into the tub of cold water. And all around: an impenetrable darkness. I'd been soaking in that tub in the evening. I'm saving electricity, so I fumble about in the darkness. Now, while I was sitting in that tub, I got very sleepy (maybe from the warm water), so sleepy that I seemed to be going unconscious. These sounds started seeping into my head, piercing it as if they were passing through cotton. They reminded me of individual syllables, and slowly they were transformed into something like words, but I couldn't understand them. All those sounds seemed so foreign to me, in my language, in Polish, but foreign, as if Polish had become a foreign language to me, completely incomprehensible. Purpossied, pwoysonnt, streeetifuld, shugcottony, brundchisy, dumisile, mournituble, lur, bg, blnkeet. Not a single Polish word in Polish. Everything in Polish but in a foreign language. I couldn't understand Polish anymore. Nothing. I don't remember when I heaved my wet backside out of the tub and fell into a deep sleep. And.

The midnight awoke me. Impediment. In the darkness, with my legs in the cold water, I sat on the bed. I got up and went through the darkness of the room on my wet legs, I went over to the door of my flat and then into the corridor. There it was brighter. Maybe lamps, maybe some other light. The cool of the corridor, a familiar sensation. I kept my right hand on the wall. Cold. I knew it well. I got to the toilet. I did what I had to and returned to my flat without encountering any obstacles. But as I was getting into bed, once more I sloshed into the cold water in the tub. I lay down with those wet feet of mine and covered myself with an eiderdown. I wanted to go away, but I had nowhere to go to (can a dead person want to die? because of the life that's passed away? can long life demand death? does it always have the right?). And I got warmer and warmer.

Enclosure in the ambit of the city, enclosure in the garret flat, which in the darkness becomes limitless, impenetrable, weakening the imagination, and finally enclosure under the eiderdown in bed. Enclosure on account of the death of a dog, on account of her absence. The city, which I am unable to leave. The flat, which I'm incapable of exiting. In my flat I wait on no one but myself. And later on, the ashes from which there's no exit at all. To be oneself in the cemetery at Tutberg. No memory of any grain of the dust spread there, blown about the old graves, the old houses, walls, and fields. The digestion of existence. The digestion of the soul. The digested soul rising aloft in ashes above the alder woods, above the birch groves and forests, above the ploughed and sown earth. No exit, never any exit.

When the darkness of the room ceased to be noticeable, dreams began to appear, and in dreams the colour of the sky, human figures and animal figures, walls, buildings, and far roads which, tangling amidst the fields and villages, lead me through Liebrade to the pastry shop I frequent for cheesecake and coffee.

I've tucked myself into a little flat in the garret. A lack of ability in the areas of addition, subtraction, and counting. A lack of comprehension of words in my own language. The words of bishops, prime ministers, ecologists, vegetarians, homosexuals, heterosexuals, mothers, fathers, psychologists, philosophers, poets, travel buffs, and culinary masters with their own television programmes, actors and directors, the directors of central agencies and bars (bars, no). A lack of reading and counting. Lying beneath the eiderdown in a tiny flat. When it began to get bright, an empty white plastic bag appeared in the freezing room. I began to fall asleep near morning. Beneath my eyelids I saw the weak light, the muddy image of brightness. The muddiness of dream and the muddiness of reality. Muddification. And.

Purpossied, pwoysonnt, streeetifuld, shugcottony, brundchisy, dumisile, mournituble – Tefil said or rather mumbled out.

I repeated something from memory.

I consolidated something, like a Hail Mary...

Or not...

I don't pray, as a matter of principle... I no longer repeat that... How dare I. Purpossied was running about in my head: pwoysonnt, streeetifuld, shugcottony, brundchisy, dumisile, mournituble.

Do you understand anything of that, sir?

As much as I do… A little. Almost nothing. I've got a hankering for something sweet.

Sugar?

Sugar…! Am I a horse?

Turns out to be the cheapest.

This might be a dream, a vertical dream, upright, about another dream. I already had something like that. It didn't add up then either. Babbling. Disconnected.

While sober.

Completely.

When I'm sober for weeks on end, sometimes I become unsober through a lack of drinking. That happen to you too, sir? Please don't answer. It's not the right moment. I don't want to hear any answer. And yet pathology is a sort of decisive… thing. Am I pathological? My head is spinning.

The sun had reached its zenith above the town. Tefil once more felt the sweat gathering on his bald head. The very same sweat was pouring down his back beneath his shirt and made him feel depressed, humiliated, fatigued, and even somewhat devoid of thought.

We need to sit down here – said Tefil. – It'd be best on that high kerb to the right, where there's a bit of a breeze. The breeze will dry us of our fatigue and our sweat. Why don't you go off to that store behind us, sir, and buy us two bottles of Sierpeckie beer?

Rozmaryn detached himself from Tefil and went into the store. Before Tefil had quite sat down on the kerb, Rozmaryn was already back with two cold bottles of Sierpeckie beer.

I don't have that dog – Tefil said. – She died over forty years ago, maybe thirty-seven. She was made of the same matter as me and you, sir. She's lying in the yard, under-

RAFAŁ WOJASIŃSKI

ground, near the tree. One, three, twelve, eight, seventeen, five, five. And again. And so on. And on. And so.

And so on. And on. And so.

Prodige died on a Tuesday. I remember. It was a fall afternoon. I dug her grave at the foot of the tree in the yard. I tied a rope around her neck, a noose just like you use to hang someone, and dragged her over to the place I'd chosen. I dug a grave a metre thirty deep. She was swollen and her mouth was open. Baring her fangs. She looked dangerous and seemed bigger than ever. All her beauty went off to hell, its place taken by immensity and power. As if she were saying: nobody will beat me now, now nobody can. Not anymore. I had only to set her in motion, set her in ageless motion. Otherwise she couldn't change her position relative to Mars or Jupiter. Her death helped me. I was rescued by a living dog and rescued by a dead one. You understand, sir? Possibility and the lack of possibility. It's the same rescue. I buried her in two shifts. The first break for a drink of water, the second for two beers. I wanted to sit as long as possible near the open grave. You could still see her head from under the dirt, her left rear paw, and a fragment of her side, her rib cage. I sat there on a little stump and stared into the grave. Then I raised my head and stared at the greying, livid sky, at the branches, at the wall of the block of flats. A couple of times.

Then a dog began to bark. Prodige! Prodiżek! Proooo-diiiiżeeek. Here girl... Here... Come on, here... Let's go, doggie, because it's getting cold... What do you want to do out here in the cold running around? Come on little girl! Little one! Come on! You can do it. Come on, stop dragging your feet, you old bat, you! Come on! You can do it.

My dear little doggie, come on. Where are you? Return from the great beyond. Come on, little girl. The world is but a province, a periphery, a forgotten old muddy scrap of land. Every little tatter of the cosmos is just a shabby province, a hole, Ignorantia. There's no reason for you to be sitting there. It's all the same everywhere. And in this is all our hope. Come on, then, because you'll get hungry and what'll you do then? You won't even find a scrap of sausage going green there that people have chucked away. Come on, because you'll just be lying about in that desert wasteland and dragging your feet around there without a drop of water, because over there maybe it doesn't even rain. To say nothing of your favourite Sierpeckie beer. It's disgusting over there... You'll perish of hunger. You'll be driven to death by overwhelming terror that there's no rodents there, neither devouring nor devoured, no me. Come on, little doggie... Prodige, get a grip on yourself and come on! Set out on the road already, come back. Prodige! Prodige! Prooodiiiige!

It began to rain. There's no way back. Sprouting. Flowers. Scent. Joy. Delight. And so on. And on. And so.

I've spilt some beer on my trouser leg. I'm all in splotches. Shirt, trousers, blazer, trench coat. I'm all spattered. It was clean duds they gave me, right? No? Soiled? And I'm schlepping about like that? And always getting soiled? Stain upon stain. Do I soil myself every day? Or only when I rope somebody in for dinner and beer in the famous restaurant? I have soiled myself on weekdays or Sundays? I soil myself at home or only out in the town?

I don't know.

I don't launder.

Stained. Ordained with beer, tripe, mustard, honey, God knows with what. Consecrated.

Holy Day. Keep it holy.

I soak my hands.

Not in the same water as my behind.

In the fountain. Same as you, sir. It's pleasant. The cool of the cold water, naturally. Constant contact with the air. No offices. No official spaces, libraries, health centres. Fresh air. The food store in the village at most. With a draught – Tefil said in all seriousness. – And in one's ears: the rustle of the wind in the birch leaves and the pine needles. Filling full the depths of one's mind, deeper than thought can do. Penetrating the skin to the very soul (the soul is inside us, constantly being consumed by beginning).

You're driving me to a state of nervous distraction, sir. It's all your fault, sir. The fault of people like you, sir. And. And on account of people like me. On account of us. Each one of us. We're quenching one another. Officials by other officials. The young by the young. The old by the young and the young by the old. Being quenched. By drunks and teetotallers, by the dying and the immortals. By hangman and victim. By chaos and coincidence. By access to knowledge and by ignorance. By the wealthy and the poor. By genius and ignoramus and complete cretin. Smoothly, inexorably, salvifically, full of elevations and love and hopes, quenching. By overpopulation and the low birthrate. By love and hatred, by a lack of cash and an overabundance of the same. By illness. And. And health. Quenching.

Everything because of you, sir. You drive me insane, sir. If only there were me and no one else. Or if only there were you, sir, and no one else. There must be someone. Someone else is crucial. Can't do without someone else. The existence of the additional is decisive. Implementation to insanity. Language. The source of the mental illnesses that prey upon us. Language is the devil incarnate. The guarantee of madness. The evil which we have never recognised and never shall recognise. It makes use of human intelligences like primitive unconscious tools in order to enchant the masses and individual wretches.

You drive me insane sir, Rozmaryn, sir. Because you are. And I am. That's how wars get started. You're killing me, sir. You are putting to death the beauty of the clothes

I have inherited from the dead, sir. The ones I wear each day. And I have nothing else of any real value.

What's that I see? What's that I see here? What's this we have here?

Why are you making such a sour face, sir? Are you insulted, sir?

No one ever really says what's really on his mind. And yet, after all, everyone has something horrid in mind for other people. Why does no one admit it, that he wishes others something horrid? And love for himself. There is no good definition of love, Rozmaryn, sir. There are no good definitions at all. Definitions are mistaken. We don't know what we're doing, even when we're admitting our guilt.

Tefil got up from the kerb. Quite gracefully. When he'd straightened up, he wanted to button his blazer, but his fingers couldn't find the button which had popped off earlier. He brushed back what remained of his hair with his fingers and extended his right hand in Rozmaryn's direction. The latter grabbed hold of Tefil's right hand with his left and stood up. They went off in the direction of November 11 Street. They had the aspect of well-rested and satisfied people. Motion. Motion to the left, motion to the right, straight ahead, backwards. Rozmaryn was walking two paces behind Tefil. He preferred the view of his lumpy back than the rest of him, which he might see from the side or from the front. They crossed November 11 quickly. And proceeded further, to Narutowicz Street. They went along the right-hand side of that street. Some fat drops of rain began to fall. The sun went down, and Rozmaryn took hope that perhaps time had begun to pass again and that everything would return to normal.

Suddenly, Tefil turned left, to quickly pass down Narutowicz again, on the left side. The two portions of the street were divided by a little square. On this square Tefil stepped in some dog crap but he wiped his shoe clean on the grass

RAFAŁ WOJASIŃSKI

with extraordinary alacrity. He pulled up in front of a little beige-coloured building with a gambrel roof, which stood at the beginning of a whole row of structures that came to an end with a food store. Behind it, divided from it by a perpendicular street, was the house of culture. Rozmaryn ran up to Tefil.

That's the first time I've seen you run, sir – said Tefil. – There was no car coming. Why did you run across the street?

Tefil tried to button his blazer because a cool wind suddenly blew up. Unfortunately, there wasn't a single button to be found on his blazer, so he buttoned his trench coat. Rozmaryn was standing right next to Tefil, to his left. So close that he probably caught the odour of the older, balding man. When Tefil moved to the left, gracefully avoiding his companion, Rozmaryn followed him. They were heading in the direction of the house of culture. Tefil pulled up after sixty nine paces, in front of the food store. On the other side of the street, or rather, the two streets meeting up as one beyond the little green square, stood the fire station that had been established in 1909. On the same side of the street stood the Lutheran church, to which seventy six years earlier a pastor would come once a month to hold services.

And – Tefil said, pointing at the church, which was falling into ruin. – Now, standing right in front of the house of culture, if we should glance to the right and cross the street, we see on our right side, and stand in front of the entrance gate to the church, through which so many people were carried out in coffins and in hope and in which many were christened in hope, we will simply be standing in front of a ruin despite the fact that the same cross is standing on the top of the pinnacle of this ruin, which stood there then. And.

It's starting to rain. Rain is falling on my head.

Rozmaryn lifted his collar. He made a somewhat sour expression with his lips, as if he wanted to smack them, but never arrived at the smacking. In his eyes there appeared impatience, along with the desire for something pleasant. Tefil stood like a statue, with his hands folded on his stomach. Rozmaryn grew very sad. Tefil took him by the arm and led him to the other side of the street. Tears welled up in Rozmaryn's eyes. They were now standing in front of the cast-iron gate leading to the grounds of the Lutheran church. Tefil passed through quickly, pulling Rozmaryn after him, moving from the gate to the large wooden doors of the church. They were open. They went inside and sat on the rearmost pew. There were only traces of the altar and the cross in the sanctuary, but the stars that had been painted on the vault were still clearly visible.

Why don't you lie down on the pew, sir – said Tefil. – for you've gone quite pale. There's no doctor here, no one is going to be curing you, nor will there be any first aid in the offing. I will not even perform artificial respiration. Anyway, human destiny is really no concern of mine. I'm completely indifferent to who's lying prone, whom I accompany on their last journey, their last mile. And. Above you, sir, there are stars painted on the vault. Not a bad view. And a true one. Those painted stars are no less real than those that collapse into themselves in our cosmos. Just as real.

Reality has many names. Falsehood is real, and truth is real. Those are two facts. False love is true and a fact. And true love is true and a fact. Is that not marvellous? As a matter of fact, anything that might occur to us is real. Phantasmagorias are real, although they are only in our heads, but our heads are real and what is born of them is real. Perhaps you can't touch it, but you know that it is. A thought is just as real as a lack of thought. Do you have any requests, sir? What sort of requests might you have, sir? You, sir, are actually but one leg... Too late. Get up, sir! Let's go! Come on then, one-two! Up, sir! Come on! Get a

RAFAŁ WOJASIŃSKI

move on, sir, before I grab a stick and whap you a solid one across your arse – what a livid welt I'd raise there! Well, come on already! And. And. Up, up, or when I thwack you... Stay! Down, boy! Stay! Jump, sir, jump! And now a little dance. Dance, sir! Now, down! Down, boy! Sir.

Tefil took off his trench coat and set it down on the pew at Rozmaryn's feet. He went on among the pews, some of which were knocked over. When he arrived at the sanctuary, where the altar had been, and stood with his back to the traces left by the missing cross, facing the empty pews and the lying Rozmaryn, suddenly, his face was transformed into the face of a priest, a cantor, an Orthodox priest, a rabbi, but it remained all the same the face of that idiot sitting in the porter's office who was constantly misplacing the keys, so often misplacing them, that it cost the lives of many animals who had been transported to the veterinary surgery following bad accidents.

In the name of... And... And... Amen – said Tefil. – Lord, sir... And... Let us apologise, that we may... And. Let us apologise to the sacrifice...

I confess... And... And... And... Through my... And... And... And... I ask... And... And... And... My brothers and sisters... And... Have mercy on us and lead us to life... And... And upon us.

Glory... And... We praise... And... We bless... And... We adore... And... We glorify... And... Thank... And... Lord... And... Jesus... And... Son... And... Who... And... Who... And... Who... And... For... And... Only... And... Only... And... With the Spirit... And... Amen.

Let us pray...
Behold... And...
Lord... And...
The Word... And...
Behold... And...
I believe... And...

the Father... And...
the Creator... And...
And... And...
the Son... And...
God... And...
True God... And...
Born... And...
He... And...
Crucified... And...
And... And...
And... And...
I believe... And...
I believe... And...
I look forward... And...
And life... And...
Amen.

Through the mystery... And...
Blessed are you... And...
Accept these... And...
Wash away... And...
Pray now... And...
Lift up... And...
We give you thanks... And...
It is truly... And...
It is truly... And...
Therefore... And...
Bless these offerings... And...
So that they become... And...
He... And...
Took bread... And...
Take this and eat... And...
Similarly... And...
Take this and drink... And...
The mystery of... And...

RAFAŁ WOJASIŃSKI

Great is the mystery... And...
We glorify the mystery... And...
Mystery... And...
In memory of the death... And...
Through... And...
Formed by divine teaching... And...
Deliver us... And...
By the help... And...
Peace... And...
Let us offer each other... And...
Behold the Lamb... And...
May the Lord bless you... And...
Go... And...

Rozmaryn got up from the pew. He did it in this way, by sliding to the left and falling with a loud rumble. Then he assumed a position on all fours and just, like a dog, took a few steps before squatting in a mysterious manner and, holding onto the pew with his right hand, he got up. A sparrow was flying about above the heads of Rozmaryn and Tefil. It couldn't find its way out of the church, even though the windows had been smashed.

Suddenly, Rozmaryn sat down on a pew. The image of Tefil grew indistinct before his eyes. On the other hand, a taste came into his mouth, a taste which had been familiar to him since childhood and which always made him feel better. It gave him the hope that, despite it all, fulfilment was something simple, independent of any complicated definition of fulfilment. It was the taste of headcheese, white headcheese, the sort his father used to make. His father's mind had to be splendid since even on his deathbed he did not submit to the illusory promises of a better world but recalled that headcheese. He died in early fall before even the furnace needed to be turned on. His father's bed stood in the foyer, where it was warm enough. The cat jumped onto the bedclothes and purred because earlier he had eaten a mouse hunted down in the shack where the grain was stored. His father purred as well. Or cleared his throat. Only Rozmaryn understood what his father said in his rumbling, throaty voice. But he was still a very small child and was only beginning to learn how to speak, so he just kept repeating to his Grandma: Dada hechee, dada hechee, dada hechee. When he died, Rozmaryn stopped repeating that 'dada hechee'. His father never got his head-cheese, dying without it.

Then that man showed up who thought himself to be his father's friend. Thought himself to be the only friend his father had in the whole village because everyone else broke off their relations with him. They avoided his glance, his words; they were unable to bear his presence. Many years after his father's death, that man exchanged a few words with Rozmaryn at the cemetery gate. Rozmaryn had been sitting on a bench at the back of the cemetery, drinking beer from a bottle. He wasn't returning from the grave of his father or his now dead grandmother at all; he just liked the peace in that place.

Your dad never had anything good from people – his father's friend told him. – Neither at work nor at home. They abased him, put him down. They laughed at his stupidity, which perhaps even was a fact, at many moments of his life. They laughed at his deteriorating, to put it in clinical terms, his dynamically deteriorating and increasing lack of competence. They laughed at what he did and what he said. They considered him to be a dolt. Probably because he always thought himself to be smarter than everyone else. That's what it's like for those who are put down and laughed at. Because it would be impossible, after all, for us to be as much of a dolt as they take us to be. But, shitass, what I'm telling you, is that it is possible. I'll say more: that's the way it is, for sure. And this is true for everybody, with-

RAFAŁ WOJASIŃSKI

out exception. Every last little human person. Not bad, eh? That's a discovery for you. I ought to get a medal for it, be honoured somehow because this is a great discovery for humanity, and it ought to be copied, published, carried all over the world. Would you believe it? No! Of course not! But that's the way it is, shitass. How could I discover something like that? How'd it occur to me, me? It's impossible, after all, that I should be so wise. It's impossible, and yet I am. Wisdom and the grace of God tread paths unknown to us.

Rozmaryn got up for the second time and saw the figure of Tefil before him, and in his left hand he felt a weight. That was Tefil's trench coat, upon which a stain of sweat from Rozmaryn's hand had already been deposited. He handed the trench coat to Tefil when the latter had come down from the altar.

Two minutes later, which passed in their pulling up their trousers, fixing their shirts, shoes, socks, and blazers, they went out into the light of day. Reaching the pavement, they turned right and set off in the direction of the small hardware store on the ground floor of a corner building. When they'd arrived there after a walk of less than two minutes, they turned right again and saw before them a road leading upward. The road was marked with grooves cut by many rainfalls. They looked like small, dry rivers. Dirt and sand, mixed with the remains of gravel that had once been carted there, made for a fairly comfortable surface.

I don't know what time it is, but it isn't late – said Tefil. It's never late.

Three minutes later they were on the sandy road which, ten metres further on, became an asphalt surface leading to Kościelna Street.

Above Rozmaryn's head, a portion of chain-link fence shone in the sun. Above the fence oak leaves were rustling.

And above the oak the heavens were spread, over which the floating clouds began to cover the sunny sphere.

You remind me of your mother, sir – said Tefil. – Despite it all, you do. I don't know how, but she's in my head, completely. It's a strange image, and I'm not too fond of looking at it. But sometimes the greatest love can be found in dislike.

What time is it, you ask?

My grandmother always kept asking me that before she died. What time, what time, what time? I told her every minute, and she'd say that much hasn't passed yet, that there's still time. Already a minute? Another minute's passed? How? How? she'd ask, and sit down on the bench, strung out on nerves. Impossible. You're lying, she says. What time is it? she asks again. I tell her five seconds have passed since last time. Impossible, she says, and again she sits down. Impossible, she says. You lie. You lie. And another minute passes, and she asks again. Already? she asks. And now what time is it? I want some soup. And then she died.

It's been a long time since I've known whether it's Monday, Wednesday, or Friday – said Tefil. – That knowledge is unnecessary to me. Ever since I retired, I don't bother with such things. At all. Blood flows through me, I breathe the air, I get up in the morning so that I might begin. And is it necessary to you, sir? Are you hungry, sir? No. Thirsty? No. Are you cold? No.

I prefer, Rozmaryn, sir – said Tefil. – I prefer to answer the questions I pose you, sir, myself. You see, sir, Rozmaryn, sir, how splendidly I can converse with you, without you, sir?

Tefil buttoned his trench coat up tightly, as it was getting even colder, and glanced at Rozmaryn.

How about a little stroll?

There's a magnificent hill not far away from here. A summit from which there's a beautiful view. Do you like beautiful views, sir?

RAFAŁ WOJASIŃSKI

They arrived at the end of the lyceum building, turned left, and went completely around the building. Behind it, a large hill was uncovered to their eyes. On its summit there stood a pine, which might have been a full six metres tall but was nearly bare of needles.

Quite quickly they climbed the summit – it took them less than two minutes – after which they sat down beneath the leaning pine.

There used to be a Jewish cemetery here, but nothing's left of it now except this pine tree – said Tefil. – There used to be windmills, too. And on that other hill behind your back, there was a Lutheran cemetery. And down there is the Catholic cemetery, which now covers many, without headstones or names on nameplates. That one still is…

Inebriate yourself with the splendid view of the roofs of this town, sir. Have a look in the other direction too in order to experience the splendid aesthetic raptures associated with the view of trees, fields, hills, and widely scattered houses. Fill yourself, sir, with these images. Absorb as much of it as you can. Delight your soul, sir, allow her to experience the cleansing, liberating, fulness of light, love, and hope of all joy. Suck it in, sir…

Beginning. Left and right. Up and down. Here, sir, lay your head in my hands, come now. Close your eyes, sir, and all will be peaceful… Three seconds… One second… And… The end of reality.

I began at eight forty – said Tefil. – and if I had to begin again, at nine forty, ten forty, or eleven forty, and descend the stairs once more, I'd have to subject myself to that beginning as do so many beings in Litental. Suddenly, the sound of an aeroplane above the roofs of our apartment blocks, our little garret flats, our little rooms in the prefabs near the stadium, above the roof of the institute for the handicapped, above the three cemeteries in which people mix up and one can no longer determine any number.

Mathematics no longer works, there remain only small humps overgrown with grass or just flat earth.

So I begin without any reason to, without the slightest sign. I descend the stairs once more, breathing in the smell of walls, wood, plaster. The smell of people of whom no traces now remain. Every day I walk over steps that lead me right onto the pavement near the pastry shop. I go to rope somebody in. To cadge a coffee, a cheesecake, or a dinner in the famous restaurant.

Beginning the euphoria of life. A huge empty space in the head. An all-embracing, eternal, and intractable ignorance. The lack of abilities. The grace of transformation. Beginning.

And fear. Is it warm enough for the dog in the shack? Is it dry for her there?

* * *

ABOUT THE AUTHOR

Rafał Wojasiński (born 1974) is a celebrated author of fiction and drama. Among his works are *Złodziej ryb* (*The Fish Thief*, 2004*), Stara* (*The Old Woman*, 2011), and *Olanda* (2018), as well as the plays *Długie życie* (*A Long Life*, 2017), *Dziad Kalina* (*Old Man Kalina*, 2018), and *Siostry* (*Sisters*, 2019). Many of his dramatic works have also been performed as radio plays; his philosophical novel *Stara* was adapted for the Polish Radio Theatre by Waldemar Modestowicz. His works have been translated into English, French, Spanish, and Bulgarian, and have been consistently nominated for prestigious literary awards, among others: the Gdynia Dramaturgical Award (for *Siostry*, 2019), the Marek Nowakowski Literary Award (also 2019, for *Olanda*), and the Award of the Capital City of Warsaw (2022, for *Tefil*).

ABOUT THE TRANSLATOR

Charles S. Kraszewski (born 1962) is a poet and translator, creative in both English and Polish. He is the author of three volumes of original verse in English (*Diet of Nails*; *Beast*; *Chanameed*), and two in Polish (*Hallo, Sztokholm*; *Skowycik*). He also authored a satirical novel *Accomplices, You Ask?* (San Francisco: Montag, 2021); his novel *At the Tone* is forthcoming in 2024. He translates from Polish (among others, Wojasiński's *Olanda* – published by Glagoslav in 2019), Czech and Slovak into English, and from English and Spanish into Polish. He is a member of the Union of Polish Writers Abroad (London) and of the Association of Polish Writers (SPP, Kraków). In 2022 he was awarded the Gloria Artis medal (III Class) by the Ministry of Culture of the Republic of Poland, and in 2023 the ZAiKS award for translations into a foreign language by the Polish Society of Authors (ZAiKS).

Glagoslav Publications Catalogue

- *The Time of Women* by Elena Chizhova
- *Andrei Tarkovsky: A Life on the Cross* by Lyudmila Boyadzhieva
- *Sin* by Zakhar Prilepin
- *Hardly Ever Otherwise* by Maria Matios
- *Khatyn* by Ales Adamovich
- *The Lost Button* by Irene Rozdobudko
- *Christened with Crosses* by Eduard Kochergin
- *The Vital Needs of the Dead* by Igor Sakhnovsky
- *The Sarabande of Sara's Band* by Larysa Denysenko
- *A Poet and Bin Laden* by Hamid Ismailov
- *Zo Gaat Dat in Rusland* (Dutch Edition) by Maria Konjoekova
- *Kobzar* by Taras Shevchenko
- *The Stone Bridge* by Alexander Terekhov
- *Moryak* by Lee Mandel
- *King Stakh's Wild Hunt* by Uladzimir Karatkevich
- *The Hawks of Peace* by Dmitry Rogozin
- *Harlequin's Costume* by Leonid Yuzefovich
- *Depeche Mode* by Serhii Zhadan
- *Groot Slem en Andere Verhalen* (Dutch Edition) by Leonid Andrejev
- *METRO 2033* (Dutch Edition) by Dmitry Glukhovsky
- *METRO 2034* (Dutch Edition) by Dmitry Glukhovsky
- *A Russian Story* by Eugenia Kononenko
- *Herstories, An Anthology of New Ukrainian Women Prose Writers*
- *The Battle of the Sexes Russian Style* by Nadezhda Ptushkina
- *A Book Without Photographs* by Sergey Shargunov
- *Down Among The Fishes* by Natalka Babina
- *disUNITY* by Anatoly Kudryavitsky
- *Sankya* by Zakhar Prilepin
- *Wolf Messing* by Tatiana Lungin
- *Good Stalin* by Victor Erofeyev
- *Solar Plexus* by Rustam Ibragimbekov
- *Don't Call me a Victim!* by Dina Yafasova
- *Poetin* (Dutch Edition) by Chris Hutchins and Alexander Korobko

- *A History of Belarus* by Lubov Bazan
- *Children's Fashion of the Russian Empire* by Alexander Vasiliev
- *Empire of Corruption: The Russian National Pastime* by Vladimir Soloviev
- *Heroes of the 90s: People and Money. The Modern History of Russian Capitalism* by Alexander Solovev, Vladislav Dorofeev and Valeria Bashkirova
- *Fifty Highlights from the Russian Literature* (Dutch Edition) by Maarten Tengbergen
- *Bajesvolk* (Dutch Edition) by Michail Chodorkovsky
- *Dagboek van Keizerin Alexandra* (Dutch Edition)
- *Myths about Russia* by Vladimir Medinskiy
- *Boris Yeltsin: The Decade that Shook the World* by Boris Minaev
- *A Man Of Change: A study of the political life of Boris Yeltsin*
- *Sberbank: The Rebirth of Russia's Financial Giant* by Evgeny Karasyuk
- *To Get Ukraine* by Oleksandr Shyshko
- *Asystole* by Oleg Pavlov
- *Gnedich* by Maria Rybakova
- *Marina Tsvetaeva: The Essential Poetry*
- *Multiple Personalities* by Tatyana Shcherbina
- *The Investigator* by Margarita Khemlin
- *The Exile* by Zinaida Tulub
- *Leo Tolstoy: Flight from Paradise* by Pavel Basinsky
- *Moscow in the 1930* by Natalia Gromova
- *Laurus* (Dutch edition) by Evgenij Vodolazkin
- *Prisoner* by Anna Nemzer
- *The Crime of Chernobyl: The Nuclear Goulag* by Wladimir Tchertkoff
- *Alpine Ballad* by Vasil Bykau
- *The Complete Correspondence of Hryhory Skovoroda*
- *The Tale of Aypi* by Ak Welsapar
- *Selected Poems* by Lydia Grigorieva
- *The Fantastic Worlds of Yuri Vynnychuk*
- *The Garden of Divine Songs and Collected Poetry of Hryhory Skovoroda*
- *Adventures in the Slavic Kitchen: A Book of Essays with Recipes* by Igor Klekh
- *Seven Signs of the Lion* by Michael M. Naydan

- *Forefathers' Eve* by Adam Mickiewicz
- *One-Two* by Igor Eliseev
- *Girls, be Good* by Bojan Babić
- *Time of the Octopus* by Anatoly Kucherena
- *The Grand Harmony* by Bohdan Ihor Antonych
- *The Selected Lyric Poetry Of Maksym Rylsky*
- *The Shining Light* by Galymkair Mutanov
- *The Frontier: 28 Contemporary Ukrainian Poets - An Anthology*
- *Acropolis: The Wawel Plays* by Stanisław Wyspiański
- *Contours of the City* by Attyla Mohylny
- *Conversations Before Silence: The Selected Poetry of Oles Ilchenko*
- *The Secret History of my Sojourn in Russia* by Jaroslav Hašek
- *Mirror Sand: An Anthology of Russian Short Poems*
- *Maybe We're Leaving* by Jan Balaban
- *Death of the Snake Catcher* by Ak Welsapar
- *A Brown Man in Russia* by Vijay Menon
- *Hard Times* by Ostap Vyshnia
- *The Flying Dutchman* by Anatoly Kudryavitsky
- *Nikolai Gumilev's Africa* by Nikolai Gumilev
- *Combustions* by Srđan Srdić
- *The Sonnets* by Adam Mickiewicz
- *Dramatic Works* by Zygmunt Krasiński
- *Four Plays* by Juliusz Słowacki
- *Little Zinnobers* by Elena Chizhova
- *We Are Building Capitalism! Moscow in Transition 1992-1997* by Robert Stephenson
- *The Nuremberg Trials* by Alexander Zvyagintsev
- *The Hemingway Game* by Evgeni Grishkovets
- *A Flame Out at Sea* by Dmitry Novikov
- *Jesus' Cat* by Grig
- *Want a Baby and Other Plays* by Sergei Tretyakov
- *Mikhail Bulgakov: The Life and Times* by Marietta Chudakova
- *Leonardo's Handwriting* by Dina Rubina
- *A Burglar of the Better Sort* by Tytus Czyżewski
- *The Mouseiad and other Mock Epics* by Ignacy Krasicki

- *Ravens before Noah* by Susanna Harutyunyan
- *An English Queen and Stalingrad* by Natalia Kulishenko
- *Point Zero* by Narek Malian
- *Absolute Zero* by Artem Chekh
- *Olanda* by Rafał Wojasiński
- *Robinsons* by Aram Pachyan
- *The Monastery* by Zakhar Prilepin
- *The Selected Poetry of Bohdan Rubchak: Songs of Love, Songs of Death, Songs of the Moon*
- *Mebet* by Alexander Grigorenko
- *The Orchestra* by Vladimir Gonik
- *Everyday Stories* by Mima Mihajlović
- *Slavdom* by Ľudovít Štúr
- *The Code of Civilization* by Vyacheslav Nikonov
- *Where Was the Angel Going?* by Jan Balaban
- *De Zwarte Kip* (Dutch Edition) by Antoni Pogorelski
- *Głosy / Voices* by Jan Polkowski
- *Sergei Tretyakov: A Revolutionary Writer in Stalin's Russia* by Robert Leach
- *Opstand* (Dutch Edition) by Władysław Reymont
- *Dramatic Works* by Cyprian Kamil Norwid
- *Children's First Book of Chess* by Natalie Shevando and Matthew McMillion
- *Precursor* by Vasyl Shevchuk
- *The Vow: A Requiem for the Fifties* by Jiří Kratochvil
- *De Bibliothecaris* (Dutch edition) by Mikhail Jelizarov
- *Subterranean Fire* by Natalka Bilotserkivets
- *Vladimir Vysotsky: Selected Works*
- *Behind the Silk Curtain* by Gulistan Khamzayeva
- *The Village Teacher and Other Stories* by Theodore Odrach
- *Duel* by Borys Antonenko-Davydovych
- *War Poems* by Alexander Korotko
- *Ballads and Romances* by Adam Mickiewicz
- *The Revolt of the Animals* by Wladyslaw Reymont
- *Poems about my Psychiatrist* by Andrzej Kotański
- *Someone Else's Life* by Elena Dolgopyat
- *Selected Works: Poetry, Drama, Prose* by Jan Kochanowski

- *The Riven Heart of Moscow (Sivtsev Vrazhek)* by Mikhail Osorgin
- *Bera and Cucumber* by Alexander Korotko
- *The Big Fellow* by Anastasiia Marsiz
- *Boryslav in Flames* by Ivan Franko
- *The Witch of Konotop* by Hryhoriy Kvitka-Osnovyanenko
- *De afdeling* (Dutch edition) by Aleksej Salnikov
- *Ilget* by Alexander Grigorenko
- *Tefil* by Rafał Wojasiński
- *Letter Z* by Oleksandr Sambrus
- *Liza's Waterfall: The Hidden Story of a Russian Feminist* by Pavel Basinsky
- *Biography of Sergei Prokofiev* by Igor Vishnevetsky
- *The Food Block* by Alexey Ivanov
- *A City Drawn from Memory* by Elena Chizhova
- *Guide to M. Bulgakov's The Master and Margarita* by Ksenia Atarova and Georgy Lesskis

And more forthcoming . . .

GLAGOSLAV PUBLICATIONS
www.glagoslav.com